When I was a kid, my parents took me to all sorts of specialists to find out what was wrong with me. I wasn't afraid of anything, not spiders, snakes, heights, wild animals—nothing. That's when they figured out that if there was a fear gene, I was missing it. So I guess you could say I'm fearless. Like if I see some big guy beating up a little guy I just dive in and finish off the big one—and I can, because my dad trained me to. He figured if I was going to keep getting myself into trouble I might as well have the skills to protect myself. And my dad knows trouble—he's in the CIA. At least I think he is. I haven't seen or heard from him since, well, since something happened that changed our lives forever.

Anyway, you'd think that because I'm fearless my life would be pretty great, right? Wrong. In fact, if I had three wishes, one of them would be to know fear. Because without fear, I'll never know if I'm truly brave. That wouldn't be my first wish, though—my first wish would be to have my dad back. For obvious reasons. My last wish . . . well that's kind of embarrassing. I'd like to end my unlucky seventeen-year stint as Gaia-the-Unkissed. Do I have anyone in mind? Yeah. But I'm beginning to think it'll never happen. . . .

Don't miss any books in this thrilling series:

FEARLESS™

Available from SIMON PULSE

FEARLESS™

Double Edition #4
Twisted (#4) & Chase (#28)

FRANCINE PASCAL

SIMON PULSE
New York   London   Toronto   Sydney   Singapore

This book is a work of fiction. Any references to historical events, real people, or real locales are used fictitiously. Other names, characters, places, and incidents are the product of the author's imagination, and any resemblance to actual events or locales or persons, living or dead, is entirely coincidental.

First Simon Pulse edition July 2003
Twisted text copyright © 2000 by Francine Pascal
Chase text copyright © 2003 by Francine Pascal

Cover copyright © 2003 by 17th Street Productions, an Alloy, Inc. company.

SIMON PULSE
An imprint of Simon & Schuster
Children's Publishing Division
1230 Avenue of the Americas
New York, NY 10020

Fearless™ is a trademark of Francine Pascal.

Printed in the United States of America
10 9 8 7 6 5 4 3 2 1

ISBN 0-689-85927-9

Twisted and *Chase* are also published individually.

TWISTED

To Johnny Stewart Carmen

There are circles in Hell.

My father—back when he still cared that I was alive and breathing—used to make me read. Not easy stuff. Even when I was a kid, there was no *Winnie-the-Pooh*, no *Little House on the Prairie*. Not for me.

It was all about the classics. *Hard* classics.

One of the moldy oldies he put under my nose was *The Inferno*, by Dante. This book was seriously tough sledding. The whole thing was written in verse, and it was full of political stuff that didn't always make a lot of sense, and the language was creaky to say the least. But there were good parts.

In this story a guy gets led all around Hell to see how everybody is punished. A lot of it is kind of like you would expect. Lots of demons with whips. Fire. Snakes. That kind of thing.

But the idea that stuck with me was the way Hell was divided up in circles. The dead guys up in the first circle don't have it so bad. It's just kind of rainy and dull up there. But the really bad people, like murderers (or members of a political party Dante didn't like), they get shoved way down to a circle where they have to run around without feet or burst into flame or get eaten by big lizards or melt like candles.

I remembered this book the other day and started thinking that my life could be sliced up in the same way as hell.

There are the little things. Finding out the deli is out of Krispy Kreme. Losing a chess game against some moron I should have schooled. That's the gloomy, first-circle sort of hell.

Then there's having to live with George and Ella. George knew my father, but I don't really know him. Ella didn't know my father, doesn't know me, and I don't even *want* to know Ella.

She's definitely a deeper level of hell.

The next level down is high school. It gets a level of hell all to itself.

Below that comes Sam and Heather. I wouldn't throw Sam in a pit by himself. I mean, Sam's the guy I want to be with. The only guy I've ever wanted to be with. But Sam is with Heather, and together they deserve pitch-forks and brimstone.

Then there's my father. My father disappears, doesn't write, doesn't call, and doesn't give me a clue about what's going on. Now we're getting really deep. Snakes and fire. Demons with weird Latin names.

And my mom. The way I feel when I think about her. When I think about her death. Well, that brings us right down to the bottom.

The way Dante tells it, the very bottom layer of hell isn't hot. Instead it's a big lake of ice with people frozen inside.

They're stuck forever with only
their faces sticking out, and
every time they cry, it just adds
another layer of frost covering
their eyes.

Put my whole life together,
and that's where I am. Down on
the ice. Some days I feel like I
have a pair of skates. Other days
I wonder if Dante didn't get it
wrong. Maybe the ice isn't the
lowest level after all.

Her big pal
gave her a
little love
pat—enough
to bounce
her from
the wall
and back to
his beefy
hand.

the high school circle

PRETTY PEOPLE DO UGLY THINGS.

It was one of those laws of nature that Gaia had understood for years. If she ever started to forget that rule for a second, there always seemed to be some good-looking asshole ready to remind her.

Jerkus High-schoolensis

She stumbled up the steps and pushed her way inside The Village School with five minutes to spare before her first class. Actually early. Of course, her hair was still wet from the shower and her homework wasn't done, but being there—actually physically inside the building before the bell rang—was a new experience. For twelve whole seconds after that, she thought she might have an all right day.

Then she caught a glimpse of one of those things that absolutely defines the high school circle of hell.

Down at the end of the row of lockers, a tall, broadshouldered guy was smiling a very confident smile, wearing very popular-crowd clothes, and using a very big hand to pin a very much smaller girl up against the wall. There was an amused expression on Mr. Handsome's face.

Only the girl who was stuck between his hand and fifty years' worth of ugly green paint didn't look like she thought it was funny.

Gaia had noticed the big boy in a couple of her classes but hadn't bothered to file away his name. Tad, she thought, or maybe it was Chip. She knew it was something like that.

From the way girls in class talked, he was supposed to be cute. Gaia could sort of see it. Big blue eyes. Good skin. Six-five even without the air soles in his two-hundred-dollar sneakers. His lips were a little puffy, but then, some people liked that. It was the hair that really eliminated him from Gaia's list of guys worth looking at.

He wore that stuff in his hair. The stuff that looked like a combination of motor oil and maple syrup. The stuff that made it look like he hadn't washed his hair this side of tenth grade. "What's the rush, Darla?" the Chipster said. "I just want to know what he said to you."

The girl, Darla, shook her head. "He didn't . . ."

Her big pal gave her a little love pat—enough to bounce her from the wall and back to his beefy hand.

"Don't give me that," he said, still all smiles. "I saw you two together."

Gaia did a quick survey of the hall. There was a trio of khaki-crowd girls fifty yards down and two leather dudes hanging near the front door. A skinny guy stuck his head out of a classroom, saw who was doing the shoving, and quickly ducked back in. Gaia had to give him some credit. At least he looked. Everybody else in the hallway was Not Noticing so hard, it hurt.

Gaia really didn't need this. She didn't know the girl against the wall. Sure, the guy with the big hands was a prime example of Jerkus highschoolensis, but it was absolutely none of Gaia's business. She turned away and headed for class, wondering if she might avoid a tardy slip for the first time in a week.

"Just let me . . . ," the girl begged from behind her.

"In a minute, babe," replied the guy with the hands. "I just need to talk to you a little." There was a thump and a short whimper from the girl.

Gaia stopped. She really, really didn't need this.

She took a deep breath, turned, and headed back toward the couple.

The easiest thing would be to grab the guy by the face and teach him how soft a skull was compared to a concrete wall. But then, smashing someone's head would probably not help Gaia's reputation.

Words were an option. She hadn't used that method much, but there was a first time for everything, right?

She could try talking to the guy or even threatening to tell a teacher. Gaia didn't care if anyone at the school thought she was a wimp or a narc, or whatever they called it in New York City. That was the least of her problems. Besides, they already thought she was a bitch for not warning Heather about the park slasher.

Before long, Gaia was so close that both partners in the ugly little dance turned to look at her. Tough Guy's smile didn't budge an inch.

"What?" he said.

Gaia struggled for something to say. Something smooth. Something that would defuse this whole thing. She paused for a second, cleared her throat, and said . . .

"Is there . . . uh, some kind of a problem?"

Brilliant.

The guy who might be named Chip took a two-second look at her face, then spent twice as long trying to size up the breasts under Gaia's rumpled football shirt.

"Nothing you gotta worry about," he said, still staring at her chest. He waved the hand that wasn't busy holding a person. "This is a private conversation."

The girl against the wall looked at Gaia with a big-eyed, round-mouthed expression that could have been fear or hope or stupidity. Gaia's instant impression was that it was a little bit of all three. The girl had straight black hair that was turned up in a little flip, tanned-to-a-golden-brown skin, an excess of eye shadow, and a cheerleading uniform. She didn't exactly strike Gaia as a brain trust.

Not that being a cheerleader automatically made somebody stupid. Gaia was certain there were smart cheerleaders. Somewhere there had to be cheerleaders who were working on physics theories every time they put down their pom-poms. She hadn't met any, but they were out there. Probably living in the same city with all the nice guys who don't mind if a girl has thunder thighs and doesn't know how to dress.

"Well?" demanded Puffy Lips. "What's wrong with you? Are you deaf or just stupid?"

Gaia tensed. Anger left an acid taste in her throat. Suddenly her fist was crying out for his face. She opened her mouth to say something just as the bell for first period rang. So much for being on time.

She took a step closer to the pair. "Why don't you let her go?"

Chip made a little grunting laugh and shook his head. "Look, babe. Get out of here," he said to Gaia.

Babe. It wasn't necessarily an insult—unless the person saying it added that perfect tone of voice. The tone that says being a babe is on the same evolutionary rung as being a brain-damaged hamster.

Gaia glanced up the hallway. Only a few students were still in the hall, and none were close. If she planned to do anything without everyone in school seeing it, this was the time.

She leaned toward him. "Maybe *you'd* better get out of here," she said in a low voice. She could feel the cheerleader's short breaths on the back of her neck. "You don't want to be late for class."

The sunny smile slipped from Chip's face, replaced by a go-away-you're-bothering-me frown. "Did you hear me tell you to go?"

Gaia shrugged. It was coming. That weird rush she sometimes felt.

"I heard you. I just didn't listen."

Now the expression on Chip's face was more like an I-guess-I'm-going-to-have-to-teach-you-how-the-world-works sneer. "Get the hell out of my way," he snapped.

"Make me."

He took his hand off Darla and grabbed Gaia by the arm.

Gaia was glad. If she touched him first, there was always the chance he would actually admit he got beat up by a girl and charge her with assault. But since Chip made the first move, all bets were off. Everything that happened from that first touch was self-defense.

Gaia was an expert in just about every martial art with a name. Jujitsu. Tai kwon do. Judo. Kung fu. If it involved hitting, kicking, or tossing people through the air, Gaia knew it. Standing six inches from Mr. Good Skin Bad Attitude, she could have managed a kick that would have taken his oily head right off his thick neck. She could have put a stiff hand through his rib cage or delivered a punch that drove his heart up against his spine.

But she didn't do any of that. She wanted to, but she didn't.

Moving quickly, she turned her arms and twisted out of his grip. Before Chip could react, she reached across with her left hand, took hold of the guy's right thumb, and gave it just a little . . . push.

For a moment Puffy Lips Chip looked surprised. Then Gaia pushed a little harder on his captive digit, and the look of surprise instantly turned to pain.

He tried to pull away, but Gaia held tight. She was working hard to keep from actually breaking his thumb. She could have broken his whole oversized hand like a bundle of big dry sticks. The real trick was hurting someone without really hurting someone. Don't break any bones. Don't leave any scars. Don't do anything permanent. Leave a memory.

"What do you think, Chip?" Gaia asked, still pushing his thumb toward the back of his hand. "Should you be shoving girls around?"

"Let go of me, you little—" He reached for her with his free hand.

Gaia leaned back out of his range and gave an extra shove. Chip wailed.

"Here's the deal," Gaia said quietly. "You keep your hands to yourself, I let you keep your hands. What do you think?"

Chip's knees were starting to shake, and there were beads of sweat breaking out on his forehead. "Who are—"

12

"Like I really want you to know my name." She pushed harder, and now Gaia could feel the bones in his thumb pulling loose from his hand. Another few seconds and one was sure to snap. "Do we have a deal?"

"Okay," he squeaked in a voice two octaves higher than it had been a few seconds before. "Sure."

Gaia let go. "That's good, Chip." The moment the physical conflict ended, Gaia felt all her uncertainty come rushing back. She glanced up the hallway and was relieved to see that there was no crowd of gawkers. That didn't stop her from feeling dizzy. She was acting like `muscle-bound freak girl` right in the main hallway at school. This was definitely not the way to remain invisible.

Puffy Lips stepped back and gripped his bruised thumb in his left hand. "Brad."

"What?"

"Brad," he said. "My name isn't Chip. It's Brad."

Gaia rolled her eyes. "Whatever." She lowered her head and shoved past him just as the late bell rang.

Another day, another fight, another tardy.

Things Gaia Knows

School sucks.

Ella sucks.

Her father sucks.

Heather Gannis sucks `big time`.

Things Gaia Wants to Know

Who kidnapped Sam?

Why did they contact her?

What was with all those stupid tests?

How could she have `let the kidnappers get away` after everything they'd done to her and Sam?

Why did Mr. Rupert use the words "all right" more often than most people used the word "the"?

Who killed CJ?

Why did she never know she had an uncle who looked exactly like her father?

Was said uncle going to `contact her again`?

Did she even want him to after he'd been nonexistent for her entire life?

Why did anyone in their right mind `choose` to drink skim milk?

Was she really expected to pay attention in class when there were things going on that actually mattered?

The Decision

EVEN BACK WHEN HIS LEGS WORKED, Ed had never been fearless.

He sat in his first-period class and stared at the door. Any moment, the bell would ring. Then he would go out into the hallway and Gaia would appear. Any moment, he would have his chance. In the meantime he was terrified.

People who had seen him on a skateboard or a pair of in-lines might have been surprised to hear it. There had been no stairs too steep to slalom, no handrail Ed wasn't willing to challenge, no traffic too thick to dare. Anyone would tell you, Ed Fargo was a wild man. He took more risks, and took them faster, than any other boarder in the city.

The dark secret was that all through those days, almost every second, Ed had been terrified. Every time his wheels had sent sparks lancing from a metal rail, every time he had gone over a jump and felt gravity tugging down at his stomach, Ed had been sure he was about to die.

And when it didn't happen, when he landed, and lived, and rolled on to skate another day, it had been a thousand times sweeter just because he had been so scared. It seemed to Ed that there was nothing better than that moment after the terror had passed.

Then he lost the use of his legs and grew a wheelchair

15

on his butt, and everything changed. A wheelchair didn't give the sort of thrills you got from a skateboard. There were a few times, especially right after he realized he was never, ever going to get out of the chair, that Ed had thought about taking the contraption out into traffic—just to see how well it played with the taxis and delivery vans. That kind of thinking was scary in a whole different, definitely less fun way.

Legs or no legs, Ed wasn't sure that any stunt he had pulled in the past had terrified him as much as the one he was about to attempt.

He stared at the classroom door, and the blood rushing through his brain sounded as loud as a subway train pulling up to the platform.

He was going to tell Gaia Moore that he loved her.

He was really going to do it. If he didn't faint first.

Ed had been infatuated with Gaia since he first saw her in the school hallway. He was half smitten as soon as they spoke and all the way gone within a couple of days.

Since then, Ed and Gaia had become friends—or at least they had come as close to being friends as Gaia's don't-get-close-to-me forcefield would allow. To tell Gaia how he really felt would mean risking the relationship they already shared. Ed was horrified by the thought of losing contact with Gaia, but he was determined to take that chance.

For once, he was going to see what it was like to be fearless.

ONE IDIOT AN HOUR. GAIA FIGURED

Sour Seventeen

that if they would let her beat up one butthead per class, it would make the day go oh-so-smoothly. She would get the nervous energy out of her system, add a few high points to her dull-as-a-bowling-ball day, and by the time the final bell rang, the world would have eight fewer losers. All good things.

It might also help her keep her mind off Sam Moon. Sam, whose life she had saved more than once. Sam, who was oblivious to her existence. Sam, who had the biggest bitch this side of Fifth Avenue for a girlfriend but didn't seem to notice.

And still Gaia couldn't stop thinking about him. Daydreaming her way through each and every class. If her teachers had tested her on self-torture, she would have gotten an A.

Gaia trudged out of her third-period classroom and shouldered her way through the clogged hallway, her cruise control engaged. Every conscious brain cell was dedicated to the ongoing problem of what to do about her irritating and somewhat embarrassing Sam problem.

It was like a drug problem, only `slightly less messy`.

It was bad enough that Sam was with Heather. Even worse was Heather getting credit for everything Gaia did. Gaia had nearly lost her life saving Sam from a kidnapper. She had gone crazy looking for him. And then Heather had stepped in at the last second and looked like `the big hero` when her total expended effort was equal to drying her fingernails.

Not to mention the fact that the kidnappers had gotten away after they spent an entire day ordering her around as if she were a toy poodle.

Gaia suddenly realized she was biting her lip so badly that it was `about to bleed`. Whenever she thought about how the nameless, faceless men in black had used her, she got the uncontrollable urge to do serious violence to something. Then, of course, her thoughts turned directly to Heather.

And the fact that Heather had sex with Sam. And the fact that Heather had taken credit for saving Sam. And the fact that Heather got to hold hands with Sam and kiss Sam and talk to Sam and—

Gaia came to a stop in front of her locker and kicked it hard, denting the bottom of the door. A couple of Gap girls turned to stare, so Gaia kicked it again. The Gap girls scurried away.

She snarled at her vague reflection in the battered door. In the dull metal she was only an outline. That's all she was to Sam, too. A vague shadow of nothing much.

For a few delusional days Gaia had thought Sam might be the one. The one to break her embarrassing record as the only unkissed seventeen-year-old on planet Earth. Maybe even the one to turn sex from hypothesis into reality. But it wasn't going to happen.

There wasn't going to be any sex. There was never going to be any kissing. Not with Sam. Not ever.

Gaia yanked open the door of her locker, tossed in the book she was carrying, and randomly took out another without bothering to look at it. Then she slammed the door just as hard as she had kicked it.

She squeezed her eyes shut for a moment, squeezed hard, as if she could squeeze out her unwanted thoughts.

Even though Gaia knew zilch about love, knew less about relationships, and knew even less about psychology, she knew exactly what her girlfriends, if she had any, would tell her.

Find a new guy. Someone to distract you. Someone who cares about you.

Right. No problem.

Unfortunately, it had only taken her seventeen years to find a guy who didn't care about her.

NAVIGATION OF HIGH SCHOOL HALL-

The Attempt

ways takes on a whole new meaning when you're three feet wide and mounted on wheels.

Ed Fargo skidded around a corner, narrowly avoided a collision with a janitor, then spun right past a knot of students laughing at some private joke. He threw the chair into hard reverse and did a quick 180 to dodge a stream of band students lugging instruments out a doorway, then he powered through a gap, coasted down a ramp, and took the next corner so hard, he went around on one wheel.

Fifty feet away, Gaia Moore was just shutting the door of her locker. Ed let the chair coast to a halt as he watched her. Gaia's football shirt was wrinkled, and her socks didn't match. Most of her yellow hair had slipped free of whatever she had been using to hold it in a ponytail. Loose strands hovered around the sculpted planes of her face, and the remaining hair gathered at the back of her head in a heavy, tumbled mass.

She was the most beautiful thing that Ed had ever seen.

He gave the wheels of his chair a sharp push and darted ahead of some slow walkers. Before Gaia could take two steps, Ed was at her side.

"Looking for your next victim?" he asked.

Gaia glanced down, and for a moment the characteristic frown on her insanely kissable lips was replaced by a smile. "Hey, Ed. What's up?"

Ed almost turned around and left. Why should he push it? He could live on that smile for at least a month.

Fearless, he told himself. Be fearless.

"I guess you don't want us to win at basketball this year," he started, trying to keep the tone light.

Gaia looked puzzled. "What?"

"The guy you went after this morning, Brad Reston," Ed continued. "He's a starting forward."

"How did you hear about it?" The frown was back full force.

"From Darla Rigazzi," Ed answered. "She's talked you up in every class this morning."

"Yeah, well, I wish she wouldn't." She looked away and started up the hallway again, the smooth muscles of her legs stretching under faded jeans.

Ed kept pace for fifty feet. Twice he opened his mouth to say something, but he shut it again before a word escaped. There was a distant, distracted look on Gaia's face now. The moment had passed. He would have to wait.

No, a voice said from the back of his mind. Don't wait. Tell her now. Tell her everything.

"Gaia . . . ," he started.

Something in his tone must have caught Gaia's attention. She stopped in the middle of one long stride and turned to him. Her right eyebrow was raised, and her changing eyes were the blue-gray of the Atlantic fifty miles off the coast. "What's wrong, Ed?"

Ed swallowed. Suddenly he felt like he was back on his skateboard, ready to challenge the bumpy ride down another flight of steps—only the steps in front of him went down, and down, and down forever.

He swallowed hard and shook his head. "It's not important."

I love you.

"Nothing at all, really."

I want to be with you.

"Just . . . nothing in particular."

I want you to be with me.

"I'll talk to you after class."

Gaia stared at him for a moment longer, then nodded. "All right. I'll see you later." She turned around and walked off quickly, her long legs eating up the distance.

"Perfect," Ed whispered to her retreating back.

A perfect pair. She was brave to the point of almost being dangerous, and he was gutless to the point of almost being depressing.

Sometimes I wonder what I would say if I were ever asked out on a date.

You'd think that since it's never happened to me, I might have had some time in the past seventeen years to formulate the perfect response. You'd think that with all the movies I've seen, I would have at least picked up some cheesy line. Some doe-eyed, swooning acceptance.

But I pretty much stay away from romantic comedies. There's no relationship advice to be had from a Neil LaBute film.

Besides, you can't formulate the perfect response for a situation you can't remotely imagine.

I figure that if it ever does happen (not probable), I'll end up saying something along the lines of "uh" or slight variations thereof.

"Uh . . . uh," if the guy's a freak.

"Uh . . . huh," if the guy's a nonfreak.

I wonder what Heather said to Sam when he first asked her out. Probably something disgustingly perfect. Something right out of a movie. Something like, "I was wondering when you'd ask." Or maybe Heather asked Sam out. And he said something like, "It would be my honor."

Okay. Stomach now reacting badly. Must think about something else.

What did Heather say when *Ed* asked her out?

Okay. Stomach now severely cramping.

So what happens after the "Uh . . . huh"?

Awkward pauses, I assume. Idiot small talk, sweaty palms (his), dry mouth (also his), bad food. (I imagine dates don't happen at places where they have good food—like Gray's Papaya or Dojo's.)

And I won't even get into what happens after the most likely difficult digestion. What does

the nonfreak expect at that
point? Hand holding? Kissing?
Groping? Heavy groping? Sex?

Stomach no longer wishes to be
a component of body.

Must stop here.

Luckily I won't ever have to
deal with any of this. Because no
nonfreak will ever ask me out.
And no freak will ever get more
than the initial grunt.

And with
those words,
Gaia's

painfully
seventeen-
beautiful

year streak

officially

came to an

end.

The Offer

THE SCHEDULE WAS A XEROX. Maybe a Xerox of a Xerox. Whatever it was, the print was so faint and muddy that David Twain had to squint hard and hold the sheet of paper up to the light just to make out a few words.

He lowered the folded page and looked around him. People were streaming past on all sides. The students at this school were visibly different. They moved faster. Talked faster. Dressed like they expected a society photographer to show up at any minute. They were, David thought, probably all brain-dead.

Still, nobody else seemed to be having a hard time finding the right room. Of course, the rest of them had spent more than eight minutes in the building.

A bell rang right over his head. The sound of it was so loud that it seemed to jar the fillings in his teeth. David winced and looked up at the clanging bell. That was when he noticed that the number above the door and the room number on the schedule were the same.

A half-dozen students slipped past David as he stood in the doorway. He turned to follow, caught a bare glimpse of movement from the corner of his eye, and the next thing he knew, he was flying through the air.

He landed hard on his butt. All at once he bit his tongue, dropped his brand-new books, and let out a sound that reminded him of a small dog that had been kicked. The books skidded twenty feet, letting out a spray of loose papers as they went.

The bell stopped ringing. In the space of seconds the remaining students in the hallway dived into classrooms. David found himself alone.

Almost.

"Sorry."

It was a mumbled apology. Not much conviction there.

David looked up to see a tall girl with loose, tangled blond hair standing over him.

"Yeah," he said. There was a warm, salty taste in his mouth. Blood. And his butt ached from the fall. At the moment those things didn't matter.

"You okay?" the girl asked, shoving her hand in her pocket and looking like she'd rather be anywhere but there.

"Yeah," he said again, reaching back to touch his spine. "I'm fine. Great."

The girl shook her head. "If you say so." She offered her hand, even as her face took on an even more sour expression.

Her tousled hair spilled down across her shoulders as she reached to him.

"Thanks." David took her hand and let her help

him to his feet. The girl's palm was warm. Her fingers were surprisingly strong. "What did I run into?"

"Me."

David blinked. "You knocked me down?"

The blond girl shrugged and released his hand. "I didn't do it on purpose."

"You must have been moving pretty fast to hit that hard." David resisted an urge to rub his aches. Instead he offered the hand the girl had just released. "Hi, I'm David Twain."

The girl glanced over her shoulder at the classroom, then stared at David's fingers as if she'd never experienced a handshake before.

"Gaia," she said. "Gaia Moore." She took his hand in hers and gave it a single quick shake.

David was the one who had fallen, but for some reason the simple introduction was enough to make this girl, this painfully beautiful girl, seem awkward.

"Great name," he said. "Like the Earth goddess."

"Yeah, well, if you're okay—"

David shook his head. "No," he said.

Gaia blinked. "What?"

"No," David repeated. "I'm not okay." He leaned toward her and lowered his voice to his best thick whisper. "I won't be okay until you agree to go to dinner with me tomorrow night."

"UH . . . HUH."

The Response

"What?" David asked, his very clear blue eyes narrowing.

He was a male. He was, apparently, a nonfreak. He was not Sam. He got the `affirmative grunt` before Gaia could remind herself of the ramifications.

"I said, uh-huh," Gaia said evenly, lifting her chin.

"Good," he said. "There's this place called Cookies & Couscous. It's more like a bakery than a restaurant. You know it?"

Of course she knew it. Any place that had *cookies* in its name and was located within twenty miles of her room automatically went on Gaia's `mental map`.

"On Thompson," she said.

"Right." He nodded, and a piece of black hair fell over his forehead. "We can eat some baklava, wash it down with espresso, and worry about having a main course after we're full of dessert."

For a moment Gaia just looked at him. He was tall. Gangly. Almost sweet looking. `Very not Sam`.

"Baklava," David repeated with a smirk. "Buttery. Flaky. Honey and nuts."

Gaia nearly smiled. Almost.

This could take her mind off Sam. The kidnappers. The uncle. Heather.

30

"When?" she said.

He smiled. "Tomorrow? Eight o'clock."

Gaia nodded almost imperceptibly.

His smile widened. "It's a date."

And with those words, Gaia's seventeen-year streak officially came to an end.

HEATHER GANNIS COULDN'T BELIEVE

The Unsaid

what she was about to do, but there was no getting around it. There were too many things that had to be said. Things that couldn't go unsaid much longer. Not without Heather going into a paranoid frenzy. And frenzy was not something Heather did well. She liked to be in control. Always.

She looked at her reflection in the scratched bathroom mirror, tossed her glossy brown hair behind her shoulders, took a deep breath, and plunged into the melee that was the post-lunch hall crowd.

Even in the crush of people it only took Heather about five seconds to spot Gaia Moore. And her perfectly tousled blond hair. And her supermodel-tall body. Before she could remind herself of how stupid it was to do this in public, Heather walked right up to Gaia and grabbed her arm.

Gaia looked completely surprised.

"We have to talk," Heather said.

Even more surprised. Gaia yanked her arm away. "Doubtful," she said.

Heather fixed her with a leveling glare as she noticed a few curious bystanders pausing to check out the latest Gaia-Heather confrontation. "Bio lab," Heather said. Then she turned on her heel and made her way to the designated room.

She almost couldn't believe it when Gaia walked in moments later.

Gaia raised her eyebrows and shrugged, tucking her hands into the front pockets of her pants. "Call me curious," she said.

Wanting to remain in charge, Heather slapped her books down on top of one of the big, black tables and rested one hand on her hip. "Who kidnapped Sam?" she asked evenly.

"I don't know," Gaia said, suddenly standing up straight.

"Right," Heather said, her ire already rising. "Then why did they contact you?"

"I don't know," Gaia repeated.

Heather scoffed and looked up at the ceiling, concentrating on trying to keep the blood from rising to her face. "Is that all you're going to say?" she spat. "You asked for my help, then you tripped me on the stairs, and I spent two hours stuck with the idiot police at NYU trying to convince them I wasn't some crazed stalker, and all you can say is, 'I don't know?'" She was sounding hysterical. She had to stop.

Gaia shrugged. It was all Heather could do to keep from clocking the girl in the head with her physics book. She took a long, deep breath through her nose, and let it out slowly—audibly. Then she picked up her books, hugging them to her chest, and walked right up to Gaia, the toe of her suede boot just touching the battered rubber of Gaia's sneaker. The girl didn't move.

"Stay away from Sam," Heather said, trying to muster a threatening tone. It wasn't the easiest thing in the world. Gaia had threatened her. Gaia had hurt her. Gaia had almost gotten her killed.

The girl was like a statue.

Heather stepped around Gaia and headed for the door. She stopped to look behind her and Gaia was frozen in place, as if someone were still standing before her speaking.

"Freak," Heather muttered. And with that, she was out the door.

Before Gaia could snap out of it and come after her.

THE PENCIL SNAPPED. IN THE silent lecture hall the noise seemed as loud as a gunshot.

Tug-of-War

Thirty pairs of eyes turned toward Sam Moon, and from the back of the hall came a muffled snicker. Sam closed his eyes for a moment, then slowly raised his hand.

"Yes, Mr. Moon," the physics professor said with a tone of tired amusement. "You can get another."

Sam closed his blue test folder and searched quickly through his book bag for a replacement pencil. All around him he could hear the quiet scratching of lead on paper as the rest of the class hurried to complete the exam. Sam's progress on the test couldn't exactly be called hurrying. There were one hundred and twenty questions on the test and exactly fifty-seven minutes to answer them all. With forty-five of those minutes gone, Sam was on number twelve.

He finally located another pencil and put the bag back on the floor. He looked down at the next question, touched the pencil to the paper. The pencil snapped into four pieces.

This time there was nothing muffled about the laughter.

The physics professor, an older man with a comb-over so complex, it was a science in itself, let loose a heavy sigh.

"Mr. Moon, if this test is causing you so much stress, might I suggest you try a pen?" he said with a sneer. "I would not want to be responsible for chopping down whole forests of precious trees just to keep you supplied with pencils."

Sam would have liked to smack the guy. He would have liked to ask him if he'd ever taken a physics midterm two days after being released by a group of as yet unidentified kidnapping psychos. He would have liked to get up and leave the room.

He didn't. Sam Moon did not shirk responsibility. It wasn't in his blood.

Ignoring the remnants of the last wave of laughter, Sam dug through his book bag a second time, extracted a ballpoint, and went back to work. Even the pen gave out a little squeak in his hand, as if the plastic was that close to breaking.

It wasn't just his recent trauma that was causing his tension, although it had less than nothing to do with the exam—less than nothing to do with frequencies and waveforms and photon behavior.

The real tension came from the tug-of-war that was going on in his brain. On one end of the rope was Heather Gannis. The lovely, the popular, the much-sought-after Heather. The Heather that Sam was dating. Assisting on her end of the rope was a whole army of good reasons for Sam to stay in his current relationship. There was beauty—which Heather certainly had. And there was sex, which Heather was willing to provide. And there was a certain reliability. Sam knew Heather. He could count on Heather. He might not always like everything about Heather, but he knew her. There were no surprises on that side.

And of course, she had saved his life.

Dragging the rope in the other direction was Gaia Moore. There was no army on Gaia's side. The girl brought nothing but frustration, confusion, mystery, and imminent danger. Technically she was a mess. And from the moment Sam met her, Gaia had seemed to stumble from one disaster to the next. But at least Gaia wasn't boring. She was anything but.

If Sam's head had staged a fair fight, Team Heather would have dragged Gaia right off the field so fast, she would have had grass burns on her face. But something inside Sam wouldn't let that happen. Something in him kept holding on to Gaia's end of the rope, keeping her in the game.

He closed his eyes for a moment and put his hands against his temples. He had to stop thinking about Gaia. Thinking about Gaia when he was already committed to Heather was wrong. More than that, the way he thought about Gaia all the time was getting to be more than a little like an obsession.

"Ten minutes, people," said the professor. "You should be getting near the end."

Sam shook his head, flinging away the rope and all

its hangers-on. He studied the next question on the test and scribbled out an answer. Then he tackled the next. And the next. When he managed to concentrate, Sam found that the answers came easily. Sometimes it was nice to have the powers of a good geek brain. He sped through a series of equations without faltering, flew past some short answers, and was within five questions of the end when the professor called, "Time."

Sam gathered up his things and carried his paper to the front of the room, relieved. At least he had cleared the Gaia fog from his brain long enough to get some work done. He hadn't embarrassed himself. Not this time, anyway.

But he wasn't sure how long that would last. The battle in his head was still picking up steam. Soon it was going to be a full-blown war.

GAIA STARED DOWN AT THE TOES OF

Maybe Connecticut

her battered sneakers and wondered how long it would be before she threw up. Or ran out of the room. Or exploded.

Accepting a date with a guy she had known all of ten seconds seemed like such a desperate thing. A total loser move. Like something a girl who was seventeen and had never been kissed might do.

The whole thing was starting to make her nauseated.

At least it had already served its purpose. She wasn't thinking about . . . all those things she didn't want to think about.

Who knew what this David guy expected out of her? Gaia the undated. Gaia the untouched. Gaia the ultimate virgin.

Maybe knocking David down had spun his brain around backward. Left him with a concussion that led to his asking out the first girl he saw.

Or maybe it was a setup. Maybe Heather and some of the certified Popular Crowd (also known as The Association of People Who Really Hate Gaia Moore) had put this guy in her way just so they could pop up at her so-called date and pull a *Carrie*.

Gaia closed her eyes and moaned. "Stupid. Definitely stupid."

"Uh, you're Gaia Moore, right?"

Gaia looked up from her desk and found a tall blond girl standing in front of her. From the way people were up and moving around the room, class had to be over. Gaia had successfully managed to obsess away the entire period.

"Are you Gaia?"

"Uh, yeah." Gaia was surprised on two counts. The first was that the girl knew her name at all; the second was that she actually pronounced it right on the first try. "Yeah, that's right."

"I'm Cassie," said the girl. "Cassie Greenman."

How wonderful for you, thought Gaia. She had noticed the girl in class before. Although she hadn't seen her running with the core popular-people crowd, Gaia assumed that Cassie was in on the anti-Gaia coalition.

"Aren't you worried?" Cassie asked.

"What am I supposed to be worried about?" Gaia wondered if she had missed the announcement of a history exam or some similar nonevent. Or maybe this girl was talking about Gaia's upcoming date. Maybe Heather and pals really were planning some horrible heap of humiliation. Maybe they were all standing outside the door right now, ready to mock Gaia for thinking someone would actually ask her out.

Not that Gaia cared.

The girl rolled her eyes. "About being next."

"The next what?" Gaia asked.

"You know." Cassie raised a hand to her throat and drew one silver-blue-painted fingernail across the pale skin of her throat. "Being the next one killed."

Killed. That was a word that definitely drew Gaia's attention. She sat up straighter at her desk. "What do you mean, killed?"

"Killed. Like in dead."

"Killed by who?"

The blond girl shook her head. "By the Gentleman."

Gaia began to wonder if everyone had just gone nuts while she wasn't paying attention. "Why would a gentleman want to kill me?"

"Not *a* gentleman," said Cassie, "*the* Gentleman. You know—the serial killer." She didn't add "duh," but it was clear enough in her voice.

Now Gaia was definitely interested. "Tell me about it."

"Haven't you heard?" Cassie pulled her books a little closer to her chest. "Everyone's been talking about it all morning."

"They haven't been talking to me."

Cassie shrugged. "There's this guy killing girls. He killed two over in New Jersey and three more somewhere in . . . I don't know, maybe Connecticut."

"So?" said Gaia. "Why should I be worried about what happens in Connecticut?"

That drew another roll of the eyes from the blond girl. "Don't you ever listen to the news? Last night he killed a girl from NYU right over on the MacDougal side of the park."

Now Gaia wasn't just interested, she was offended. The park in question was Washington Square Park, and that was Gaia's territory. Her home court.

From the chessboards to the playground, all of

it was hers. She used it as a place to relax and as a place to hunt city vermin. Gaia had been in the park herself the night before, just hoping for muggers and dealers to give her trouble. The idea that someone had been killed just a block away. . . .

"How do they know it was the same guy?" she asked.

"Because of what he . . . does to them," her informant replied with an overdone shiver. "I don't know about you, but I'm dying my hair jet black till this guy is caught."

"Why?"

Cassie was starting to look a little exasperated. She pulled out a lock of her wavy hair and held it in front of her face. "Hello? Because all the victims had the same color hair, that's why. You need to be careful, too."

"I'm not that blond," said Gaia.

"Are you nuts? Your hair's even lighter than mine." The girl gave a little smile. "It's not too different, though. In fact, ever since you started here, people have been telling me how much we look alike. Like you could be my sister or something."

Gaia stared at the girl. Whoever had said she looked like Gaia needed to get their eyes checked. Cassie Greenman was patently pretty. Very pretty. There was no way Gaia looked anything like her.

"You're nothing like me."

Cassie frowned. "You don't think . . ."

"No."

"I think we would look a lot alike," insisted Cassie, "if you would . . . you know . . . like, clean up . . . and dress better. . . ." She shrugged. "You know."

All Gaia knew was that all the cleaning up and good clothes in the world wouldn't stop her from looking like an overmuscled freak. She wished she was beautiful like her mother had been, but she would settle for being pretty like Cassie. She would settle for being normal. "Thanks for giving me the heads up on this killer."

Cassie wrinkled her nose. "Isn't it creepy? Do you think he's still around here?"

"I wouldn't worry too much." Gaia stood up and grabbed for her books. "If he's still here, he won't be for long."

Not in my park, she thought. If the killer was still there, Gaia intended to find him and stop him.

Suddenly she felt pinpricks of excitement moving over her skin. For the first time all day she felt fully awake. Fully engaged. Fully there. She needed to make a plan. She needed to make sure that if this guy attacked anyone else in the park, it was Gaia.

As terrible as it was, in a weird sort of way the news about the serial killer actually made Gaia feel better. At least she had stopped thinking about her date.

"A SERIAL KILLER," ED SAID SLOWLY.

Dead Already

Words he never expected to say unless he was talking about some movie staring Morgan Freeman or Tommy Lee Jones.

Gaia nodded. "That's right."

"And you're excited about this?" Why was he not surprised?

"Not excited. It's more . . ." She tipped back her head and looked up at the bright blue sky, her breath visible for one split second each time she exhaled. "Yeah, well. Kind of."

Ed stopped talking as they moved around a line of people waiting for a hot dog vendor, then took up the conversation again once he was sure no one was close enough to hear. "Don't you think that's a little—"

"Crazy?" finished Gaia.

"That wasn't what I was going to say." Ed stopped in his tracks and looked up into her eyes, rubbing his gloved hands together. Early November in New York City. Almost time to put away the cotton gloves and whip out the leather. "But since you said it—yeah, it seems more than a little Looney Tunes."

Gaia was silent for a moment. She walked a few steps away and stood next to the fence that bordered the playground. Ed followed.

As usual, the equipment was overrun with bundled-up kids. Anytime between dawn and sunset the playground was packed with screaming children. A little thing like someone getting killed in the park wasn't enough to empty any New York jungle gym. They were too few and far between. The sound of laughter and shouting mixed together with traffic around the park until it was only another kind of white noise – the city version of waves and seagulls at the beach.

"This is important," Gaia said at last. "I have to get this guy."

Ed stared at her, trying to read the expression on her beautiful face. Usually that was easy enough. On an average day Gaia's emotions ran from mildly disturbed to insanely angry. But this expression was something new. Something Ed didn't know how to read. "Does this have something to do with Sam's kidnapping?" he asked. "Why exactly do you have to . . . get him?"

Why and you being the operative words.

Gaia pushed at her tangled hair to get it out of her face but only succeeded in tangling it further. "Because I do," she said, looking down at him. "And I don't think this has anything to do with Sam. This guy is killing blond girls, not college guys. But this also isn't just some loser snatching purses or some asshole junkie waving a knife to feed a crack habit. This is serious."

"Some of those assholes kill people," Ed pointed

out, tucking his hands under his arms. "Stopping them is important, too."

"Yeah, but not like this. This guy, this *Gentleman,* he's killing people because he wants to do it." She stared out at the kids on the swing sets, and Ed saw that her ever-changing eyes had turned a shade of blue that was almost electric. "This guy likes what he's doing."

Ed was chilled to the bone. He blamed it on the sudden, stiff breeze that picked up dead leaves and general city debris all around them. But he knew it was more about Gaia's words.

"What do you know about this guy?" he asked.

Gaia shrugged, hooking her bare fingers around the metal links of the fence. "Nothing, really. He kills blond girls. I'm not sure how many."

"Why is he called the Gentleman?" Ed asked.

"I don't know that, either. I don't really know anything about him . . . yet."

There was one particularly loud playground scream, and Gaia's eyes darted left, searching for possible trouble.

Ed ignored the kids and stared at Gaia's profile. Looking at her was something he always enjoyed, but this time he was looking with a purpose. He hadn't known Gaia for that long, but he had never seen her back away from anything she set out to do. From what he could read of the expression on her face, Gaia was determined to stop this killer. Ed could either get behind her or get out of the way.

"Maybe I could help you," he said.

Gaia shook her head. She didn't even look at him. "I don't want you getting hurt."

Ed tried hard not to be insulted. "Hey, we've been through this before. I'm not going to be out here playing Jackie Chan. That's your job. I just thought I could help you fill in the holes."

"Holes?"

"Holes." He tilted his head in an attempt to catch her eyes. "Like I did with Sam."

She blinked, and her grip on the fence tightened. There. She couldn't deny he'd been indispensable when Sam was kidnapped. He'd figured out where they were holding Sam—not that the information had played a role in rescuing him. But he'd helped Gaia get the key to Sam's room from Heather—not that they'd needed it. But he *had* caused a distraction so that Gaia could sneak into the dorm. Of course, if he hadn't been there, she probably wouldn't have needed a distraction in the first place, but—

"Ed—"

"Let me at least read up on the guy," Ed interrupted before she could shoot him down. "Maybe I can figure out what he's about. What he's got against girls with pigment-challenged hair."

Gaia turned away from the kids and knelt down

next to the chair. It was a move that usually made Ed angry—he didn't want people bending down beside him like he was a three-year-old—but anything that brought Gaia Moore's face closer to his own was an okay move in Ed's book.

"Okay," she said. "But you do research. *Only* research. I do the . . . other. Maybe together we can exterminate this guy."

We. Together. Ed liked the sound of that. It wasn't just Gaia going after a killer. It was Gaia and Ed. Batman and Robin. Partners.

"All right," he agreed. "I'll dig into the Net. Maybe stop by the library."

"Good," Gaia said. She smiled. In a strained way.

Forced or not, two smiles in one day from Gaia Moore had to be a record. Still, something about this whole thing had Ed moderately wiggy.

"Want me to call you tonight?" he asked.

"I'll call you," Gaia said. She started walking again, and Ed hurried to keep up. "If you can get some info in the next couple of hours, maybe I can bag this loser before he moves on to a different neighborhood."

She made a sound that might almost have been a laugh and ran the long fingers of her right hand through the heavy mass of her tangled hair. "Besides, I'm busy tomorrow night."

"What's tomorrow?" Ed asked.

"I've got a date." Gaia glanced over at Ed. For a split second she looked small, vulnerable. Like what he was about to say mattered. Unfortunately, Ed's heart was in his mouth, temporarily making speech impossible.

"A date," Ed replied finally. "Wow." Articulate, it was not, but he was pleased to hear that his voice sounded normal. He even managed to keep a smile on his face.

But if the serial killer came for him, Ed wouldn't have to be afraid. He felt dead already.

Girls I have liked:
Jenn Challener
Aimee Eastwood
Raina Korman
Ms. Reidy
Jennifer Love Hewitt (Okay, I was fourteen)
Storm, Rogue, Jubilee, Jean Grey
The lady behind the counter at Balducci's

Girls I have loved:
Heather Gannis
Gaia Moore

Girls who have ripped out my cardiovascular muscle and squashed it under their feet:
Heather Gannis
Gaia Moore

Anyone besides me sensing a pattern around here?

One glance
from afar
was all he
needed. But
he needed it
like he
needed
oxygen.

**the
gaia
flu**

THE PARK WAS JUST A SHORTCUT.

Give in to Insanity

The fastest way from point A to point B.

Besides, cutting through the park would take Sam past the chess tables. Not that he had time for a game, but it never hurt to see who was playing. He had to keep up on the competition. See who was new. Check out who was winning, who was losing. It wasn't like he was looking for anyone in particular. Nope. Not at all.

Except that he was.

Truth? Sam was sneaking through the park, looking for Gaia. Not to meet her, not to talk to her, just to *see* her. One glance from afar was all he needed. But he needed it like he needed oxygen.

Before Sam met Gaia, the park had seemed like the one safe place in his life. Sure, it was a hangout for muggers and junkies, scam artists, aging hippies, and gang members. If you wandered off the path on the wrong day or stayed too long on the wrong night, you could be beat up, maimed, or even killed. Every place had dangerous people, but Washington Square Park had more than its share.

Sam knew about that firsthand.

But none of that stopped him from loving the place. When he was hanging out in the park, he could relax. Nobody at the chess tables cared if he wore the right things, said the right things, or hung with the right people. Playing chess in the park was one situation where Sam could lean back and let his inner geek rise to the surface.

Gaia had ruined that.

From the first time they played, Sam had developed this weird kind of spastic tick. No matter who he was playing, every ten seconds Sam had to look up from the board to see if he might catch a glimpse of blond hair flying loose in the wind or a beautiful face centered around a scowl.

Sam had seen plenty of stories about obsessive-compulsive people. People who can't leave the house without locking the door ten times or who wash their hands a hundred times a day. He just hadn't expected to become one of those people. Glance at the chessboard, look around for Gaia. Move a piece. Check for Gaia. It was more than sick. It was pathetic.

What was worse was that he had no idea how he really felt about Gaia. Sam had good reasons to hate her—had once even told her he hated her—and the kidnapping should have only made him hate her more.

The kidnapping. Something Sam was trying so hard not to think about even though the questions kept flashing through his mind at warp speed.

Why me?

What did they want?

Did they get it?

Who were they?

Why did they let me go?

And, of course, what did Gaia have to do with the whole thing?

He'd been chasing Gaia when it happened. And he had the vague, possibly imagined memory of Gaia's named being mentioned by one of the kidnappers while he was semiconscious and half dead on a concrete floor. That was the thought that always gave him pause.

Kidnappers mentioning Gaia = kidnappers knowing Gaia = Gaia having something to do with the torture he was put through = Sam should hate Gaia.

But Sam was pretty sure that wasn't how he felt. If it was hate, it was a weird kind. Still, this obsession couldn't be love. It was more like an illness. The Gaia flu. Gaia-itis.

If she had anything to do with what happened to him, she must have been just as much a victim as he was. That had to be it.

Suddenly Sam found himself carefully scanning the park.

He was looking for her now—going out of his way and looking. This wasn't just the possibility of a random encounter anymore. And he was supposed to be on his way to meet his girlfriend.

Sam tucked his chin and kept walking. Eyes down. Hands in pockets. Too bad he didn't have side blinders like the horses that drew carriages through Central Park.

He needed a cure for this disease. Brain surgery. `Strong anti-Gaiotics`. At the very least, a good psychiatrist.

When he got to the chess tables, Sam found them almost deserted. Only a handful of regulars were playing, taking money from the usual mix of naive college students and overconfident businessmen who strolled through the park. A couple of would-be players were sitting across from empty seats, hoping for fresh victims.

No Gaia.

Sam felt `a swirling mixture of disappointment and relief`. It was kind of like the feeling he got when someone else took the last scoop of Ben & Jerry's. It was probably good for him to skip that ten zillion additional calories; it just didn't feel good at all.

Zolov was at his table, of course. He was in the middle of a game, so Sam didn't stop to talk. Not that talking would have bothered Zolov. Zolov might be a little crazy, but he knew how to concentrate on chess.

A middle-aged Pakistani looked at Sam with a hopeful expression. "You want a game, Sam?"

He shook his head. "Not today, Mr. Haq. Sorry."

"Oh, sit down and play," the part-time taxi driver, full-time chess hustler said. "It won't take long."

When Sam considered the way he'd been playing lately, that part was probably true. "Sorry, I really don't have time."

Since Sam had become Gaia infected, he had become Mr. Popularity at the chess tables. Everyone wanted to play him. He had lost money to people he used to put down in ten minutes.

Past the chess tables, Sam picked up the pace. Heather wasn't the kind of girl who took well to waiting.

Sam slipped through the not-so-miniature marble Arc de Triomphe at the center of the park and was almost out of the park. Then he saw her.

Gaia was thirty feet away, talking to a guy in a wheelchair. He recognized the guy. It was Ed Fargo, Heather's ex. But Sam didn't spend any time looking at Ed. That would be a waste of Gaia time.

Her hair was light and golden in the sunlight. Sam couldn't tell what Gaia was saying, but her face was incredibly animated. Even from where he was standing, Sam imagined he could see the deep, shifting blue of Gaia's eyes. A little gray in the center. Streaks that were almost turquoise. It was only imagination, but he had a very good imagination when it came to Gaia.

For just a moment another image of Gaia started to seep into Sam's mind. An image of Gaia in the dark, leaning over him, urgently whispering to him. Sam's heart froze in his chest.

The kidnapping.

He knew that couldn't be right. It was Heather who had come in at the last second to save Sam and give him the insulin he so desperately needed. Not Gaia. Still, there was something about the events that scratched at the insides of his skull.

The path Gaia was walking angled away from Sam. If he stood there for another ten seconds, she would be out of sight. To keep up with her, all he had to do was take ten fast steps. Another ten steps and he would catch her.

All he had to do was forget Heather, forget everything, and follow Gaia. All he had to do was give in to insanity.

Sam took the first step.

HEATHER LOOKED AGAIN AT THE

watch on her wrist. Time. Time and then some.

She stretched her neck, looking around for Sam. Heather wished he hadn't asked her to meet him at the entrance of the park. She didn't have to go inside, but even the sidewalk was still way too close.

Heather didn't like the park. She had been cut

there, almost killed by some maniac. Since then she had looked at the clumps of trees and clutter of equipment as hiding places for thieves, murderers, and worse. It didn't surprise Heather that some brainless girl had gotten herself killed there. She was only surprised that it didn't happen more often.

The park held monsters. She was sure of it.

Heather checked her watch again. Ten minutes late. If it had been anyone but Sam, she would have left. She was beginning to wonder if she had the place or time wrong when Sam suddenly stepped into view. Heather put on her best smile and raised her hand in a little wave.

Sam didn't respond. He was walking right toward Heather, but he didn't even seem to see her. There was a distant, distracted look on his face. His curly, ginger-colored hair seemed a little more mussed than usual. Even his normally crisp tweed jacket looked wrinkled. Heather didn't appreciate the change.

Sam had been ill, and of course, there was the whole kidnapping thing, but still. He needed to take better care of himself. After all, appearance was very important. Sam knew that.

Sam took two more steps, stopped, and looked into the park.

For a moment Heather worried that Sam might really be sick again. Or maybe he had been attacked. There was a confused, stunned expression on his face.

Maybe some lunatic in the park had hit him on the head. Maybe he was hurt.

Heather started walking toward him quickly. She was almost close enough to touch him when Sam moved again. But he didn't come toward Heather. He stepped off the path and into the grass.

Heather frowned. "Sam?"

Sam jumped. He whipped around and stared at Heather with wide eyes.

"Um. Uh." He stopped and cleared his throat. "Heather."

The way he said it made it seem like he was surprised to see her. Heather couldn't put her finger on it, but something about his expression irritated her. A slight blush tinted her cheeks. She crossed her arms over her chest.

"What's wrong, Sam? Are you okay?" She tried to sound concerned and earnest. It came out as defensive and accusatory. Luckily, Mr. Oblivious didn't seem to notice.

Sam nodded quickly. "Yeah, sure. I just . . ." His face suddenly flushed an incredible bright red. "I just got lost in thought."

Heather's eyebrows scrunched together. She tried to smile again, but it was more difficult this time. "Oookay," she said. "C'mon. Let's get out of here."

Lacing her fingers with Sam's, Heather started to lead him out of the park. He was coming out of the bizarre stupor—walking like a normal person instead of shuffling like he had moments before. In fact, within seconds he was practically pulling her arm out of its socket.

What was with him? He was acting like something had him spooked. Heather glanced back in the direction Sam had been looking when he'd stopped in place. For a fraction of a second, a moment so short it might have been imagination, Heather thought she saw someone stepping behind a group of trees—someone with pale blond hair.

Heather's blood went cold and hot at the same time. It had only been the barest glimpse, but she knew who that blond hair belonged to. Gaia Moore. And Sam didn't want Heather to see her.

"Sam? What's the rush?" Heather said, just to see if he would tell her the truth.

"Nothing," he said, still pulling.

Heather felt a familiar feeling of humiliation, mixed with anger and tinged with fear, slip through her veins. God, she hated Gaia. Heather hated Gaia more than she had ever hated anyone in her whole life. More than everyone she had ever hated in her life put together. Times ten.

Sam stopped pulling when they reached the far corner, but Heather kept her hand locked together with his as they strolled down the sidewalk. Sam was saying something to her, making suggestions about where they might go, what they might do. Heather gave vague, one-word answers to his questions without really hearing them. It was her turn to be distracted.

Since her first encounter with Gaia, Heather had been burned, humiliated, stabbed, hospitalized, ego bruised, deprived of her boyfriend on various occasions, and detained by the NYU security force.

None of that came close to the reason Heather hated Gaia. It was the way Sam acted around Gaia. Like he couldn't think or breathe. Like he'd never seen anything like her.

And then there was the fact that Gaia was beautiful. She was beautiful without even trying. And that brought Heather to the real heart of it. Not the beauty. Heather hated Gaia because she didn't seem to try, didn't seem to care what others thought of her. Gaia dressed like a refugee. She said whatever she wanted. She never even seemed to notice how guys turned around to watch her when she went by. Gaia acted like she didn't think she was pretty, but Heather knew better than that. Gaia had to know. She just didn't care.

It was driving Heather mad—in every sense of the word.

Sam suddenly stopped walking. His grip on Heather's hand tightened to painful intensity.

Heather came out of her daze and struggled against his tight grip. "Sam? Sam, what's wrong?"

"Nothing," he replied in a harsh whisper. He

stopped again and shook his head. "Nothing. Don't worry about it."

Heather stared at him. For a moment she had a terrible premonition that everything between them was over. Ice went down her spine, trickling slowly over every lump in her backbone. *He's going to tell me he's dumping me. Dumping me for Gaia Moore.*

But Sam wasn't even looking at Heather. She followed the direction of his gaze and saw a newspaper stand. Right away Heather spotted the thing that had captured Sam's attention.

Splashed across the front page of the *Post* was a color photo of a young blond girl. Under the picture was the caption KILLER TAKES 6TH VICTIM.

Heather untangled her fingers from Sam's and went in for a closer look. From a distance, the girl in the picture looked a lot like Gaia. A tabloid twin. This had to be the girl that the serial killer had murdered the night before, the one that everyone had been talking about at school.

It wasn't Gaia. Still, Heather felt a little thrill go through her. As sick as she knew the thought was, the idea of Gaia and murder just seemed so right.

ANOTHER BLOND BEAUTY DEAD

GENTLEMAN KILLER PLANTS BLOODY KNIFE IN HEART OF NYC

After a killing spree that has left victims scattered from Connecticut to New Jersey, the serial killer known only as the "Gentleman" has taken his act off Broadway—slicing up an NYU coed just a block from the school's campus.

Carolyn Mosley, 20, a freshman at NYU, was found dead this morning by maintenance workers at Washington Square Park, say city officials. The manner of death points to a connection with the string of killings committed by the infamous serial killer, the Gentleman, according to officials.

Police have been reluctant to share details of the killer's technique, but sources have confirmed that this Gentleman is no gentleman. Death in the Gentleman's victims has been brought about by numerous knife wounds, according to information released by New Jersey police. Victims have received multiple stab wounds and have suffered "extreme violence and extensive damage," according to reports on the previous victims.

"Their throats were cut so badly, they were nearly decapitated," said Stanley G. Norster, a detective who investigated the Gentleman's killings in Connecticut. "There's an incredible amount of anger in these killings. A rage."

Police have admitted to withholding some details of the Gentleman's actions in previous crimes. The FBI has been involved in this investigation for several weeks, and a psychological profile of the killer has been prepared, but this profile has not been made available to the public. Sources inside the coroner's office indicate that the bodies show evidence of torture. The killer apparently administered dozens of cuts and other injuries before the killing blow. The killer didn't stop with death. Other signs

Continued on page 12

NYU Student Killed in
Washington Square Park

NYU—A New York University student was found dead early this morning only two blocks from the university campus, according to police. Carolyn Mosley, 20, a freshman at NYU, died as a direct result of blunt trauma and numerous stab wounds, officials say.

The body was discovered in the southwestern part of Washington Square Park by maintenance workers responding to a report of a gas leak. No leak was found, but Ms. Moser's body was found at the location of the alleged leak. Police spokesmen refused comment when asked about the possibility that the gas leak was reported by someone involved in the murder.

Mosley was last seen leaving a restaurant on MacDougal Street around 11 P.M., according to officials. The student worked part-time at the restaurant and worked her regular shift there the evening of her death.

No suspects have been named; however, the condition of the body has led to speculation that the case may be related to a series of killings in Connecticut.

Police have scheduled a press conference for 3 P.M. to discuss the case. Case files from the possibly related murders in other states have been requested, according to police.

From: E.
To: L.

Last night's events confirm Delta presence.
High probability of encounter with primary subject and subsequent risk. Advise.

From: L.
To: E.

    Continue to monitor activity. Do not intercede at this time. Will personally visit site within twenty-four hours.

    I want to see what happens.

They had nothing
in common at
all—nothing

numbering

except a general **the**
similarity
of features **dead**
and the fact
that they were
all dead.

ONE AFTER ANOTHER, THE FACES

Pretty Girls

and names of the Gentleman's victims appeared on the computer monitor.

Debra Lemasters—more cute than beautiful, with her hair pulled back in a ponytail and wide blue eyes that stared out from a yearbook photo.

Amanda Loring—older, taller. Holding a track trophy aloft while teammates cheered.

Susan Creek—eyes more gray than blue, thinner than the rest. She looked so sad, it was almost as if she knew what was coming.

Clarissa Richardson—very pretty but looking awfully uncomfortable in a tight, off-the-shoulder formal gown and a paper crown that proclaimed her queen of the junior prom.

Paulina Dree—sitting on horseback, her father standing beside her, both smiling. She had a great smile.

And finally, poor Carolyn Mosley, posing in cap and gown, a high school diploma rolled in her hand. Valedictorian of her class. Her family's pride and joy.

The youngest of them was fifteen, the oldest, twenty. They were six young women from three different states. None of them had known one another. Most but not all were good students. Most but not all had participated in some sort of organized athletics. They shared no common hobbies. They didn't read the same books, or like the same music, or share the same dreams.

They had nothing in common at all—nothing except a general similarity of features and the fact that they were all dead. And blond hair.

Gaia's hair, thought Tom Moore. He scrolled through the pictures again.

If he looked closely, he could see a little of Gaia in each of the dead girls. It was far more than the hair. The dead girls weren't identical, but they shared a similar bone structure—wide eyes, strong cheekbones, high forehead. Pretty girls, all of them. Of course, Tom was sure that none of them was as pretty as Gaia. But then again, Tom might be more than a little prejudiced—he thought his daughter was the most beautiful young woman in the world.

Six dead girls who all looked a little like Gaia Moore.

"What have they done?" Tom whispered to the empty room. He leaned back from the monitor and stared into the shadows. "What have *we* done?"

IT NEVER GOT DARK IN THE CITY.

Not really dark the way it had in other places. Like Connecticut.

He strolled down the sidewalk, careful never to touch

Warm-up Exercises

70

anyone he passed. He didn't like to touch people. He didn't like to be touched.

The sun was already going down, but the sky overhead only shifted from blue to a kind of dingy yellow as the lights came on. It wasn't anything close to real darkness. After only three days in the city, he still thought the dirty, nearly starless sky seemed terribly odd.

He craved the darkness.

He moved off the sidewalk and headed down the curving path that led out under the trees. A handful of children were still indulging in a few last minutes of play, but there were parents on hand to watch and a policeman standing at the edge of the playground. A pair of street musicians were putting away their instruments and counting up handfuls of change and folded bills.

They were scared. All of them were scared of the coming night.

He could feel it, almost taste it. For a moment he had a desire to rush into the center of them, screaming and waving his arms, just so he could watch them scatter. He fought down that desire.

No matter how fun it might be to see them run, it wasn't his reason for being in the park. There was important work to be done—a higher purpose. Nothing could be allowed to get in the way of that purpose.

He walked on, passing two more policemen on his way to the chess tables. Like the playground, the boards were almost deserted. Two men still squinted at a game in the failing light. At another table an old man slowly packed away his chess pieces.

The old man looked up as he passed. "You wanting game?" he said. "I will play you."

"No, thanks, Gramps." The idea of playing this guy actually made him smile. The man was ridiculously ancient, with sun-spotted skin and flyaway tufts of white hair. Beating him at chess couldn't possibly be a challenge.

Killing him would be even easier.

It would be a mercy, really. Put the old fool out of his misery. Maybe he would do it. Not as a main course for the evening, but just as a warm-up exercise. Something to keep his fingers busy.

The old man shuffled away, and the moment passed. Pointless, anyway. It was no fun without a real struggle.

He moved away from the tables and down the tree-lined paths. Even in the middle of the park there was nothing that approached true darkness.

But under the trees and in the shaded places, it was dark enough for his purposes.

The form on
the ground
didn't even
look like a
girl. It **chalk**
barely
looked like
a person.

DEATH DIDN'T LEAVE MUCH OF A

permanent stain. Not on the park, at least.

Gaia reached out and caught a strip of the yellow tape in her hand. Crime Scene—Do Not Cross.

Stalking a Stalker

As if yellow tape created some magical force field that could keep everyone away. Gaia wondered if police tape had ever stopped anybody in the history of the world from jumping into the middle of a crime site. The temptation was just too much. Even when you weren't stalking a stalker.

Considering how everyone had been talking up the murder at school and in the papers, Gaia had expected to find the park swarming with cop types. She had thought there would be uniforms keeping back the crowds. Whole squadrons of trench-coat-wearing detectives combing the ground, examining every blade of grass for a clue like a flock of investigating sheep. There should have been technicians spreading fingerprint powder. Flashing lights. Enough doughnuts to soak up a swimming pool of coffee.

Instead there was only this dark patch of grass. If there had been detectives, they were long gone. There wasn't a single cop left to keep people from ignoring the warning on the flimsy yellow tape. No one had even left behind a doughnut.

Losers.

Still, Gaia had a hard time stepping over the line. It wasn't like she was afraid of getting caught. Gaia didn't do afraid.

Maybe it was some new desire to be a law-abiding citizen. She wasn't sure. But the idea of going across the tape, going to the place where the body had been, made Gaia feel weird. Like something way down inside her wasn't quite as solid as it should be. Squishy.

She stood there and took a few deep breaths of evening air before the squishiness started to fade. After all, there was nothing out there but grass.

Gaia ducked under the tape. Inside the magic line the ground was all dented and bumpy—like it had been walked on by a herd of elephants. Maybe there really had been hundreds of detecto-sheep here after all.

The grass in the field was soaked with dew. By the time she'd taken a dozen steps, Gaia's sneakers were soaked through and cold water was making little burping noises between her toes. A lovely way to start a long evening.

Almost dead center in the field she saw the rough outline of a body marked in white. Just like in the movies. Only this line wasn't made from tape. It was powdered, chalky stuff, like they use to mark the baselines at a ball game.

Somewhere in the back of Gaia's head, random associations started to fire.

`Strike three. You're out. Game over.`

When she considered where she was standing, this seemed more than a little sick. But Gaia had never claimed to be in complete control of what went on in her head.

She stood with the toes of her wet sneaks almost touching the crumbling chalk line. The form on the ground didn't even look like a girl. It barely looked like a person. It was just a rough outline with something like a hand pointing one way and two blocky leg things shooting off the other end.

Despite all the violence Gaia had seen in her life— `despite all the violence she had caused`—there was something about this scene that gave her pause. She wasn't scared; she just felt ill. Ill and numb and . . . responsible. And sad. Where there had been a girl with warmth and memories and a smile, there was now just chalk and dew. It was almost too much for her.

Gaia turned away, wanting to block out the images of premature dying, but her eyes were drawn back as if some unseen thing were pulling her.

Gaia was no big believer. `She didn't go in for ghosts, or voodoo,` or little leprechauns with colored marshmallow cereal. If people wanted to call themselves witches, that was cool with Gaia as long as they didn't expect her to believe in witchcraft. She might be an overmuscled, fear-deprived, jump-kicking freak girl, but Gaia didn't skim the tabloids for predictions or use a Ouija board to communicate with the dead. For all the weirdness in her life, she knew where to draw the line between what was real and what was not. Or at least, she thought she did.

But the area inside the police tape gave Gaia a bad feeling. Something worse than a mugging or robbery had happened there. And Gaia could still feel it.

She looked up from the line on the ground and did a quick check of the trees around her—just in case any werewolves or zombies were approaching. Then she laughed at herself.

Still, he could be out there. Right there.

There was that whole bad film noir/cheesy paper-back theory that criminals return to the scene of the crime.

It sounded like an idea dreamed up by a lazy detective or by some writer who didn't know where to go with the plot. Just sit on your ass, and the killer will come to you. In Gaia's book that was way too easy to be true.

There was no real reason to think the killer might come back to this place. None at all. Gaia had the whole park to patrol. She couldn't stand here all night, staring at an empty field. Glaring at the trees made about as much sense as her Sam obsession.

But when she looked again, something was out there. Right at the bottom of a bunch of little ash trees, stuck in a chunk of shadow was—something. Maybe someone.

The all-over sickness she had been feeling started to turn into the more familiar `let's-go-kick-some-ass buzz`. Gaia took a slow step toward the shape in the shadows. She squinted until her eyes watered. Was someone really there? She couldn't be sure. She took another step. It was so hard to see. The shape in the shadows could be a crouching person, or it could be a shrub or a trash can.

Then the shape moved.

HE WAS UP AND RUNNING BEFORE

she had a chance to blink. There was no reason to run, really. He could just kill her now.

`He wasn't afraid of her.`

No Killing Tonight

But he was in the mood for a challenge. He wanted to run. Run until it hurt. Until the air coming in and out of his lungs burned the delicate flesh of his throat.

He wanted her to feel the same thing.

And so he ran. There was no way she would catch up to him. Which meant no killing tonight. But that was okay.

He wanted to see what she could do.

GAIA'S LEGS WERE PUMPING EVEN

Gaia vs. Bad Guy

before her brain had finished realizing that it really was a person out there. Someone had been there in the shadows, watching her. Now the person was running. So was Gaia.

She made it out of the chewed-up field and jumped the police tape on the far side. For a moment she stood there, frustration tightening her throat. It was a terrible thing to be ready for a fight and not find anyone to punch.

Then she saw the shadow guy again. He was a hundred feet away, cutting across the grass by the side of the path. Gaia started after him.

Then something strange happened.

The average Gaia-versus-bad-guy race lasted all of five seconds. It wasn't that she was Ms. Olympic Runner, but the same thing that made Gaia strong also made her pretty damn fast in a sprint. Her father said it was part of being fearless. That little regulator that keeps people from pushing their muscles to the absolute limit was absent without leave in Gaia. She could push her legs a hundred percent. Maybe further. Gaia could even push her muscles so hard that she broke her own bones.

Disgusting but true.

There was a price to pay for beating herself up like that, but the upside was irresistible—before Gaia began to fade, most losers were on the pavement.

Not this guy. Shadow Man was fast. More than fast. A real speed demon.

Gaia and the shadow whipped along the path through the heart of the park, jumped a hedge, and skirted a gnarled old oak. Gaia didn't gain a step. She could never get close enough to see more than a hazy form in the distance. Several times she almost convinced herself that nothing was out there but shadows—no man at all. But she didn't stop.

By now Gaia was solidly in the zone. Nothing mattered in the world but catching the guy in the shadows. The chessboards came and went in a blur. The playground. The sprinklers. Then they were out of the park, powering north on Fifth Avenue.

In the back of her mind nagged the vague thought that she had no clear reason to pursue him except for the fact that he was running away from her. But the chase was on, and her instincts pushed her hard to catch him.

She zipped past knots of people and saw startled faces turning her way. A woman jumped back as Gaia thundered past. A guy dropped a bag of groceries, and apples went bouncing along the sidewalk.

Gaia didn't slow. They had been running now for a solid minute at a speed that would have been impressive for a ten-second sprint. Her chest heaved in and out as she tried to draw in all the air in New York.

Then she realized she was gaining on the shadow. Not much, but the gap was definitely closing.

Another hundred yards and she had gotten close enough to see that he was wearing some kind of long, floppy black coat. Not a trench coat, but something from a cowboy movie. A duster.

How could he run this fast in that thing?

Gaia followed as the duster flapped past the trendy crowd waiting outside Clementine's, past the glowing signs at Starbuck's, and on across fourteenth Street without even looking at the streams of passing traffic. Her heartbeat seemed to move up through her body with every step. One moment it was pounding against Gaia's ribs. The next it was beating in her throat. The next it was throbbing in her skull.

Shadow Man took a hard right onto a side street, then ducked down an alley. Gaia was right behind him. The gap between the two runners had closed to no more than fifty feet. Forty.

A mesh fence blocked one end of the alley. Gaia slowed a step, getting ready to fight, but the guy in the black coat didn't hesitate. He jumped up, landed one foot on a Dumpster, and sprang from there to the top of the fence. Two steps and he was over the ten-foot barrier. He hit the other side running.

"What?" Gaia gasped.

She might not get scared, but she was still quite capable of being amazed.

Gaia ran up to the fence, looped her hands in the mesh, and flung herself upward. She flipped head over heels and her feet came down on the top of the gate. A very slick move.

Then the top of the gate sagged, and she fell.

The pavement wasn't friendly to Gaia's knee. She hit with a force that sent jolts of fire running up her thigh and set off flares of white light in her head.

Gaia stayed there for the space of two breaths. Then she got on her feet and ran again.

Black Coat had widened his lead on Gaia to a good hundred feet, but she soon had it back to fifty. He cut right again, this time along University Place. Gaia followed.

The pair sprinted past a series of nightclubs. The door of each one spilled out different music, but Gaia went past them so fast, they blended like notes in some insane song. Disco high C. Jazz G. Bass blues.

Thirty feet.

Shadow Man was wearing running shoes. Gaia could see them now. The off-white soles flashed at her under the flapping hem of his long coat. She found something comforting about the shoes. At least it was nice to know he wasn't running so fast in penny loafers.

Twenty feet.

A policewoman shouted at Gaia as she dashed across Fourteenth Street and headed south. She didn't bother to stop. If the policewoman wanted Gaia, she had better start running.

Now Gaia realized the man had brought her right back to Washington Square Park, and they ran through shadows cast by huge oaks and ghost white birch.

Ten feet.

Gaia could almost reach out and touch the flapping coat. Almost. The air in her throat tasted like fire, and there were little sparks of white light dancing in her eyes. In another ten seconds this psycho was hers.

Then somebody screamed.

Gaia thought for a second it was her. She was hurting badly enough to scream.

Then the sound came again from somewhere off to her right.

Five feet.

All Gaia had to do was keep running and she could catch the black coat. But what if she caught him and he turned out to be innocent? Really fast, but innocent.

What if the Gentleman was killing someone else in the park right that second? Gaia tried to get her oxygen-starved brain to make a decision. Another scream.

"Oh, shit," she wheezed through her breathing.

Gaia turned right, leaving Black Coat to run on into the night, and dashed toward the commotion.

It didn't take her ten seconds to find who was doing the screaming. Standing under a pool of light was a young girl in blue jeans and a black sweater. Tugging on her purse strap was a potbellied, long-haired guy with a tangled brown-and-gray beard that went halfway down his chest. The girl had both hands clamped to her purse and her feet well planted. She was putting everything she had into it. The guy might outweigh her by a good fifty pounds, but she was giving him a fight.

"Let go!" the girl cried.

The guy laughed. "Come on, baby. I need it worse than you."

Gaia didn't think either one of them saw her coming. By then she was running at roughly the speed of a 747 pulling out of JFK. Gaia didn't slow a bit as she tucked in her head, lowered a shoulder, and smashed into Brown Beard.

The impact was enough to make Gaia fall to her bruised knee and send fresh neon bolts of pain ripping through her body. The bearded guy was knocked at least ten feet. He lay facedown on the grass with one hand stretched out over his head and the other trapped under his body. For just a second Gaia flashed back to the chalk outline on the ground. Hand up, legs spread.

She shook her aching head to clear away some of the fog and climbed to her feet. It seemed like a long way up.

"Y-You . . . ," Gaia started, then took a breath and tried again. "You okay?" she asked the girl.

The girl nodded. Gaia couldn't see her clearly, but she was very tall and very slim. Delicate looking. And she was definitely young. Way too young to be walking around the park alone at night. Of course, who was Gaia to talk?

"Who are you?" the girl asked.

"I—" Gaia couldn't think of a good answer. If she even had a name, she had misplaced it somewhere.

Somewhere back along the long minutes and longer miles of her run. Gaia turned around and staggered back the way she had come.

"Where are you going?" the girl called.

Gaia didn't bother to answer. There wasn't enough air to talk and run.

She put up her arms, drew in a deep breath, and started back to the spot where she had last seen the shadow man.

Gaia made maybe three whole steps before the ground jumped up and gave her a hard slap in the face.

You'd think that I wouldn't have a very vivid imagination. I'm a science geek, right? I play chess. It's all analytical. It's all about numbers, proofs, strategies.

Solid definitions.

There's no room for imagination.

But sometimes I don't even believe what my mind can come up with. There are things living in my head I'm sure any shrink worth his cheap spiral notepad would kill to delve into.

My imagination is especially vivid when it comes to Gaia Moore.

And not in the way you think. I'm not a total pervert. Although . . . Well, yes, the brain does travel in those circles, but I'm a guy. You have to forgive it.

I'm talking about the sick side of my mind. The dark side. The side a lot of people probably have but don't talk about. And

ever since this afternoon, that
side has been transmitting Gaia
pictures. Not pleasant Gaia pictures.

Pictures of Gaia dead. Pictures
of Gaia cut. Pictures of Gaia
bleeding and crying and gasping
and sputtering. They only last
for seconds at a time before I
drive them away. But in those
seconds they scare me to death.
They arrest every functioning
part of my body and take the
breath out of me.

Why?

Because they could become reality.

Ed stared at
the handset in
confusion.
"Who is this?"

the
connection

"Sam Moon,"
said the voice.
"I'm trying to
reach Ed."

ED HIT THE KEYS ON HIS COMPUTER

so hard, the whole desk started shaking. The words on the word processor screen glowed back at him.

Serial Killer Junkie

```
     LOSER. LOSER.
LOSER. BIG LOSER. ALL THOUGHT AND NO ACTION MAKES
ED ONE GIANT LOSER. LOSER. LOSER.
```

Somewhere, three screens' worth of LOSERs away, there was a letter that started with "Dear Gaia." It was a letter that explained everything. It was a letter that put into words all the things Ed wished he could have said that morning.

LOSER, Ed typed one last time, moving his fingers slowly across the keys and striking each one as if he meant to knock a letter from the keyboard.

```
     L. O. S. E. R.
```

He closed his eyes for a moment and rubbed at his temples. It turned out that losing, or at least not getting the woman you loved, caused a massive headache. Three aspirins had gone down his throat and Ed still felt like his skull was going to bust wide open. He almost wished it would.

With a sigh he moved the mouse up to the corner of his document and clicked the close button.

Save changes? the machine asked.

Ed clicked on the No button and watched as both his letter to Gaia and his three-page tribute to self-pity blinked into nothing.

He took in a deep breath, turned his back to the computer, and rolled over to the heap of books lying on his bed.

He had braved the snarling stone lions and endless wheelchair ramps at the main public library to come up with this stack. Six books, all of them about serial killers and murderers. Ed wondered if the librarians would add his name to some list they kept behind the counter. Serial killer junkies. Murder geeks. Or maybe Hannibal Lecter wanna-bes.

It was possible they even suspected that he was the Gentleman. But Ed doubted that. Sometimes being in a wheelchair was a weird kind of being invisible—no one ever looked at the wheelchair guy as a threat.

Ed grabbed the first book off the stack and flipped open the pages to the introduction. Staring back at him was a wild face framed by wilder hair. It was a woodcut picture of a killer from the Middle Ages—a man who had killed dozens of children near a small village in France. In the picture the man held a child in one hand. Not all of a child. Part of the body had already been eaten.

A quick flip of the page and Ed was facing newspaper sketches of a shadowy Jack the Ripper stalking the streets of Whitechapel in a cape and top hat. Across from the sketch was a diagram of a woman who had been dissected more completely than Ed's frog in freshman biology.

Another page and there was a black-and-white photo from the 1930s. This time the killer was a calm-looking man from Germany who had ground some of his neighbors into sausages. Flip.

He was looking into the fantastically mad eyes of Charles Manson.

On the next was the dumpy face of John Wayne Gacey.

Flip. Jeffrey Dahmer.

Flip. A middle-aged Russian guy with thick-framed glasses. Maybe he had killed fifty. Maybe it was a hundred. No one knew for sure.

Ed tried to read more of the text around the pictures, but he was having a hard time concentrating. And for an admittedly frivolous reason, when he considered the subject matter in front of him.

Gaia had a date. Ed's chance had been there. All he'd had to do was roll up to Gaia, open his mouth, and tell her how he felt. She had been right there. Right there.

Of course, she could have shot him down. Absolutely *would* have shot him down in flames. A girl like Gaia. Ed had to be crazy to think he could ever be more than friends with Gaia. He should be glad she even noticed him.

Ed looked down at his book and stared into the face of the Russian killer. A world that could put Ed in a wheelchair and have Gaia making a date exactly at the wrong moment seemed like just the kind of world that could produce a serial killer. They were probably as common as cockroaches.

The phone rang.

Ed stared at it with mixed emotions. It was a little early, but he had no doubt that it was Gaia on the other end. Usually, he called her, but since she was going to be out patrolling, and he was going to be fact-finding, she'd said she'd call him when she got in.

On most nights Ed looked forward to the late-night Gaia call. She was never exactly a blabbermouth, but compared to the way she was at school, Gaia was far more open on the phone. The phone calls were the only times when she really spilled her thoughts. Ed loved it. He just wasn't sure he could take it right now. Not after everything that had happened. He didn't think he could sit there and make happy noises while Gaia talked about her upcoming date. The thought made his blood curdle.

Who was this date-worthy guy, anyway? Where had he come from? And what gave him the right to ask out Perfection Personified?

The phone rang again. If Ed didn't answer, he wouldn't have to hear about the mystery guy. He wouldn't have to kick himself for being such a gutless wonder.

Of course, if he stopped answering, Gaia might never call again.

Ed scrambled for the phone.

"Hey," he said as he lifted the receiver, "I know why they call him the Gentleman."

"Is this Ed Fargo?" said a voice on the other end of the line. A guy's voice.

Ed stared at the handset in confusion. "Who is this?"

"Sam Moon," said the voice. "I'm trying to reach Ed."

Sam Moon.

Ed knew who Sam was. They had even spoken a time or two, but that certainly didn't make them friends. Back in the days when Ed had traveled sans wheelchair, Heather had been his girlfriend. Now she was Sam's.

"What do you want?" Ed's voice came out a little rougher than he had intended.

"It's about Gaia Moore," said Sam.

Wonderful. Did Sam have a date with her, too? Maybe she'd lined up the football team for the weekend. Open wound. Salt at the ready. "What about Gaia?"

"It's just that . . . well—"

Ed wasn't breathing. "Well, what?"

"You're her friend, right? I've seen you together."

"I'm her friend," Ed agreed. And that was probably all he was ever going to be. Once again tiredness and anger got the better of him. Still, it was nice that Sam had noticed. Maybe he was even j e a l o u s . "If you're looking for tips on asking her out, you better talk to someone else because—"

"I'm not calling about anything like that," Sam said quickly.

"Then what do you want?"

Sam took a deep breath.

"I want you to help me save Gaia's life."

"ARE YOU AWAKE?"

Quite Contrary

Gaia looked up. Or tried to look up. All she could see was dark and slightly less dark. Neither one of them seemed to form any shape that made sense.

"Don't worry," said a voice from the not so dark. A girl's voice. "I'm going to go call an ambulance."

95

"Uhh," Gaia grunted. She struggled to move her rigid jaw muscles. "Nuhhh."

No. Don't do that.

"Do you want me to stay with you?"

What Gaia wanted was for this disembodied voice to go away and leave her alone so that she could recover.

It was the most irritating thing—the real price of stressing her body in ways that no human being was built to take. For a few seconds, at most a few minutes, Gaia could push herself way past the limits of normal human strength and endurance, but when that time limit was up, Gaia's body went on strike. Her muscles stopped talking to her brain, and her body stopped moving. It would pass soon enough, but until it did, Gaia was absolutely helpless.

It was a feeling she didn't cherish.

"Look," said the voice. "I don't know what's wrong with you, but I don't think you're dying."

Great diagnosis, Doc.

"So I'm going to sit here with you and make sure you're okay." Gaia felt a warm body next to her arm. It didn't feel all bad, but she didn't want it there. "If you're not, I guess I better call an ambulance."

"Gooo way," Gaia managed to whisper. Gradually her muscles were waking up again, but she was still embarrassingly weak. She could probably get up; she just didn't want to try it in front of this girl.

Just how long had she chased the man in the black coat? Had they run two miles? Three miles? More than that? Every second of the run had been at a dead sprint. Add in a badly bruised knee and a shoulder that just might be dislocated, and Gaia felt like crap. Tired, abused crap.

Finally Gaia pushed her scraped hands onto the pavement and stood up shakily. She'd only been out for seconds, but it felt like an eternity to her.

"I think you really are going to live," said the girl.

Gaia licked her lips. "You sound surprised," she said in a harsh voice.

The girl shrugged. "Well, I've seen a lot of things, but I've never seen anybody kick ass one second and go into a coma the next. What are you on, anyway?"

Gaia started to laugh at the absurdity of the question, but it turned into a cough. A harsh, racking cough.

"You sure you don't want to go to the hospital?" the girl asked, reaching for Gaia's arm. "St. Vincent's is right down the street."

"No." Gaia shook her head. "I'll be all right. Really."

"Whatever you say," the girl said, eyeing her with disbelief.

Gaia turned her head and had to fight down a fresh wave of dizziness. "Where is he?"

"The guy who was after my purse?"

Gaia nodded.

"Don't know," said the girl. "He ran off. The way you hit him, I'd be surprised if he's not on his way to the nearest emergency room with a half-dozen cracked ribs."

All the systems in Gaia's body were coming back into action like a computer being booted up after a long sleep. Unfortunately, her nerves were waking up along with her muscles. There was pain everywhere.

Gaia thought she heard something behind her and turned quickly. Nothing was there, but the head rush that overtook her was so overpowering, she momentarily stumbled. The red-haired girl reached out for her.

"I've got . . . oof!" The slim girl stood in close and held Gaia with both arms. "Damn, girl. You're solid."

Solid. That was a nice way to say she weighed as much as a water buffalo.

"I'll be okay," she said. "Just go on. Let me sit here a little longer, and I'll be fine."

"Nope. If you're not going to let me take you to the hospital, you at least have to let me buy you a cup of coffee," the girl said. "Not that you need to add caffeine to whatever weird substance you've got running through your veins."

Gaia closed her eyes. "I don't think—"

The girl shook her head. "Come on. A double latte is the next best thing to surgery."

Gaia started to laugh, but it was still a bad idea. It made too many things hurt too much. Maybe sitting and sipping would be the best things for her right now. Besides, if Shadow Man came back, she couldn't be sure she could defend herself.

"All right," Gaia agreed. "Coffee."

HE WATCHED FROM THE BEST

Perfectly Pathetic

darkness he could find. Sweat poured down from his temples. His back. His underarms. His lungs felt like they'd been roasted over an open flame. Bent at the waist, holding his hands above his knees, he fought for breath. She was good. He had to give her that. But the scene in front of him made his pulse race faster than any sprint ever could.

She was also down. And she wasn't getting up. Couldn't, apparently. Not without help.

It was all he could do to keep from laughing through his gasps. How pathetic. How perfectly pathetic.

A skinny girl with tangly red hair was aiding the one. The target. The ultimate trophy.

His eyes narrowed into slits as his breath started to slow. He could take them both. Two for the price of one. He could practically smell them from here. The fear would smell even better. He licked his lips. He could almost taste it.

As the girls shuffled off, he straightened his back. There would be `no satisfaction` in taking her now. Not when she couldn't even walk on her own. The side dish wasn't enough to sweeten the deal.

He wanted a fight.

`He would have what he wanted.`

But there were too many cops around. Too many pissants. There would be no more girls in the park tonight.

Unless, of course, he dragged one there.

Once, when Gaia was a baby, she was playing in a sandbox in Central Park. It was a sunny day in early spring. I remember because Katia was picking buttercups and tickling Gaia's chin with them.

We turned our backs on Gaia for one moment. Just to clean up our picnic before retrieving her and heading for home.

Suddenly, out of nowhere, a crazed pit bull came charging at Gaia. She was two. Only two. Sweet. Small. Seemingly helpless.

Before I could blink, the pit bull was bearing down on Gaia and her playmate. With the attack instinct of an animal, my lovely daughter leaped at the wild dog and sank her baby teeth into the dog's hind leg.

That was when we knew we had a very special girl on our hands.

TOM MOORE

There was a
distinct
possibility **mary**
she could
like this
girl.

Sharing Stories

GAIA'S ARM WAS FLUNG AROUND THE red-haired girl's shoulders as they stumbled their way across the winding pathways. The muscles in Gaia's knee felt like they had been stomped flat, stripped raw, and rubbed in coarse salt.

They neared the entrance of the park and found a young policeman with an unlikely handlebar mustache standing guard over the end of the pathway. Gaia made an effort to stand up straighter, putting less of her weight on her smaller companion. The last thing she wanted was for the cop to think she was drunk or on some kind of drugs.

"What do you two think you're doing in there?" the policeman called as they approached.

"Just taking a walk," the red-haired girl said.

The cop gave a snort. "You picked a bad place for a walk. Didn't you hear what happened in the park last night?"

"They're only slicing up blonds," the girl replied. "It's in all the papers."

"I wouldn't be too sure about that." He paused and looked them over. "Besides, your . . . *friend* is about as blond as they come."

There was something about the way he said *friend* that caught Gaia's ear. Maybe it was because she was so tired, but it took her a moment to put the idea together.

103

Two girls. Walking alone. Arms around each other.

This guy thought they were lesbians.

Gaia leaned harder on her companion and smiled. Might as well give him a show. His already ruddy face darkened, and there was a spark of interest in his eyes.

Men. So predictable. He quickly glanced away.

"We're leaving the park now," Gaia said. "So we'll be okay."

When the policeman looked at them again, he seemed a little irritated. "Be careful," he said. "If you have to come back this way, go around the outside of the park."

"Sure," said the girl. "Thanks for the profound advice."

They moved away and turned down Sullivan Street toward a row of cafes. Tired as she was, Gaia watched the stream of people moving in and out of the buildings with interest. Living in the city that never slept certainly had its high points. Getting coffee and doughnuts at any hour of the day or night was civilization at its peak.

Now that there were other people around, Gaia thought again about her weakness. She pulled her arm away from the red-haired girl's shoulders. "I can make it on my own now."

"You sure?" The girl kept her arm at Gaia's waist for a few steps, as if measuring her steadiness, then let her go. "For someone who was unconscious five minutes ago, you've made a miraculous recovery."

"I heal fast," said Gaia.

"Let's hope so." The girl stopped by a narrow building with a red door and a long list of coffees displayed in the window. "Come on—I'm buying."

Inside, the place showed signs of being in the middle of a theme change. There was a blackboard over the counter that read Coffee Cannes and a big-screen TV stood in a corner playing some film with subtitles, but the framed movie posters had all been taken down and stacked in a corner. In the front half of the shop the tables had been removed along both walls, and even though it was after eleven at night, workmen were busily installing computers and workstations in their place.

The red-haired girl found a table as far from the chaos as possible—which wasn't very far—and dropped her slim body into a cane-bottomed chair.

"I'm going to stop coming to this place when they're finished with the remodeling," she said. "It was cool to get my coffee with a Bergman flick. Caffeine and data is not my mix."

Gaia carefully bent her swollen, tender knee and eased herself into a chair across from the girl. "You don't have to buy," she said. "I've got cash."

"Save it." The girl slid her purse from her shoulder and dropped it in the center of the table. "If it weren't for you, I wouldn't have any money to pay for this, anyway. The least I can do is buy you a cup."

Gaia looked up at the board above the counter. Coffee and milk appeared in every possible combination. "Coffee," she said. "Just coffee. Nothing fancy."

The red-haired girl grinned. "I know exactly what you need." She twisted in her seat and shouted to the man behind the counter. "Hey, Bill, bring two cups over here. And none of that weak-assed Colombian. Bring the *stuff*."

The man behind the counter gave a tired nod and turned to a row of gleaming steel machines. A few moments later he dropped two huge mugs on the table, then turned without a word and went back to his post.

The coffee in the mugs produced tall plumes of steam, but that didn't stop the red-haired girl from lifting her mug and taking a long gulp. She shivered as she lowered her coffee. "Ahhh, as long as there's coffee, life goes on."

Gaia took a tentative sip. It was strong, bitter, and blazingly hot. It also seemed to carry a caffeine kick that rivaled espresso. Gaia could almost feel the coffee circulating in her veins. Perfect.

The girl reached a small hand across the table. "I'm Mary," she said.

Gaia took the hand. "Gaia."

"Gaia." The girl squeezed her fingers for a moment before releasing them. "Cool. Like the goddess."

Gaia blinked. Was it just her, or were people around here getting smarter? "Hardly a goddess."

"Well, you were certainly a powerful force of nature tonight," said Mary. She lifted her cup and took another slug of hot coffee, then she planted her elbows on the table and looked at Gaia. "Wait a minute—I know you."

Gaia's shoulders tensed.

"You do?"

Mary nodded. "I saw you at a party. You were there with Ed Fargo." She stopped and grinned. "Heather Gannis went nuclear on your ass."

Gaia rolled her eyes. It figured. "Yeah, that was me."

"Cool," said Mary. "So, you know Ed?"

Gaia nodded. She suddenly felt even more self-conscious. Ed was one of the few people who had seen her in the middle of a postfight collapse. Pretty soon the two of them would be sharing stories.

"Uh," Gaia mumbled. "Can I ask a favor?"

"You don't have to ask," said Mary. She made a dramatic sweep of her hand. "As an ass-kicking goddess, anything you want is yours."

"Cool. I mean, okay." She took a breath. "Could you please not talk about what happened tonight?"

"Not even with Ed?"

"Especially not with Ed," said Gaia.

Mary looked disappointed. "Well, all right." A mischievous smile crossed her face. "It would make a hell of a good story, though. The way you hit that guy, I thought—" She shook her head. "I don't know what I thought."

Gaia took another careful sip of the hot brew and studied the girl across the table. She was tall, at least as tall as Gaia, ridiculously thin. But her features weren't "elegant." Mary had a short, narrow nose set above full lips. Her eyes seemed almost too large for her head and were colored an intense green, with hardly any traces or flecks of other colors. Her skin was pale and freckled, yet there was something exotic about the angle of her big eyes. But the feature that really caught the attention was the hair. Surrounding Mary's face and tumbling down her back was a tangled mass of curls, curls, and more curls. She kept pushing them out of her face, and they would bounce right back.

She was oddly beautiful.

"Where did you come from, anyway?" Mary asked. "What were you doing in the park?"

Chasing a supersonic serial killer.

"I was just out for a run," Gaia lied. "I heard you yell and thought maybe I could help."

Mary nodded, a smile on her lips. "You definitely helped. You probably saved my life."

"I didn't save your life."

"How do you know?"

Gaia shook her head. "That guy you were fighting was just an ancient hippie. He probably wanted some money for drugs."

"That guy was an ancient hippie with a *gun*," Mary said.

"Gun?" Gaia frowned and tried to think back. "I didn't see any gun."

"It was there," said Mary. "He had it in one hand and pulled on my purse with the other. I thought he was going to kill me."

"Why didn't you let go of the purse?" asked Gaia. She hated the question as soon as it was out of her mouth. People were always saying that. Sit still. Don't fight. Give the bad man your purse like a good victim.

"No one gets my purse," said Mary. "All my shit's in there." She stopped for a second, then lowered her voice. "Actually, I guess there's nothing in there that's worth dying for, but I was just pissed off. I hate not being able to walk across the park without someone bothering me."

Now that was a sentiment Gaia could fully agree with. "You really think that guy had broken ribs?"

Mary grinned broadly. "I sure hope so."

Gaia half smiled. There was a distinct possibility she could like this girl.

But she wasn't making any promises.

THE BLACK MERCEDES PULLED UP

behind a long line of police cars, the early morning sunlight glinting against their windshields. A few of the officers standing by gave it a glance, but no one moved to order the car away. Slowly the rear window rolled down.

Pile of Cattle

Loki looked out. It was ridiculous. Absolutely ridiculous. There had to be at least fifty policemen in the park. They were everywhere, from uniforms standing guard by the gate to technicians literally up in the trees.

Loki couldn't stop himself from laughing. It was all so silly. If there ever had been any clues in this place, this herd of cattle had destroyed them. Not that he expected the police to catch the killer. Not this killer.

Loki raised his window and pushed open the door. "I'm going to go over and take a closer look."

"Do you want me to come with you?" asked the woman in the front seat.

"No. Wait here. This shouldn't take long."

"Yes, sir," said the woman.

Loki climbed out and started toward the park.

A tall, African American officer blocked his way. "I'm sorry, sir. No one is admitted to the park this morning."

"Official business." Loki reached into the pocket of his overcoat and pulled out a badge case. He flipped open the case and held an FBI identification card up for the policeman to see. It was a fake, of course, but it was a very good fake. It came from the same machines that produced badges for actual FBI agents.

The officer looked from the card to Loki and back again. "Maybe I should get my lieutenant," he said uncertainly.

"There's no reason to do that," said Loki. "Just move out of my way."

The policeman stepped aside.

Loki moved on up the path. The day had started out overcast, and low clouds still blocked the rising sun, but as he approached the actual crime scene, Loki put on a pair of dark sunglasses. There were still a few men left in the NYPD who had once worked with him as a young government agent. It was many years in the past, and even that identity had been false, but in case any of those men happened to be on the murder investigation team, Loki didn't want to be part of an uncomfortable reunion.

The crime scene was in a grassy field near the corner of the park. A pleasant enough place, with benches, trees, and gray squirrels that dodged around the policemen's feet. Pleasant, but utterly boring.

Loki ignored several other policemen who tried to talk to him and walked straight to where the body lay crumpled on the ground. It was a young girl, as expected, with long blond hair splayed out in a fan around her head. There was blood matted into the hair. More blood on the ground.

"Can I help you?"

Loki looked around and saw a plainclothes officer. From the man's cheap coat and old-fashioned hat, he had to be a homicide detective.

"I'm Frank Lancino, Connecticut state police," Loki said. He reached into his coat and produced another identification card. Just as fake. Just as good. "I've been called in to consult on this one."

The detective nodded. "I heard they were talking to your guys." He jerked his head toward the body. "What do you think? Same asshole you had up your way?"

Loki knelt next to the body. The girl had been killed with a knife, but not with a single wound. There were cuts on the arms. Cuts on the legs. Puncture wounds that went all the way through the body and a long slice that cut halfway around her neck. "Yes," he said. "Yes, this certainly looks like the work of our boy."

The detective sighed. He jammed his hands into his tweed overcoat. "What are we going to do about this? Any ideas?"

Loki straightened. "First you need to talk to your

technicians." He pointed at the ground. "If they can't do a better job outlining a body than that, who knows what else they missed."

"That outline's not from this body."

"It's not?" Loki looked at the detective curiously.

"That's from the previous victim," said the detective. "It looks like the killer did this one on the same spot as the one from the night before."

Loki had to fight back a smile. It was a nice touch. A very nice touch. He squinted at the trees around them. What were the odds that the subject of this investigation was out there right now, watching them? Loki thought it was very likely. Every artist wants to see the reaction to his work.

"Can I ask you some questions about the cases you've seen?" asked the detective.

"Later," said Loki. "I need to get to the station house. I'm sure I'll see you there."

Loki quickly retraced his steps and retreated to the car. The woman hustled around to open his door for him, then jumped back behind the wheel to steer the big sedan away from the curb.

"It's going to be interesting," said Loki.

The woman's green eyes were reflected as she glanced at him in the rearview mirror. "When do you think they'll meet?"

"Soon." He glanced out the window at the passing scenery. Rushing pedestrians. Colorful awnings. A man hosing down the sidewalk. It was another world. "Even now they could be moving toward a meeting."

"And when they meet?"

Loki gave a quiet laugh. "It will be one unbelievable fight."

"What if she dies?" the woman asked, her voice tight.

"Well, then, she's failed," Loki said. If she couldn't handle this, she was of no use to him, anyway.

"She has more training," the woman said. "You've seen how she can fight."

"Yes," Loki agreed. "But he has another advantage. He knows what he is. He knows what he's capable of."

"What is he capable of?" asked the woman.

"Anything."

GAIA WOKE UP, THEN WISHED SHE
hadn't.

She rolled over and sat up in the bed with a groan. Even before she peeled back the covers, she had a good idea of what she was going to find, and the real thing didn't disappoint.

Dress for Distress

Her right leg was bruised from thigh to ankle. Her knee was one big scab, and every color of the bruised-and-abused rainbow decorated her leg—all the way from battered purple-blue to super-sickening yellow-green.

There was still a lingering whole-body soreness from her adventures the night before, but it wasn't as bad as she had predicted. Gaia was relieved to find that despite how awful her leg might look, it wasn't too stiff. She could walk without a problem, but it was going to be a while before she was up for another run like last night's.

She grabbed a pair of scuffed jeans from the back of a chair and carefully worked them up her injured leg. Then she pulled a hooded sweatshirt out of the closet and slipped it on. One glance in the mirror told the story. Gaia Moore, girl geek.

Why should today be any different from every other day?

She started toward the bedroom door, then had a startling thought. Today was different from every other day. Today she had a date.

Gaia groaned, limped back to the mirror, and took a longer look. She wasn't encouraged by what she saw.

Would there be time to change after school? Maybe. But what if David saw her in school? If he saw her like this, he would want to cancel.

Which would probably be a good thing. She

shouldn't have said she'd go out with him in the first place.

But that thought hadn't even made it across her brain before another one chased it.

What was wrong with going out with a guy? Couldn't she just allow herself to be normal for five seconds?

Gaia shook her head. It was too early in the morning to start arguing with herself. It was *always* too early to argue with herself. She half expected a little devil and angel to pop up on her arms and start debating.

"I'm going," she said aloud. "I'm going, and that's it."

"If you're talking about school," said a voice in the doorway, "then it's about time."

Gaia spun around and saw Ella standing in the doorway. As usual, Ella looked like she was dressed for an evening at the clubs. Even at eight in the morning the *über*-bitch looked ready for dancing. Or an affair. Probably whichever option presented itself first.

This morning her ensemble was a short, glossy leather skirt topped off by a green blouse with a neckline that showed the top of her breasts. Her scarlet hair was swept back from her face, worked into an elaborate coif that Gaia couldn't have reproduced given an entire week.

"Ever heard of knocking?" Gaia asked.

Ella arched one perfectly plucked eyebrow. "Not in my own house, I haven't." She waved a lacquered nail at Gaia. "What are you doing up here talking to yourself? School starts in ten minutes."

"Then I'm not late yet."

Ella gave a sigh that held all the exasperation in the world. "Just don't expect me to give you a ride. I have a business appointment this morning."

Gaia nodded. "Getting started a little early today, aren't we?"

The comment brought a frown to Ella's cherry red lips. "And what is that supposed to mean?"

"Nothing," said Gaia. "It's only that I noticed that you had a . . . business appointment last night, too. One that kept you out pretty late. Seems like you've had one every night since George went out of town."

Now Ella's lips pressed together so hard that Gaia was sure she'd have to reapply her lipstick. "Careful, Gaia." For a moment Ella looked almost dangerous. "George has done a lot for you. Your father meant the world to him. It would be ungrateful to insult his wife."

Gaia was about to make a reply to that when she noticed something odd about Ella's choice of words. "'Meant'?"

"Pardon?" Ella replied.

Gaia took a step toward her. "You said my father

meant something to George." Did Ella know something about him? Had something happened?

"Did I?" The sarcasm in Ella's voice was so acid, `it could have eaten through steel.`

Gaia was amazed to find that her throat was getting tight. She had trouble speaking. "Yes, you did." She was angry at herself. She'd shown Ella too much vulnerability.

Ella gave a sly smile that would do any cat proud. "Just a slip of the tongue, I'm sure." She turned away. A few seconds later, Gaia could hear the tapping of Ella's pointed heels down the stairway.

For several long moments after that, Gaia could only stand there, trying to catch her breath and get her thoughts under control. Her father had left her. He didn't care anything about her, so why should she care about him? Still, the tightness in her throat didn't want to leave.

"He's not dead," she told herself.

Ella was just trying to screw with her. That was all. `Superbitch` in action.

Gaia looked again at the girl in the mirror. Now she saw not only a beast with tree trunk legs and lumberjack shoulders, with tangled hair, dressed in tasteless clothes. Now the beast had bloodshot eyes, too.

There wasn't much Gaia could do about the legs or shoulders, at least not in ten minutes, but she could try to do something about the clothes. She stripped off

the worn jeans as fast as she could without descab-
bing her knee and tossed them on the bed. The
sweatshirt followed. Then she confronted the dreaded
closet.

The trouble with Gaia's wardrobe was that nothing
inside the closet looked much better than the things
she'd been wearing. Gaia had a pair of capri pants, but
they did nothing but accentuate her she-hulk hips
and legs. There were a few dresses wrapped up in dry-
cleaner plastic. Gaia hadn't worn them in years.

Besides, any sort of skirt was out. Unless she wore
it with jet black hose, the Technicolor glory
of Gaia's bruised leg was bound to show. Even with
black tights there was the possibility of blood and
ooze and . . . nope. No skirt.

Gaia finally settled on a pair of drab olive draw-
string pants. They weren't too attractive, but at least
they were clean—and they hid her legs. Gaia fumbled
through crumpled sweaters and sweatshirts before settling on a slightly less baggy black sweater.

She studied the results in the mirror. Lumberjack
shoulders. Tree trunk legs. Tangled hair.

Unless the grunge look came back before first period, Gaia was as fashion-free as ever.

But serial killers were different. They weren't run-of-the-mill **genuine** killers **monsters** who happened to get away with it more than once.

ED HAD DONE STUPIDER THINGS

Odd Couple

in his life—most of them on a skateboard, surfboard, or other so-called extreme-sport implement, but this was high on his list of "I can't believe I'm doing this" moments.

He was skipping first period—cutting school—to see a guy who had stolen his old girlfriend. Worse than that, he was cooperating with a guy who obviously loved Gaia. Ed wasn't an idiot. Sam could spout that "oh I only want to help her" bullshit all day and into the next, but the truth was that Sam was seriously into Gaia. Worst of all, Ed knew that Gaia was seriously into Sam. The whole situation tied his intestines in knots. Big ones.

The assigned meeting place for their little get-together was the chess tables in the park—neutral ground. But the police still had the park closed off, so that spot was out. Instead Ed was patrolling the sidewalk along the north border, hoping to intercept Sam. And if he missed him, that was just too bad.

"Ed?"

Ed turned and saw Sam walking toward him. "What's wrong? Don't they have clocks in college? I was about to give up on you."

Instead of answering the question, Sam hooked his

thumb toward the park. "What's going on? Why the big crowd this morning?"

"Haven't you heard?" Ed asked, glancing at the organized mayhem. "The Gentleman made another call last night."

Sam's eyes flicked toward the trees at the edge of the park, and the tan went out of his square-jawed face. "You don't think . . . I mean, it couldn't have been . . ."

Ed seriously considered letting him stew for a moment, but his conscience got the better of him. "It wasn't Gaia."

"You're sure?"

"Yep," Ed said with a nod. "The TV guys say this one happened before eleven last night. I talked to Gaia after that."

Sam still looked concerned, but the concern was tainted by obvious envy. Score one for the Ed-man.

"Was she okay?" Sam asked.

"She was fine." Actually, the conversation had been disappointingly short. Gaia had said she was tired, and she hadn't wanted to talk about the murders. But Ed liked the idea that he knew more about Gaia than Sam did. Sam might be on Gaia's short list for sex, but Ed was the one Gaia talked to every night.

Sam fiddled with the collar of his oxford shirt. "Are the police any closer to catching this guy?"

Ed shrugged. "If they have any suspects, the papers aren't mentioning it. Except the *Post*—I think they've pinned it on Elvis, or aliens, or a coalition of brunettes jealous of all that fun blonds are supposed to have."

Sam only nodded. "I'm worried about Gaia."

That was the heart of the matter. That was what had convinced Ed to cut school and meet with a guy who he barely knew—but who he hated on general principle.

Sam was afraid because of how closely Gaia resembled the first girl killed in the park. For Sam it was about protecting a girl he feared was in danger.

For Ed it was a different story. Ed knew the big secret, and from the way Sam talked, he was pretty sure that Sam didn't. Sam apparently loved Gaia, but he didn't know that Gaia was Wonder Girl. He didn't know she could slice and dice Bruce Lee without breaking a sweat.

Ed was proud to be in on it. But it gave him more reason to be scared for her. Gaia wasn't just the killer's ideal victim; she was actively seeking the killer's attention. She was all set to find this demon, shove his teeth down his throat and his arms up his nether regions, then put in a call to the police. Case over. City saved.

It had seemed like a good idea. There wasn't much Gaia couldn't handle.

But Ed was no longer so sure. Between the phone call from Sam and his stack of serial killer bios, Ed worried that maybe Gaia was in over her head. Sure, she could land a roundhouse kick with the best of them. He had seen her take out three thugs in one go. But serial killers were different. They weren't run-of-the-mill killers who happened to get away with it more than once. These guys were strange, creepy. They were genuine monsters.

Ed was pretty sure that Gaia wasn't experienced in taking on monsters. When it came to these guys, she needed just as much help as the next person. Problem was, Gaia would never recognize the fact that she might need help—let alone admit it.

"What have you found out?" asked Sam.

Ed nodded toward a bench along the perimeter of the park. "Let's go over there where you can sit down," he said. "I'm tired of looking up at you."

Sam followed instructions. He went to the bench, sat, and waited for the Ed report.

"You know the basics, right?" Ed asked.

"Six victims," Sam started, then he turned his head and looked over his shoulder. "Seven now, I guess. Connecticut, New Jersey, and here. All of them stabbed, all of them blond, all of them around Gaia's age and size." He stopped and ran one hand through his ginger-colored hair. "That's about all I know. I don't even know why they call him the Gentleman."

"I do," said Ed. "It's from an old movie, *Gentlemen Prefer Blondes*."

Sam nodded slowly. "I've seen it. Marilyn Monroe, right?"

"Bingo."

Sam looked down at the ground and shook his head. "That's not much help. How are we going to catch this guy before he has a chance at Gaia?"

"We're not," Ed replied.

Sam's head jerked up sharply. "What do you mean?"

Ed rolled slowly back and forth in front of the bench. Wheelchair pacing. "You're the college guy. Isn't it obvious that if three states' worth of cops can't catch this guy, we're not going to do it?"

Sam's frown grew deeper. "Then why are we even talking?"

"Because," said Ed. "We don't have to find the killer." He raised one hand and pointed in the direction of the school. "We only have to stick to Gaia."

GAIA WAS THIRTY MINUTES LATE

Empty Chairs

to first period. Even compared to some of her previous arrival times, it was a new achievement in nonpunctuality. Even so, her teacher decided to ignore her.

Gaia had barely started at this school, and already she had been the butt of so many jokes, people were getting tired of it.

It was a good plan. Give them so much to laugh about that it `wears them out`. Too bad she hadn't actually *planned* to do it.

Gaia settled into her seat and the public address speakers crackled to life.

"May I have your attention, please?" said the voice of an unseen school office worker. "This is a school-wide announcement."

The last event deemed worthy of a schoolwide announcement had turned out to be a pep rally. `Earth-shattering stuff.`

"Due to recent events, the school will be closing early today. The last period will end at one P.M. Additional counselors will be on hand in the lunchroom for any students who feel they would benefit from a counseling session. School hours will return to normal tomorrow. Thank you." The voice ended with another squirt of static.

The announcement of an early end to the school day drew a few muted cheers but didn't get nearly the reaction that Gaia had expected. She leaned toward a skinny, red-haired guy at a nearby desk.

"What events are they talking about?" she asked. "Why let us out early?"

The redhead nodded his pointy chin toward a desk at the front of the room. `An empty desk.`

Gaia stared at the desk, trying to remember whose body normally filled it. It wasn't Hateful Heather. Heather was in her usual place of power at the center of the room. It wasn't Ed. Ed wasn't in this class. Gaia frowned as she tried to remember. It was . . . It was . . .

Cassie Greenman. The girl who had told Gaia about the killing the day before. The girl who had said they looked alike.

Gaia turned to the red-haired guy again. "What happened to Cassie?"

Redhead moved his lips to form a single word. Gaia didn't have to be much of a lip-reader to make it out. Gentleman.

The headache that had only threatened in Gaia's bedroom suddenly came on with full force. "Where?" she asked.

The guy looked toward the teacher and tried to avoid Gaia's attention.

"Where?" she said again, more than a little louder. "Where did it happen?"

"In the park at eleven o'clock," the redhead shot back. He picked up his book and opened it, angling the pages so they formed a screen to ward off Gaia.

It didn't matter. Gaia had asked all the questions that mattered. She closed her eyes and tried to fight back waves of nausea and confusion. It was too coincidental, too weird. Cassie knew about the murderer. Why in the world would she be any-where near the park at eleven o'clock at night?

How could Gaia have failed a second time? It almost felt like this killer was taunting her. Once again he had struck right under her nose. And this time it had been someone Gaia knew.

Gaia had thought she could catch this guy before he did any more damage. She had maybe hoped there was something good in being fearless. Maybe even something good in being a muscle-bound freak. Something that made her life worthwhile.

Obviously she was wrong.

I make friends pretty easily.
I'm fun. I'm loud. I know how to
have a good time.

People are drawn to me.

But I'm not always drawn to
them.

But this Gaia person? I genuinely like her. She intrigues
me. That's why I gave her my number and told her to call if she
ever felt like hanging out.

It's obvious she never will,
but it's a gesture. And when you
make a gesture, sometimes people
feel they owe you something. And
when people feel they owe you
something . . . Well, that can
come in handy from time to time.

The sooner
the informa-
tion reached
Sam, the **simple**
better the
chance of **job**
saving Gaia.

a

Murphy's Law

TOM MOORE TUGGED DOWN ON his brown cap and did his best to shade his face. He had no reason to suspect that anyone would recognize him on the campus of NYU, especially dressed as he was in the brown uniform of a package delivery-man, but it didn't pay to take chances.

Years of experience had taught Tom that Murphy's Law was always in full operation when you were undercover. If anything could go wrong, it would. Even when nothing could go wrong, it went wrong, anyway.

Today's expedition into the city seemed like a simple thing—drop off a package, run, and hope that the person getting the package knew what to do with the information it contained. That only made Tom more cautious. It was the simple jobs that turned into nightmares.

He felt a little odd, walking between the square buildings along Washington Place. Part of it was the feeling that any older person gets visiting a college or high school. An out-of-place feeling. Only Tom didn't need to be surrounded by kids to feel out of place. He was out of place just being alive.

He reached the gray concrete steps of the dorm and hurried inside. Put on the right uniform, and you can get anywhere. Show a little paperwork, and people will even point out the right door.

Three minutes later, Tom had walked through a disheveled common room and was rapping his knuckles against a dented oak panel marked B4. He'd hand the boy the box and go.

A feeling of guilt added to Tom's uneasiness. This boy's relationship to Gaia had already led him into serious trouble. Involving him further might well get the boy killed.

Tom shoved away the guilt. He had to do what he could to protect Gaia. It would be impossible to get the information directly to her—Gaia was under almost constant observation. If Tom tried to get close, he would only get himself killed. And more to the point, Gaia as well.

There was no response to his knock. He tried again, rapping a little harder this time.

"Package," he called through the closed door. "Package for Sam Moon."

One of the doors on the other side of the common room opened, and an overweight young man, his hair shaved down to a dark stubble, stuck out his head.

"He's not here," he said, a strong southern accent in his voice. "I saw him leave about half an hour ago."

Tom frowned. "Do you know where he could be?"

The stubble-haired neighbor shook his head. "He

usually comes back here between classes. You want me to hold on to that for him?"

Tom's fingers instinctively tightened around the package. He ran through the possibilities. He could try to find Sam elsewhere. He had pulled the boy's class schedule off the Internet, and he could always wait for Sam outside a classroom. Unfortunately package delivery companies didn't usually ambush people in hallways.

He could try coming back later, but that had its own set of risks. The sooner the information reached Sam, the better the chance of saving Gaia.

Tom looked at the boy with the shaved head. There was no reason to think he couldn't be trusted. No reason except that he appeared to have about as many brain cells as a ceiling beam.

"If I give it to you, will you be able to give it to him today?" Tom asked.

"As soon as he shows up," the boy promised.

Tom hesitated a moment longer, then nodded. "Sign here," he said. He passed a clipboard over, watched the boy sign it, and then—reluctantly—handed him the box.

The boy stepped back and started to close the door.

Tom grabbed the edge of the door and held it open. "This is an important package," he said. "You need to see that he gets it right away."

"Yeah," the boy replied, obviously perplexed. "Sure." He pulled on the door, and Tom let it go.

"Tell him it's from Gaia," Tom said to the closing door. "An important package from Gaia."

The door closed with a click, and a moment after, Tom heard the sound of one, two, three locks being set. He stared at the old, scratched wood door for a moment, then turned and started out of the building.

He was aware that he hadn't acted like a deliveryman. It didn't matter. Sam's neighbor could think anything he liked.

As long as he delivered the package.

GAIA NEVER KNEW A PIECE OF furniture could scream.

It was there in every class she had shared with Cassie Greenman. A desk. An empty desk.

It was just a plain desk, scratched up and written on by so many students, it was hard to even make out where one set of initials stopped and the next one started. A couple of pieces of plastic, some plywood, and twisted-up metal. But every time Gaia looked at it, she heard this weird kind of wailing down deep in her brain.

She wondered if she was going crazy—even more crazy than usual. But Gaia didn't think she was the only one who heard the screaming.

All day, other people kept glancing over at the desk. The Empty Desk. And every time they looked that way, they'd get this expression on their faces. Instantly zoned. Even the teachers seemed to be looking at it as if they expected the desk to answer a question or make a comment on the class.

It was profoundly weird.

Gaia knew they cut a couple of hours off the day, but by the time the last bell rang, she would have sworn that she had been in school for at least three weeks.

If anybody had asked her what had been covered in her classes that day, Gaia couldn't have repeated a word. Not that she was ever Ms. Perfect Attention. But ever since the morning announcement the only sound track in Gaia's head was the screaming desk and a running loop of her conversation with Cassie.

As far as Gaia knew, it was the first time she had ever talked to Cassie. And the last.

The thing that really bugged Gaia, the thing she just could not get around, was this:

What in hell was Cassie Greenman doing in Washington Square Park at night? It didn't make any sense. Cassie had seemed genuinely scared of the killer. She had even talked about dyeing her hair to take her off the victim list. Cassie Greenman might not have been a rocket scientist, but anyone smart enough not to play on subway tracks would have known better than to go into the park.

Except Gaia, of course, but that was different.

Gaia took a last took at the screaming desk as she staggered out of class. It had eyeball magnetism, that desk. It was like a tooth missing right in the middle of someone's smile. You couldn't stop looking at it. Gaia wondered how long it would be before someone else sat there and filled in the gap. She was willing to bet that desk was going to be empty for a long time.

Gaia made it down the hall, pounded her locker into submission, and shoved her stuff inside.

Why hadn't she seen Cassie in the park? It wasn't exactly teeming with people. How could Gaia have missed her?

Thoughts of Cassie grew so thick, it was like walking around in a literal fog. Gaia trudged slowly along the hallway, lost to the world. Then she started around the corner by the school office and ran smack into what felt like a concrete wall.

She gave a mumbled "sorry" and started to move on.

"It's all right. At least this time you didn't knock me down."

Gaia looked up at the voice. "Huh?"

"Hi," said David. "Remember me? David Twain, boy obstacle."

Gaia blinked away the tangle of twisted thoughts. David hadn't felt like a wall yesterday. Last night must have taken more out of her than she thought. "What are you doing here?" she asked.

David grinned. "It's school. They make you go."

"I mean . . ." Except Gaia didn't know what she meant. Her brain was still deep in the Cassie zone, and she was having a hard time getting it back in the real-world dimension.

"I'm going to have to start wearing football pads," David said, rubbing at the back of his neck. Gaia watched his forearm where he'd rolled up his sleeve. He was better looking today. Somehow the thought pissed her off.

"Sorry," Gaia said again, stepping around him. "I'm not all here at the moment."

"Yeah, I've seen the studies," David said, shoving his hands in his pockets. His binder was tucked under his arm with one book. There was no backpack. Gaia brought her hand to her forehead, confused by her inadvertent observations. Since when was she interested in this kind of thing?

"What studies?" she asked, focusing in on the little space of skin between his dark eyebrows.

"About you," David replied. "Four out of five

doctors warn that you're a major source of bruises."

Gaia shook away the last of the Cassie fog and tried to concentrate on what David was saying. Some part of her brain told her that she had just missed a joke, but she was in no mood to go back and figure it out.

"Whatever." Another brilliant response from Ms. Gaia Moore, ladies and gentlemen.

David smiled. Dimples. Annoying.

"Well, *whatever* you are or aren't, I *was* looking for you," he said. "In fact, looking for you was my number-one objective for the afternoon."

"Why?" The fog was rolling back in.

"The date, remember?"

Gaia blinked. Date. For a moment the words belonged to a foreign language. Something they might say in the jungles of Borneo or maybe on the far side of the moon. Then she remembered. Coffee. Baklava. Her first ever genuine date. It was amazing what a little thing like murder could make you forget.

"Look, David," she said. "Maybe we shouldn't. You know, because of . . . Cassie and all."

His face was quickly overtaken by an expression of concern. "I'm sorry. Were you two close?"

"No. It's not that. It's . . ." Gaia wondered how David would react if she explained to him that she was the ugly sister of Xena, Warrior Princess, and

Cassie was one of the `helpless peasants` Gaia was supposed to protect from the rampaging hordes. "It bothers me."

David nodded. "It bothers me, too." He gave a quick look around the hallway. "I just moved here last week. Everybody keeps saying that New York is this really safe place, that there's not nearly as much crime as people say. They act like it's all in the movies. But I get here and there's this big murder thing going on."

Gaia shrugged. "They're only killing blond girls. You shouldn't have to worry."

That `off-center smile` crept back onto his face. "Yeah, but I kind of like blond girls," he said in a low voice. "I want to keep them around."

It wasn't the smoothest response in the world. On the Skippy scale, Gaia marked it `closer to regular than extra creamy.` But he was trying.

"Okay," she said. "Maybe we could go somewhere. Just for a little while."

"Anywhere you want," he replied. "If you don't feel like dessert, maybe we could just go over to Googie's and grab a burger."

Googie's. Yet another spot on Gaia's Guide to the Village. It was a place so tacky, it was ... `really tacky.` "For a guy who's only been here a couple of days, you sure have homed in on prime sources of empty calories."

David patted his disgustingly flat stomach. "I have

a list of priorities whenever I move." He raised his hand and started ticking off the points. "First, locate an immediate source of sugar. Two, find a good greasy burger. Three, pin down a decent pizza." He lowered his hand. "Once all that's done, you're ready to move on to number four."

Gaia raised an eyebrow. "What's number four?"

The dimples retreated, and David looked at her for the first time with a completely serious expression. "Find the right girl to share it with."

Gaia had to give him credit. He was Not Sam, but he was good. She did a quick top-to-bottom survey. Chinos: pressed, but not too neat. Khaki shirt over black T-shirt: again, looking a little less than perfect. Just an average guy. And average was okay with her.

Gaia did a little mental arithmetic. If what she had heard was right, then both victims had died in the park in the middle part of the evening, somewhere before midnight. If Gaia was in place by nine-thirty, ten at the latest, she should be ready to tackle the killer if he came back for thirds—not that she would be the only person looking for him there tonight. She'd still have time for a quick dinner, a change of clothes, and working her way past Ella.

Not that the last part was hard. Ella had been off doing Ella things every night for a week.

"You're sure you want to go out with me?" Gaia

asked. She knew it was tempting fate, but she felt like she had to give him a final chance to back out.

David nodded. "Absolutely."

"Then here's the deal. Meet me at Third and Thompson at six, and we'll eat."

"What's at Third and Thompson?"

"Jimmy's Burrito." Gaia gave him her best excuse for a smile. "Even greasier than Googie's."

SAM LEANED AGAINST THE COOL STONE

A Simple Plan

of the Washington Square Park arch. He looked around to make sure that no one was watching, then pulled a small yellow radio from his pocket and squeezed the trigger on its side. Even alone, he still felt like an idiot.

"Do you see her?" he asked. He let go of the trigger, then quickly pressed it again. "Over."

There was a moment of silence before Ed's voice came back. "Yes, I see her. I'm in a wheelchair. I'm not blind. Over."

"Which way is she going? Is she heading toward the park?"

`Static.`

"Ed? Is she going toward the park?"

`Static.`

"Ed?"

"You're supposed to say 'over' when you're done."

"Over, for God's sake. Is she going toward the park? Over," Sam snapped.

`Static.`

"Ed? I said over."

"I heard you. I was just moving to keep up with Gaia. Have you ever tried to roll and use a walkie-talkie at the same time?" he hissed. "Next time you decide to steal radios, I suggest you get one with a headset. `Over.`"

Sam pushed the trigger again. "I didn't steal these. I paid for them."

It was at least temporarily true. They were good radios, guaranteed to have at least a two-mile range and fourteen channels, and they had fancy built-in scrambling so no one else could listen in on the conversation. Very nice radios. Also very expensive.

There was no way Sam could afford to keep them. So he had paid for them at an electronics store with a thirty-day return policy. As soon as `Operation Protect Gaia` was over, the radios were going back. At the moment they were paid for.

"Which way is Gaia going?" Sam asked again. "Over," he added quickly.

"It looks like she's going home," Ed's voice replied. "Probably to get ready for her date. Over."

Sam stared at the radio in his hand. He had to have heard that wrong. "Say again."

Static.

"Ed?"

"You didn't say 'over.' Over."

Sam squeezed the radio, envisioning Ed's neck between his fingers. "Can you forget the stupid 'over' and just repeat whatever it was you said?"

"I said, she's going home." There was a hint of laughter in Ed's radio voice.

Sam gripped the radio. "Not that part."

"Then what . . ." Static. "Oh, you mean the date."

"What date are you talking about?" It took all his effort to release the talk button so he could listen for a response he was sure he didn't really want to hear.

"Don't you know about the date?" More glee. Obvious this time.

Sam was glad there was at least a mile of space between them. If Ed had been close enough to reach, the Gentleman wouldn't be the only one in the park committing murder.

"Obviously I don't know about the date," Sam said slowly. "If I knew about the date, would I be asking about the date?"

"Gaia has a date tonight," Ed's voice replied. His

voice had changed. There was resignation in it now. "She warned me about it yesterday."

No one had warned Sam. Of course, Gaia and Sam weren't on the best of terms. They had basically no reason to speak at all. But Sam still felt blindsided by the enormity of Ed's announcement.

Gaia had a date. *She's not yours,* he reminded himself. *She was never yours.* Somehow he still felt betrayed.

"Who is she going out with?" Sam asked.

"A new guy," Ed replied flatly. "David something." Sam was about to ask another question, but before he could, Ed's voice came again. "I need to move again if I'm going to keep her in sight."

Sam pushed himself away from the cold marble of the arch. "All right. Call me if she comes back out. We'll work out positions."

"Roger," said Ed. "Over and out. Ten-four. Copy tha—"

Sam switched off the radio. He flicked a switch that would make it ring like a telephone if Ed called, then dropped it into his jacket pocket.

Sam went through a mental list of questions about the date, but he couldn't think of how to ask them without sounding jealous. Was he jealous? He thought about it for a moment and decided the answer was yes. He might not be able to define his own feelings about Gaia, but he was sure about one thing—he didn't want her going out with anyone else.

With Gaia gone back to her brownstone to prepare for the unthinkable date, Sam wasn't sure what to do. He could hang around the park for the afternoon, maybe get in a game. But losing a game of chess didn't seem very appealing without at least the chance of seeing Gaia.

After a few moments of indecision he turned to go back to his dorm. This was probably the only chance he was going to get to shower, eat something, maybe even grab a quick catnap. He would be back on duty soon enough.

Sam strolled across Washington Square North and headed uptown. The plan he and Ed had worked out was a simple one—until the Gentleman was caught, killed, or had moved on to another state, they would keep Gaia under close observation. Close observation defined as spying on her night and day.

There were two upsides to this plan. First, it would keep Sam occupied, thus keeping his mind off the obsessive kidnapping questions. Second, the plan involved seeing Gaia. A lot.

For today both Sam and Ed would both be on duty. If Gaia appeared, they would stay close. If Gaia got in trouble, they would help her. If they made it through the first day, they would switch over to working in shifts. Ed would watch Gaia during the school day; Sam would take over in the afternoons. It seemed like a simple plan.

Sam only hoped the killer was caught before Sam died from exhaustion.

A group of skateboarders went past, headed for the park, followed closely by a knot of laughing kids. The police had kept Washington Square locked up for most of the morning, but now that the barriers were down, the usual park population was rushing in to fill the void.

Sam cast a sideways glance as a barrel-chested man in a Greek fisherman's hat strolled past, a newspaper tucked under his arm. The man didn't seem familiar. He definitely wasn't a regular. Maybe he was the killer.

Another man went past. This one had a narrow, hatchet-shaped face and wild, bushy eyebrows. Killer material for sure.

There was a middle-aged Asian woman wearing a long, dark coat—an awfully heavy coat for a day that was pretty warm. She could have hidden anything under that coat. After all, even if the press called the killer the Gentleman, there had been no witnesses to the killings. Who was to say this Gentleman wasn't a Gentlewoman?

Sam was looking at another man when he realized how crazy this was. Of course these pedestrians didn't look familiar. Fifty thousand people must walk down Fifth Avenue to Washington Square on any day of the week. Maybe more like a hundred thousand. Sam couldn't possibly recognize them all.

It was time for Sam Moon to stop playing Sam Spade. A blast of sugar laced with caffeine, some sack time, and an icy shower were all required. Any order would do.

He managed to make it back to his dorm without spotting any more serial killer wanna-bes on the streets. But that didn't mean there wasn't still one out there. Maybe Sam could just have the caffeine and the shower. The nap would take too long. He couldn't leave Gaia out there alone while he snoozed. So no nap.

That decision made, Sam actually felt a tiny bit better. He walked through the common room and was about to open the door to his bedroom when he heard another door open.

"Hey, Sam," said a voice at his elbow. "Think fast."

Someone who had gone through high school playing basketball would have had an instant response to those words. Sam played chess. He turned around just in time to take a cardboard box between the eyes.

"Ouch," he said as the small package bounced off his forehead and thumped to the floor.

"You got bad hands, Moon." Sam's suite mate,

Mike Suarez, leaned back against his door frame, grinning.

Sam reached for the package. "My hands are okay; it's my head that's slow." He picked up the box and turned it over in his hands. "What's this?"

"Delivery guy brought it for you this morning," Mike replied. "That's all I know." He shrugged and winked. "You better work on those hands."

"Right." Sam returned the smile, although he felt more like smacking Mike's head right back.

Sam turned to the door and pushed it open, reminding himself for the umpteenth time that he really had to get that lock fixed. As soon as he was inside, he looked at the package again, wondering who might have sent it. It was a small box, little bigger than a stack of index cards, and the label had no return address.

There was only one way to find out. He grabbed the paper at the edge of the box and started to tug.

"Sam?"

This time the voice came from inside his room. Sam looked up in surprise and saw Heather sitting on the edge of his bed. "Heather! Jesus, you scared me."

Heather smiled at him. "We didn't have the best night last night," she said. "I thought I would try to make it up to you."

Sam opened his mouth to say something else, but

148

the subject slipped away before it could get to his tongue. Heather's long, rich brown hair had been set loose to spill around her shoulders. She was wearing a short, black skirt that ended well above her knees and a white shirt. A big white shirt.

"That's my shirt," he said.

Heather nodded. "I borrowed it." Her lips pursed into a pout. "I'm sorry. You want me to take it off?"

"No, I—"

The pout on Heather's lips was replaced by a sly smile. "I was hoping you would say yes." She raised her fingers to the top button and slowly slipped it open. Then she moved down to the next. "I think we should try again, Sam," she said. "The last time didn't end so well, did it?"

Her tone was inviting, but her eyes conveyed a whole other message. She was giving him a chance to make it up to her. Make up for chasing after Gaia and leaving her naked. Alone. Unsatisfied. One chance.

There was no way Sam was stupid enough to disappoint her. He didn't want to.

He quickly shoved the little package into his coat pocket next to the yellow plastic radio and closed the door.

Apparently there would be no nap, no shower, and no caffeine.

"Soon I'll be
through the
main course."
He looked at
Loki **stranger**
over his
shoulder. "I
think I'll take
up brunettes
for dessert."

The Thing

"YOU MIGHT AS WELL COME OUT," Loki said calmly. "I know that you're following me."

The boy stepped out from the trees and stood in the dry grass at the edge of the sidewalk. "Well, if it isn't my dear uncle Loki," he said in a cheerful tone. "Whatever brings you here?"

Loki kept his hand in his pocket and closed his fingers around the comforting bulk of his 9-mm pistol. "You couldn't resist, could you?" he said. "You had to come and watch."

The boy shrugged. "I admit, there is a certain pleasure in watching all the little bugs scurry around." He waved his hands extravagantly. "The police run here. The FBI runs there. And you run in between."

"Do you think this is funny?"

"Oh, very," the boy said. "But that's not why I'm here."

"Then why are you here?" Loki took a half step back. He tried to judge the odds. His skills with a firearm weren't as polished as they had been ten years before, but he was still quite fast. He could pull his semiautomatic pistol and get off ten rounds before most men even realized he had moved. But against this boy . . . Loki thought his chances of surviving were no better than fifty-fifty.

The boy turned and looked back through the

screen of trees at the people passing through the park.

"Actually," he said, "I was only taking in the menu. Picking out a little something for tonight." He gestured at a group of girls laughing near the fountain. "There are so many possibilities here."

Loki studied the boy as if he were a stranger. It was almost true. A year before, the boy had been just that—a boy. A boy with an unusual predilection. Then he'd been unsure of himself. Awkward. Looking to Loki and others for guidance.

A year could change everything. The man—the thing—that Loki faced had as little relation to that uncertain boy as a kitten did to a tiger. In every way that counted, he was a stranger.

"I didn't think any of that group would be to your taste," Loki replied, glancing at the gaggle of young women.

"No?"

"I thought you were only after blonds."

The stranger with a familiar face laughed. "So true," he said. "But that was only the appetizer. Soon I'll be through the main course." He looked at Loki over his shoulder. "I think I'll take up brunettes for dessert."

Loki frowned. He wasn't squeamish. He never had been. One life lost, a hundred lives lost, what did it matter? But there were things he cared about: years of work, research, effort. Those things should never be wasted.

Against his better judgment he took a step forward. "Come back," he said. He thought about touching the stranger's shoulder but decided against it. "Come home."

"Home?" The boy made a noise that might have been the start of laughter but quickly turned into something more like a growl. "Home," he said again. His face twisted into a sudden sneer, and he began to pace back and forth between the trees and the edge of the concrete path, his black coat billowing in the wind. "Couldn't you find a better word than *home?*"

"It was your home," Loki said in his most reassuring tone. "For most of your life you were—"

The boy whirled. His eyes were sharp. "Oh, don't say happy," he snapped. "It was an experiment. A rat cage. A prison. Not a home. And I was never, ever happy in that box." He raised his arm and pointed an accusing finger at Loki. "That place is the reason I'm here. The reason for everything."

Loki sighed. It was a sad, tired sound, the sound of an old man who was past his prime and weary of the world. It was a sound Loki had practiced.

"All right," he said. "I don't suppose there's anything I can say to make it better now." Hidden in the pocket of his coat, his hand tightened on the grip of the pistol. He began to raise the barrel.

The boy blinked, and as quickly as it had come, his

rage seemed to evaporate. A broad smile returned to his face.

"Don't tell me you're going to shoot me," he said. "Not after you've come so far to ask your poor prodigal son to come back to the farm."

For ten seconds they stood in silence. Loki had no idea what the boy was thinking, but his own mind was playing over scenarios as fast as a chess computer trying out moves. In this game there were only two opening moves: Leave the boy alone or kill him. Each of those moves had its possibilities and its dangers. Loki made a quick glance around and judged his distance from the other people in the park. There were no police nearby, and the risk of auxiliary damage was low. Now was the time.

"I was wrong to let you out," said Loki. "You're undisciplined. Unready. You have to come back with me."

"Or you'll kill me," said the boy.

Loki nodded. "Yes."

The boy was fast. Incredibly fast. One moment he was ten feet away. The next Loki's hand was hit by a rock-hard blow that sent the automatic pistol spinning away. Before he could react to that first attack, a fist cracked against his chin. He reeled backward, red fog swirling in his brain.

Strong hands caught Loki by the shoulders and spun him around.

"You made me the way I am for a purpose," the boy hissed in a low whisper, "but I've got my own objectives now. The first one is to kill your golden child." The fingers tightened. "And then I'm coming for you."

The boy released his grip, stepped back, and smiled. It was almost serene. He touched one finger to his forehead in a mock salute, then turned and strolled casually across the park.

Loki watched him go. In a way, he was greatly relieved that he hadn't managed to kill the boy. He couldn't be certain if it was the right decision.

But he would know soon enough.

THE BEST THING ABOUT HAVING A

A Happy Gaia

date at Jimmy's was that it had all the ambiance of a shoe box. Maybe less.

That didn't mean Gaia didn't like it. Ambiance came way, way down on the list of her requirements in a restaurant. Way below sour cream and globs of melty cheese.

Besides, no ambiance equaled no need to dress up. No need to dress up equaled no need to worry about changing clothes. No need to worry about changing clothes equaled a happy Gaia.

That was the theory. In the real world she decided to make a change.

What she really needed was something dark. Something nice. Cool. Something sort of Matrix-like. Something that would hide stains.

Fat chance of finding it in her closet. This was depressing. For a split second Gaia thought of the redhaired girl. Mary. The smudged number on the crumpled coffeehouse napkin in the pocket of last night's jeans. Had Mary meant it when she said to call her? Was that what girls did? Call for advice before dates?

Right. Like that was going to happen.

Gaia went back to the black jeans she had looked at in the morning and decided to give them another try. They fit a little snug—snugger than she would have liked across her bulging butt. Still, they didn't look too bad.

She stared a few minutes longer, then closed her eyes, reached in, and selected a hanger at random. Gaia opened her eyes to peek. A big denim shirt. Not an inspired choice, but at least a choice.

She gave her hair a few strokes, pulled it back, and slipped it through her one and only scrunchie. There. She was dressed, and the whole thing had taken less than half an hour. It had to be a new record.

Gaia checked the clock. Plenty of time to cruise by the park, lose a game to Zolov, and still be early for her date.

Date.

Gaia felt a shimmery feeling in her legs. Not a major quake, but at least a 3.5 on the do-I-really-want-to-go-through-with-this scale. The date was only a couple of hours away, and she still couldn't get a good handle on the idea. Gaia was going to a restaurant. With a guy.

It wasn't a completely unknown situation. She had been out on social occasions before. Of course, the last time was probably when she was twelve. It wasn't completely unheard of. Except this time the guy was actually coming because of Gaia. He would look at Gaia. And talk to Gaia. Worse, he would expect Gaia to talk back and be interesting for minutes on end.

She wondered if she could just keep her mouth full of burrito and let him talk. Guys liked to talk. That's what she had heard, anyway.

With this stellar plan in place Gaia started downstairs, sure that she was on her way to end her status as the world's oldest undated girl. It was possible that she would even break the great kiss curse.

But a new obstacle was waiting for Gaia before she reached the ground floor. She closed her eyes and sighed.

She'd forgotten about the Wicked Witch of the Wonderbra.

Ella looked at Gaia over the rims of her purple-tinted sunglasses. "Where are you going?"

"Nowhere," Gaia replied.

Ella smirked. "Then maybe you shouldn't go. It's getting late."

"Late?" Gaia pointed at the window beside the staircase. "It's barely after four. It's broad daylight out there."

Ella pursed her glossy lips. "I know, but with all those murders going on, I really think you need to stay in. It's just too dangerous."

The person on the stairs looked like Ella. The perfume drifting toward Gaia in invisible clouds certainly smelled like Ella. But her mind had clearly been replaced by the mind of someone else—someone who cared if Gaia kept breathing.

Or at least bothered to pretend to care.

What the hell was she supposed to say? Part of her just wanted to walk out like she normally would, but some morbid part of her was tempted to play along.

"I . . . uh . . . won't stay late." That was at least partially true. Gaia could circle back by the brownstone after her early date with David. Then she could slip out again as soon as Ella got over this caring fit.

Ella waited a few seconds, then nodded. "All right," she said, "but whatever you do, stay out of the park.

And try to get home before eight. It's a school night."

Gaia stared. Body snatchers were definitely at work. This whole conversation could not be occurring. Not with Ella.

She tried to answer but could only manage a nod. Ella's behavior had baffled Gaia beyond the ability for rational speech.

SAM WONDERED IF YOU COULD

Timing Is Everything

drown in hair. Heather's hair was long and lush and altogether beautiful to look at. Breathing through it was a different story. No matter how Sam turned in the narrow bed, he seemed to end up with a suffocating curtain of brown spilling over his face.

Heather murmured something and snuggled against him. Her soft skin felt extraordinarily warm against his legs and chest.

Like Heather, Sam was nearly unconscious in a postsex daze. It was amazing. Sex was like the greatest sleeping aid in history. One minute he was more charged up than he had ever been in his life, the next minute his arms and legs seemed to weigh a thousand tons. Each.

Sam pushed open a gap in Heather's hair wide enough to permit a breath of air. He couldn't allow himself to actually sleep. With the serial killer working the neighborhood, Heather's parents would panic if she was out late. And Sam had something to do. Something important. But for the moment he couldn't remember exactly what it was. He settled himself against Heather's warm softness and began to slide toward sleep.

This wasn't so bad. He could live with this. Having a beautiful girl naked in your bed was about as close to perfect as life could get.

For the moment, at least, Sam's obsession with Gaia seemed distant. Silly. There was nothing wrong with Heather. So what if she didn't know what a rook was? So what if she had a small cruel streak? It would be okay. It would work out. He was sure that he could love Heather.

Except, as his drowsiness pulled him down the slope toward true sleep, he brushed his lips against Heather's brown hair and imagined it was gold.

A buzzing alarm began to sound. Sam groaned and flapped his arm at the clock on the bedside table. He smacked the button over and over, but the noise kept coming.

"Mmmm." Heather rolled over and brushed her

lips against his face. "Turn that off," she whispered.

"I'm trying." Sam propped himself up on one elbow and picked up the clock. He pressed the button again. He slid the alarm switch to off, but the noise didn't stop. He stared at the clock blankly for a few seconds longer, then realized what was wrong.

The sound wasn't coming from the clock.

Sam scanned the room, searching for the source of the noise. It wasn't the phone. It wasn't the stereo. It was . . . a coat.

Across the room Sam's jacket was lying folded across the back of a chair—not the neatest fold in the world, but then, he had been in sort of a hurry to get undressed. For some reason, the coat was buzzing.

"Sam," Heather called. "Please. That's so annoying."

"Sure. Right." Still more than half asleep, Sam carefully eased himself away from Heather and rolled off the side of the bed. He stumbled over discarded clothing, banged his knee against his desk, knocked over a stack of books, and made it to the coat without generating any more noise than a rogue elephant in a bell factory. He fumbled in the pocket of the coat and grabbed something. What he pulled out was a bright yellow plastic radio.

Sam's heartbeat slammed to a stop.

Oh, yeah. The radio.

Free of the coat, the buzzing noise was louder than ever. Sam flipped the radio over and over in his hands, searching for the switch. At last he located the trigger on the side and pressed it. The buzzing stopped.

Sam breathed a low sigh of relief. He would call Ed back as soon as he could, but in the meantime at least the radio was quiet. The last thing he wanted to do was explain to Heather what he—

"Sam?" said a loud voice from the radio. "Sam, are you there?"

Panic shot through Sam. All remains of the after-sex sleepiness were blown away in an instant. He looked at the bed, trying to ascertain whether Heather was waking up, then he squeezed the trigger on the radio.

"I'm here," he said as softly as he could.

"Took you long enough," Ed's voice replied. "I've been sitting here buzzing you for the last five minutes. I was about to give up."

Sam wished he had.

Heather rolled over on the bed and stretched her hands above her head. "Sam," she said in a voice that was half a yawn. "Who's on the phone?"

"Nobody important," Sam replied with forced cheerfulness. "Go back to sleep." He lowered his voice and spoke into the radio. "Look, can you call me back later?"

"Hey, this thing was your idea." The quality of the radio was plenty good enough to pick up the irritation in Ed's voice. "Are you going to help me or not?"

"What's happening?"

"She's in the park," Ed answered. "She's been playing chess against that old guy. The Russian."

"Zolov," said Sam. "He's Ukrainian."

"Whatever. The game's over, and she's leaving."

Heather raised her head and rubbed at her eyes. "Sam . . ."

"Just a minute." Sam walked across the small room and stood as far from Heather as he could. "Look, can't you follow her?" he whispered to the radio.

"I'm too obvious," Ed replied through a crackle of static. "If I leave the park, she's going to see me."

Sam sighed and closed his eyes. They should just let her go. This whole business was seriously screwed up.

Sam squeezed the trigger, ready to tell Ed to pack it in.

For a full five seconds Sam held down the little button, but the words wouldn't come. If he gave up and something happened to Gaia, Sam would never be able to live with himself. That much he knew.

"All right," he said in a low tone. "Watch her as long as you can. I'll be right there."

"Hurry."

Suddenly Sam noticed a small plastic switch at the top of the radio. He flicked it, and the speaker inside went dead.

He'd found the off switch. Great timing.

Heather sat up and held the white sheets against her chest. "What's wrong?" she asked.

"Um, nothing," Sam said. He moved across the darkened room and found his clothes lying on the floor. Still trying to be as quiet as he could, he picked up his pants and began to slide them on.

"Where are you going?" asked Heather. There was a lingering fog of sleep in her voice, but it didn't hide an edge of irritation. "Aren't you going to stay with me?"

Sam ran a hundred excuses through his mind, but all of them seemed too lame to speak.

He could always tell her the truth. On the other hand, he wasn't ready to die.

"I have a class," he said.

"Now?" Heather pushed her hair back from her face and frowned at him. "I thought you had a short day on Tuesdays."

"It's a lab," Sam replied. He dragged out his shirt and began to put it on as fast as he could. "A . . . um, makeup lab from one I missed earlier."

"How long will it take?"

That depends on Gaia.

"A couple of hours," he said. "Three at the most." He finished with his shirt, dropped into a chair, and started putting on his shoes.

Heather stretched her long, bare legs but didn't get up. "Then I guess I better get dressed, too. I have to get home."

"Okay," said Sam. He stood up. "I've got to run, or I'll be late."

Heather pulled the pillows together and leaned back against them. "All right," she said. "Mind if I use your shower before I go?"

Sam smiled. "No problem. I wish I could stay."

He did wish he could stay. Although the decision to watch over Gaia was already made, Sam felt a fresh wave of indecision.

After all, the last time he'd left Heather to chase Gaia, he'd ended up kidnapped and half dead.

It would be nice if he could stay here. It would be nice if he could think of nothing but Heather.

It would probably be a lot safer, too.

But the undefined feelings he had for Gaia Moore were too hard to ignore.

Sam picked up his jacket and put it on. As he did, he noticed the small package still nestled in the right-hand pocket. He took out the box and held it up to the light. Small box. Brown paper. Nothing special. He started to leave the package behind, then he changed his mind and dropped it back into the pocket. If he ended up on a nightlong Gaia stakeout, he would at least have something to look at.

"Well, I guess I'm going," he said as he moved toward the door. "Are you going to be all right going home by yourself?"

"I'll be fine."

There was a new tension in Heather's voice that caught Sam's attention. He turned back to her and looked at her lovely face. "Are you sure?"

"I'm sure," said Heather.

Sam wanted to ask her more, but Ed was waiting and Gaia was moving. If he was going to catch up to them, he needed to get outside. "Okay, then, bye."

He turned and grabbed the doorknob. He was halfway into the hall when Heather called again.

"Sam?"

"Yes?" he replied without turning.

"Does this have anything to do with her?"

Heather named no names, but Sam didn't bother to ask for a definition of "her."

"No," he said in a hoarse voice. He cleared his throat and tried again. "No, it's just class."

He waited a few seconds more, but Heather said nothing else. Sam stepped through the open door and left.

"I fear nothing," David said. "That's another of my special powers."

david

AT FIRST GAIA WAS FEELING FAIRLY
pleased with herself. She was
handling this date thing okay.
No pressure. She had even kept
it together in her game against
Zolov. She'd lost, of course, but
she always lost to Zolov. At least
this time she had come close.

The Wild Burrito

She tugged at the scrunchie in her hair as she walked. There was absolutely no reason to get tense about this dinner. They were only going to grab fast food from a cheap restaurant. Nothing fancy.

She was fine—right up until she turned the corner onto Thompson. The closer Gaia got to Jimmy's, the more she could feel a pressure pushing her backward. It was as if there were this weird wind coming from the restaurant. It blew harder as Gaia got closer until every step toward the restaurant was like pushing into a gale. Other people walked down the sidewalk with no trouble, but Gaia felt like any moment the wind might grab her and send her flying back across the park.

Gaia slowed. Jimmy's Burrito was only a dozen steps away, but they were hard steps to take. She steeled herself, squared her shoulders, and walked to the door.

Lightning didn't strike. No earthquakes shook the ground.

Gaia took a deep breath. She glanced inside, scanned the tables and booths. No sign of David.

Maybe he wasn't coming.

David had probably wised up at the last moment. Maybe he had talked to someone else at school. Maybe he had finally come to his senses. Whatever the case, it was clear he had realized that dating Gaia was a big mistake.

Disappointment settled into Gaia's empty stomach like lead, but there was an equal amount of relief. No David. No date. There was still some chance of potential irritation if the story "How Gaia Got Stood Up" became part of the next day's grind of boring school gossip. But Gaia doubted that would happen. The story was too dull, considering what was going on.

"So what do you recommend?" a voice asked.

Gaia turned to find herself face-to-face with David. She struggled for something witty to say, but her well of wit was experiencing a drought. "I, um . . . I see you found the place."

David tapped a finger against the tip of his nose. "Able to detect taco sauce at a hundred paces." He held up his arms and pretended to flex huge muscles. "It's one of my secret powers."

Gaia forced a smile. She actually *wanted* to smile, but her face wasn't responding to her brain, so she had to force it. "You have others?"

"Too many to number," David said. He crowded in close to Gaia and leaned forward to look at the menu taped up against the window. "What's good here?"

"Depends on what you think is good." He was very much in her personal space. Gaia stepped aside, hoping it wasn't the wrong thing to do. He didn't even blink.

"Anything," he said. "As long as it's hot."

"They have plenty of hot," Gaia said. Another smile. This one didn't take as much effort.

"I am the terror of hot peppers everywhere." David stepped past Gaia and pulled open the front door. "Jalapeño parents tell stories of me to frighten their children."

This time Gaia actually laughed. Suddenly all the tension she had felt about this date seemed completely stupid. David was just a person. A funny person who, for some reason, seemed to like her. None of those things was bad. Not everything she did had to turn into a disaster movie. Did it?

She stepped through the open door and waited for David to follow. "I'm not talking about wimpy peppers like a jalapeño," she said as he entered.

"Jalapeños are wimpy?"

"Extremely," she said. She was bantering. This was banter. Who knew?

They walked past the newsstands inside the door. Gaia picked out a booth off to the side of the restaurant and slid her butt across the red vinyl seat.

"They serve serious peppers here," she said. "They don't mess around."

David dropped into the seat across from her and pulled a plastic-coated menu from between two bottles of hot sauce.

"So what makes a serious pepper?" he asked. "I'm ready to do battle with any vegetable in the place."

"Good." Gaia reached across the table and plucked the menu from his hand. "Then I'll order for us."

"Go ahead," said David. "I'm not afraid."

Gaia looked at his blue eyes. Something weird was going on. She actually felt, well, almost comfortable. This was not her. This was some other girl who actually knew how to talk to other human beings.

A waitress approached, and Gaia delivered the order. David picked up the menu again after the waitress left. "What's the special burrito?" he asked.

Gaia snatched the menu a second time. "Just a burrito."

David's eyes sparkled. "But what's so special about it?"

"You'll see," said Gaia.

Much to her own surprise, Gaia was actually enjoying herself. So far, at least, she hadn't suffered from a brain fart causing her to say something inexcusably stupid. It was only a matter of time, of course, before she was revealed as a hopeless social outcast, but at least she was enjoying a few moments of normal life.

"So . . . ," David said.

Gaia stared at him. "So . . ."

They lapsed into silence. Uh-oh. This was getting less good. Gaia pressed her hands against the sticky vinyl. Was she supposed to say something? Was *he* supposed to say something?

That was when the emergency cop-out system flipped into action. Gaia stood up, nicking the edge of the table with her bad knee.

Ow.

"Where are you going?" David asked.

Gaia took a deep breath. "Bathroom."

"SO YOU'VE PROVED YOU'RE AN IDIOT with nothing to say," Gaia told her dripping reflection. The cold-water-in-the-face splash had done nothing for her spirits. It had only served to form huge blotches on her shirt and soak the hair around her face. Lovely.

Not Quite Normal

She might as well go back out there and seal the deal. Send him `running for the hills`. If the city had any.

Gaia opened the door and was headed back down the dark, grimy hall past the kitchen when she heard a huge crash, followed by a bloodcurdling scream. She stopped in front of the open kitchen door.

There was a fire. `A big one.`

This could really put a damper on her already dampered date.

Without hesitation Gaia strolled into the kitchen, took the phone out of the hand of a trembling fry cook, and hung it up before he could dial 911. She grabbed the fire extinguisher and yanked it off the wall, walked over to the searing, leaping flames, and doused them with one good squirt.

`The sprinkler system didn't even have time to kick in.`

Gaia turned and looked at the three white-clad, grease-stained kitchen workers who were huddled in the corner, looking like they'd fallen there out of shock. From the way they were gaping at her, she could have been an angel plunked in the middle of their crusty linoleum floor directly by `the hand of God.`

Gaia flushed. Sometimes she forgot her reactions to danger weren't quite normal.

She took a deep breath and tried to smile. "Uh . . . you can still make the burritos, right?"

"EVERYTHING OKAY BACK THERE?"

David's face wore a worried expression as Gaia returned to her seat.

"Fine," she said, averting her eyes. She cleared her throat noisily. "And dinner is on the house."

Family Stuff

He glanced past her toward the kitchen, a question obviously forming. "Why did they—"

"So how do you like New York?" she interrupted, placing her hands flat on the table. Lame question. Better than trying to deal with his.

He narrowed his eyes at her, obviously mulling his options. Which line of questioning was better/safer/more intriguing? Finally he leaned back into his bench, resting one arm across the top.

"I'm not sure yet if I like it," he said.

Gaia smiled, glad he'd made the right choice.

He looked toward the windows at the front of the restaurant. "It's great to get a burger anytime you want," he continued, "and to find an open bookstore at three A.M., but I think it's just too crowded for me."

"I like crowds," Gaia said, watching a group of people standing in line to pay their bill. "It's easy to get lost in them. Go unnoticed."

She felt her skin flush. She stared at the chipped tabletop. She hadn't just said that, had she?

174

"I can't imagine you'd go unnoticed anywhere," David said.

Gaia blushed more deeply. He hadn't just said that, had he?

"Anyway, I don't know if I'll be here long enough to adapt," David said.

Gaia glanced up. "You just got here. Why would you be moving?" Why wouldn't he be moving? She'd waited seventeen years for a first date. She'd probably be waiting another seventeen for a second.

"You know." David shrugged. "Family stuff." For the first time he looked a little uncomfortable.

"Following your parents' jobs?"

Now David looked down at the table. "My parents are . . . I'm not with my parents."

Gaia felt a nearly irresistible urge to touch him. "That's something we have in common," she said. "My parents are gone, too."

David raised his head. "That's weird, isn't it?"

For a moment they just looked at each other. This silence wasn't nearly as uncomfortable as the first.

"What is this?" David asked.

"What?" Gaia asked back.

David pointed up. "This music," he said.

A song played from invisible speakers. Gaia hadn't noticed it until that moment. She strained to hear.

Her waiting dark heart,
The violence in her eyes,
The hunger in my body,
The things she denies.

"It's this band called Fearless," Gaia replied, shaking her head slightly. "They play around here."

"Fearless?" David repeated, raising his eyebrows.

Gaia confirmed with a nod. At one point when she'd first moved to New York, it had seemed like this random band with this ironically appropriate name was following her around. It was almost too bizarre. But now it didn't even affect her. She was used to it.

The waitress came back with two oval platters loaded with burritos, corn flour tacos, and heaps of seasoned rice and beans. Gaia took her plate and dug in quickly, sweeping together a blob of sour cream, rice, and a chunk of steaming burritos. The combination of flavors was almost too good.

David eyed his plate. "What are all these little brown peppers?"

"Ever heard of *habañeros?*" Gaia asked through a mouthful of food.

His eyebrows scrunched together. "I don't think so."

Gaia grinned at him. "Good luck."

David picked up one of the peppers between his fingers, examined it for a moment, then tossed it into his mouth. Gaia heard it crunch between his teeth. A moment later David's blue eyes opened so wide, they looked like they might fall out of their sockets.

"Wow," he whispered.

"Pretty hot?" asked Gaia.

He nodded. "I don't think I'm really tasting it. It sort of made my ears ring."

Gaia took another bite of her own meal and watched as David chewed his way through a second pepper. "Most people are scared to death of those things."

David took a third pepper and crunched it. A red flush spread over his face, and he trembled.

"I fear nothing," David said. "That's another of my special powers."

Gaia looked at him. Maybe they had more in common than she thought.

SAM MOON WAS AN IDIOT.

Nope. Even *idiot* didn't sound bad enough. It was an insult to idiots everywhere.

The Other Guy

He had started out in situation A. In situation A he was lying in bed with a beautiful girl. A beautiful naked girl. A beautiful naked girl who wanted nothing more than to be with him. A girl with whom he had just had sex.

But from there Sam had proceeded straight to situation B. In this case he was up, out of bed, and running off to chase a different girl. Only this girl didn't want him. Probably hated him. Definitely didn't want to have sex with him.

Oh, yeah, and she was on a date with someone else.

As Sam crossed the street and stopped in the middle of the crowded sidewalk, he hoped his parents would someday have another son. He would be wrong ever to pass these pitiful genes along to the next generation.

Sam stood across from Jimmy's Burrito and watched Gaia eat her dinner with the guy she was dating. The back of the guy's head was nothing special. From what Sam could see, the pair were eating, talking, and even laughing.

Gaia was laughing.

Sam's heart squeezed. He tried to think of all the times he had been with her—which weren't many. Now that he thought about it, Sam wasn't sure he had ever gotten her to smile, much less laugh.

Gaia was having a good time. Meanwhile Sam was miserable in every way possible. He felt guilty. Tired. Jealous. Foolish. You name it. If it was bad, he felt it.

Sam leaned back against a brick wall and tried to

keep his head down. He didn't have a hat, or a big trench coat, or even sunglasses to make him harder to recognize. If Gaia looked out the window and saw Sam looking back, it would be `the perfect end to a perfect day.`

The radio buzzed in his pocket. Sam hated the sound. First thing in the morning these suckers were going back to the store. He dragged out the radio and squeezed the trigger.

"What do you want? *Over.*"

"A report," Ed replied. "You haven't even told me if you found her."

Sam said nothing.

"Sam?"

He smirked. "You didn't say '*over.*'" He sounded like a child. He didn't care.

"Over," Ed said.

"I found her," Sam replied. "She's okay. They're eating."

"Where?"

"Jimmy's Burrito."

Gaia laughed again. Another slice to the heart.

"Jimmy's?" Ed laughed. "Man, he got off cheap."

Sam glanced across the street and saw that Gaia was washing down a bite of something with her drink. He also saw that `at least two people` were giving him odd looks.

Sam turned his back to them. "Ed, I have to get off," he said.

"I need more details," Ed replied. "Booth or table?"

"Booth," Sam said through clenched teeth. He braced his free hand against the wall. "I'll talk to you later."

"Same side or across from each other?"

Sam rolled his eyes. "Across from each other."

"What are they eating?"

"Ed!" Sam shouted into the radio. "I can't tell what they're eating, and I don't read lips, so don't bother to ask what they're talking about. I'll call you if anything happens."

He snapped off the radio before Ed had a chance to reply and shoved it back into his coat pocket. His fingers brushed against the little box. Sam took it out. It didn't look like much.

Sam took a glance at Gaia, then tore at the paper on the outside of the box. Whoever had wrapped it had used plenty of tape. It took him a lot of tugging and tearing to get the paper unraveled. Once the paper was crumpled in his pocket, he was left with a featureless box of gray cardboard. He snapped a couple more pieces of tape and lifted off the lid.

The first thing Sam saw inside was a piece of folded paper. At the top of it was written *Sam Moon*. He picked it up, unfolded it, and started to read.

Sam—

I know that you have some connection with Gaia Moore. I hope that you continue to feel affection for her and that you will take the concerns expressed in this letter seriously.

Gaia is in danger. If I could take direct action to save her, I would, but circumstances prevent my appearance.

Instead I am passing this information along to you in hopes that you will know what to do with it. Watch out for Gaia. She is stronger than she appears to be, but she is not as strong as she believes. She can be hurt.

She needs you, Sam. Don't let her down.

Don't reveal the existence of this package or note to Gaia. For her own safety there are things she cannot know.

By the time he was done reading, Sam's heart was pounding in his ears. He read through the note again, clutching the page. There was no signature, no clue as to who had sent the package.

This little scrap of typing paper was about the weirdest thing Sam had ever run into in his life. Sure, he had been standing on the street playing undercover cop, but this note was straight out of some spy novel.

His immediate suspicion was that Ed had sent the package. Who else could have known that he was involved in any way with Gaia? It had to be a joke. If he called Ed on the radio, Sam could probably get Ed to confess.

But the longer he stood there, the less Sam believed in his own theory. Certain words in the note kept drumming against his brain.

Gaia is in danger.
She can be hurt.
She needs you, Sam.

He folded the note and shoved it back into his jacket pocket. Then Sam looked inside the little box again. There was another folded sheet of paper. With shaking hands Sam pulled it out and found that it was some kind of information form. Name. Age. That sort of thing.

Only this form had been attacked by someone with a big, fat black marker. Whole lines of the form were completely blacked out, but Sam could still read a few things.

Eyes: Blue

Several lines below that was another clear line.

IQ: 146

So whoever this sheet belonged to, they had blue eyes and they were smart. Sam wondered for a second if the sheet was about Gaia, but then he spotted another piece of uncovered info.

Height: 6'2"

Gaia was tall for a girl, but not anywhere close to that tall.

The biggest area of readable type was a box of text marked Evaluation.

Subject demonstrates almost complete lack of empathetic response. Does not act under social

constraints. Does not operate in a frame of be-
havioral mores. It is our opinion that this subject should be considered deeply sociopathic.
Extreme caution is recommended.

Sam glanced back up at the glowing windows of
the restaurant. What did any of this have to do with
Gaia?

Sam put away the sheet. All that remained in the
box was a small black-and-white photo. Sam pulled it
out and raised it closer to his eyes.

Sunset was coming on fast, and the street-
lights were just beginning to flicker. In the gloom Sam
had to squint to make out the grainy, low-quality photo.

The guy in the photo was young. He had short, wavy
black hair and a squared-off chin. There was a flat, angry
expression on his face. He seemed a little familiar. Sam
knew that he had seen the guy in the photo before.

Then he remembered where.

Sam let the box fall out of his fingers and ran right
through the traffic on Thompson. He drew a chorus
of horn blasts as he darted between the cars, and a
couple of people had to slam on their brakes. Sam
didn't care. He charged up the steps into Jimmy's,
shoving people out of the way as he went.

But when Sam got inside, the booth at the side of
the restaurant was empty. Gaia was gone.

His eyes
narrowed, and
his teeth
clenched
together so **double**
hard, Gaia
could see the **dare**
muscles bulge
at the corner
of his jaw.

"WHAT TIME ARE THEY CLOSING

David the park?" David asked.

"I heard they were closing it at seven," Gaia responded. "Both the killings happened sometime around eleven or twelve. They probably want to make sure they get everybody out well ahead of that."

She took a deep breath and watched the fog it caused disappear into the night sky.

"Let's go," David said.

Gaia looked at him. There was no way to know what he was thinking. His expression conveyed nothing.

"It's almost seven," Gaia said. "The police probably won't let us in." Not that that mattered to her.

"Are you scared?" David asked.

A challenge. Interesting. Gaia felt the skin around her eyes draw tight.

"I'm not scared," she said.

"Then let's go." David pointed. "If they have the gates blocked, we can always sneak over the fence."

Gaia stopped, hands in pockets. She looked him directly in the eyes, giving him a chance to back out. "If we go into the park, we'll probably get caught."

"So?" He kept walking. She followed.

"So, they'll put us in jail," she said. "Aren't you scared of that?"

"No." He turned to look at her, walking backward. "I guess I'm just naturally fearless."

"WHAT DID YOU SAY?"

Gaia stumbled to a stop on the sidewalk and leaned against the iron fence that guarded the park's south side.

Two Davids

David shrugged. "I said I was naturally fearless." He struck a dramatic pose, chin lifted, chest out, eyebrows lowered. "Intrepid explorer David Twain, ready and able to penetrate the deepest mysteries of unexplored regions."

Coincidence. That's all it was. It wasn't like *fearless* was a word reserved just for her. "You really aren't scared to go in the park?"

"Not me," he said. He folded his arms over his still puffed-out chest and raised an eyebrow. "What about you, little lady?" he said with a Hollywood cowboy accent. "You a-feared to go in that thar patch of woods?"

There was something odd going on here. Something had shifted.

This seemed like the same funny, talkative guy Gaia had shared burritos with back at Jimmy's. Obviously it was the same David. Only now it seemed like there was somebody else there, too. Like there were two completely different people looking at her with those dark blue eyes.

"All right," Gaia said, refusing to tear her gaze from his. "Let's go."

"Cool," David said. He stood up on the tips of his toes and looked over her head. "But there's already a cop down by the entrance. You're probably right that they won't let us by."

Gaia looked up at the fence. "So I guess we'll have to go in this way."

She braced herself, bent low, and jumped. Gaia's beat-up right knee protested, but she still managed to grab the top of the fence. A few seconds later she was over and in the bushes on the other side.

David clapped in rapid applause. "I think you're doing the wrong thing by staying in school," he said through the fence. "You should definitely run off and join the circus."

"I'll think about it," Gaia replied. "Are you coming over here, or are you too much of a chicken?"

There was nothing funny about David's reply this time. His eyes narrowed, and his teeth clenched together so hard, Gaia could see the muscles bulge at the corner of his jaw. He wasn't happy.

He jumped for the fence. With his longer arms he had no trouble grabbing the iron crossbar at the top. It took him a little longer to pull himself up, and he wasn't nearly as smooth working his way over the top, but less than thirty seconds later he dropped to the ground beside Gaia.

"I told you," he said. "I'm fearless."

Gaia started to wonder if maybe he was telling the truth.

"WHERE'S THE SPOT?"

"This way," Gaia replied. She circled a small fountain and pushed south past the makeshift stage where bands sometimes played on the weekends. She was moving fast. She wanted to get there and get it over with. "Why do you want to see it, anyway? You're not some kind of murder groupie, are you?"

Absolutely Fearless

David laughed. A normal laugh. "No. Absolutely not. I just wanted you to know I wasn't afraid."

"You keep saying that." She looked toward him, then back at the path, her ponytail of golden hair flipping back and forth as she moved. "Why are you so worried about not being afraid?"

David took a couple of quick steps and moved up to walk beside her. "I just think it would be cool, that's all. Not to be afraid of anything."

"Why?"

"Because then you'd really be free, wouldn't you?"

Gaia blinked. Interesting theory.

They passed under a group of oaks, and the shadows thickened around them. "Being fearless wouldn't make a person happy."

David reached up and snapped off a small dead limb. "Why not?" he said. "It's being afraid of things that makes people sad."

Gaia shook her head. "That's not true. Even without fear you still get lonely, or angry, or depressed."

"There's nothing wrong with angry," David said. "Sometimes you have to be angry. Sometimes it's what you need."

Gaia couldn't argue with that. "And what about the others?"

"What? Sad and lonely?" David shrugged. "I don't really feel those things."

Gaia reached the edge of a concrete path and stopped. "It doesn't sound like you feel much."

"All I need."

For a moment the two of them stood in silence, then Gaia turned her back on him, raised a hand, and pointed at the open space on the other side of the path.

"This is it," she said. "This is where they found the bodies." She turned back to look at David. She met his gaze dead-on. "But I think you already knew that."

DAVID REACHED BEHIND HIS BACK and pulled out a long knife. The blue-steel blade was almost black in the dim light, but the sharp **Painless** edge caught the glow from distant streetlamps and threw off glittering sparks.

Damn, he loved that.

"You're smarter than I anticipated," he said. "I like it." He stretched out a hand to Gaia. "Come on, I'll make it painless."

"No, you won't," Gaia said.

David grinned. "You're right. This is going to hurt like hell."

There was a
wildness in
his eyes. **the**
gentleman
How had she
not noticed
it before?

"I'M NOT THE ONE WHO LET HER
get away," Ed's voice
crackled through the
radio.

The Rescue Party

Sam glared at the lit-
tle yellow transistor. "I
was distracted," he said.
"Besides, it doesn't mat-
ter now. We've got to find a way into the park."

"I'm with you on that," Ed replied. "So, what's the plan?"

Sam looked across the street. There were now two policemen standing by the nearest entrance to the park, and he didn't think for a moment that the officers were just going to step aside and let them in.

"I'm going to have to go over the fence," Sam said after a few seconds' thought. "I don't see any other way."

"What about me?" asked Ed. "I don't know if you've noticed, but I'm not very good at going over things."

The thought had already occurred to Sam, but he didn't have a solution. "I need your help so I can get in. You come down here and distract the police."

Ed sighed. "That's me. Ed Fargo, distraction specialist."

"What?" Sam asked, confused.

"Forget it," Ed answered. "Distract them how?"

Sam glanced around and winced. Every second counted. There was no time to argue. "I don't know. Ask directions. Fake a heart attack. Just get them looking the wrong way long enough for me to climb the fence."

He didn't wait for Ed's reply. Instead he switched off the radio and dropped it into his pocket. He darted across the intersection, took a last longing look at the gate, then walked quickly toward the corner where the police would be far away and nearly out of sight.

Sam was only halfway to the corner when he got a break. The sounds of yelling and of running feet came from the direction of the entrance. Sam turned and saw the policemen wrestling a man with a potbelly and a stiff, graying beard.

It was the best chance Sam was going to get. There was no point in waiting for Ed when there was already a perfect distraction. He hurried across the sidewalk, bent low, then jumped for the top of the fence. His fingers managed to catch the square bar at the top, but the metal bit painfully into his palms. He started to bleed. Gritting his teeth, he slowly pulled, kicked, and scrambled his way to the top.

He stopped there for a second to catch his

breath. Down at the entrance the police were busy putting handcuffs on the bearded man. No one was looking.

Sam smiled. He had made it. Now he only had to find Gaia before it was too late.

He started to jump, but his foot slipped and his jump turned into a fall. The cuff of his pants caught on one of the points at the top of the fence. Sam pendulumed back and smashed against the fence with bone-jarring force. He kicked his feet, but the thin strip of fabric held him in place as firmly as a rope. He grabbed at the bars and tried to pull himself back up.

A hand grabbed Sam by the collar and jerked him away from the fence. Upside down, he found himself staring into a stern face topped with iron gray hair and an NYPD cap.

"What do you think you're doing, son?"

"I've got to get into the park," said Sam. "There's this girl, and she's in danger."

"Really?" The policeman grabbed Sam's arms and pulled them roughly behind his back. A moment later Sam felt hard, cold steel close around his wrists.

"What are you doing?" Sam shouted.

"My job," said the policeman. "What's your name?"

"Sam . . . Sam Moon."

"Well, Sam Moon, you're under arrest."

GAIA ALMOST LAUGHED.

You Die

She'd always thought she had perfect bad-guy radar. How wrong she was.

"What are we going to do now?" she said. There was a wildness in his eyes. How had she not noticed it before?

He looked at Gaia as if she were completely brain-dead. "Oh, please!" He pointed his nose up in the air and put on a thick British accent. "That should be immediately obvious to the most casual observer." Then he looked her directly in the eyes. "You die."

He was about to lunge. But Gaia wasn't going to take on a knife. "What's the matter? Scared to fight me hand to hand?"

David paused. He looked at the knife. His knuckles turned white. "I fear nothing from you," he said. He placed his weapon on the ground.

Gaia had to struggle to watch him and not look at the knife. Watch the opponent's every move. Every twitch. It was a basic rule of fighting, something her father had told her a thousand times.

But she couldn't stop herself. She checked the position of the knife. And that's when David hit her.

Gaia had been hit before. You didn't make it through the belts in any martial art without having your ass handed to you a hundred times. Gaia's nose had been bloodied by the best. But she was sure she had never been hit harder than that first blow from David.

He hit her with a `straight left` that knocked Gaia all the way across the path. She snapped through the stupid plastic police tape at the edge of the field, slipped on the grass, and fell.

Judo saved her life. To the naked eye, judo seems to be all about grabbing people by the arm and flipping them in the air. That wasn't it at all. `Judo was about falling.`

Gaia was falling backward. If she fought against that kind of fall, she would only spin her arms in the air and still end up sitting on the grass. Instead Gaia went with it. She pushed off hard, threw back her hands, and took the fall, using her arms as `shock absorbers.` Another quick push and Gaia was back on her feet.

David was almost on top of her. He swung again, but this time Gaia caught his wrist and pulled it past her.

For a moment they were almost face-to-face—so close, all Gaia had to do was move her lips to end her long kissing drought. The thought turned her stomach.

David pulled left, then quickly back to the right. It was an elementary move, and Gaia was braced for it, but David was very strong. Gaia was great at keeping her balance, but not even she could keep her balance when both of her feet were off the ground. That wasn't a rule of judo—that was a rule of gravity.

She didn't go down, but it was close. Before Gaia could recover, David drove a pile-driver fist into her side so hard, Gaia imagined she could hear her ribs crack. Maybe it wasn't imagination.

David grabbed at Gaia. He took her arm, jerked her back toward him, and threw another punch. Gaia blocked with a forearm and drove a knee into his gut at the same time.

David released his grip on her and fell back a step. Gaia didn't let him.

She took a quick step forward and delivered a kick that took David across the hip. Another that struck him in the thigh. He staggered and stepped back again.

This was more like it. Gaia spun, trying to deliver a solid kick to the body.

David blocked it easily. He took the blow against the flat of one palm, pushed sharply to throw Gaia off balance, then followed the push with a straight left that took her right between the eyes.

This punch was even harder than the first. The sound of his knuckles hitting her skull was amazing. It was like somebody had broken a rock with a sledgehammer. Like an ax biting into a tree.

Sparks of red light swarmed through Gaia's eyes. Her ears started to ring. All at once her arms and legs gained fifty pounds each.

She tried to get her hands up to block, but they didn't listen to orders. Another punch whistled in and hit her on the temple. This one was a right hook. That was another thing Gaia had learned early about fighting: If you're going to get hit in the face, get hit by a straight punch. Straight punches hurt, but if you get hit from the side, `hurt doesn't even come close.`

The night flashed into bright shades of yellow and blue. There was a sound in Gaia's ears like the roar from a hundred seashells.

She backpedaled fast and managed to avoid the next shot. Another punch came. Blocked. Another. Dodged. Another. It glanced off the top of her head without shooting any fireworks through her skull, but this time she felt `the warm flow of blood` across her forehead.

Gaia kicked out wildly and was lucky to hit David in the side. She didn't think it really hurt him, but at least it made him back off.

"Getting scared yet?" David taunted.

Somehow David knew about her, but this wasn't the time to figure out how.

Gaia didn't waste breath on talking. Her head was starting to clear, but the blood from her forehead was dripping into her eyes. Gaia's ribs ached, and the knee she had messed up the night before was starting to get in on the complaints. If she was going to end this on her feet, Gaia had to end it soon.

David launched another punch, but it was a long overhand right, and Gaia had time to get out of the way. She feinted a punch with her left, ducked his response, and stepped back. Did the same thing with the right and took another backward step.

There was a rhythm to David's fighting. If Gaia could work it out, she could time her shots and plaster him without taking blows of her own. All she needed was time.

Suddenly David lunged forward and grabbed Gaia with both his arms. Grabbing like that was a really stupid move—unless you were as strong as a gorilla. David could have made gorillas beg for mercy.

He squeezed the breath out of Gaia in a painful rush, and this time she knew the cracking sound had to be at least one of her ribs turning into a two-piece. She kicked her feet along David's shins, but he didn't let her free. So Gaia lowered her head and butted him in the face.

David howled. His nose exploded in blood. He lost his hold on Gaia and clamped a hand over his face.

Gaia drew a painful breath and jumped forward. She got off a kick to the chest, and David was staggering.

Then a kick to his side, and he groaned. His hand came away from his face. Blood spilled over his lips and dripped from the point of his chin. In seconds his shirt was stained by a spreading pool of darkness.

He punched. Gaia blocked and counterpunched. It wasn't a perfect hit on his solar plexus, but it was good enough to make David gasp for air. She hit him again, driving her fist into his gut so deep, Gaia wouldn't have been surprised to feel his backbone.

David made a wild, flailing punch. Gaia blocked it easily. He threw another, and she turned it aside. He stepped back. He was breathing hard, and Gaia could hear air whistling through his smashed nose.

"What about you?" she said. "Still fearless?"

"I . . . don't . . . have . . . anything to fear from you," he said.

It was time to end this thing. Gaia started forward, planning to put her foot where David's face was, but something grabbed her by the ankles. She glanced down. Tape. Stupid yellow police tape. Somehow yards of it had become tangled around her legs. It snapped easily enough, but it distracted Gaia for a second.

A second was too much to give up in the middle of a fight.

When she looked up, David's fist was six inches from her face and coming in fast. Gaia tried to dodge, but the blow still caught her on her right jawbone.

This time Gaia didn't just see sparks. This time she went someplace. Someplace where squirrels played banjos and the trees were cotton-candy pink. The seashells were roaring again, and this time they were joined by a brass band. Gaia tried to put out her hands and catch herself, but for a second there she couldn't even tell if she had hands. Gaia didn't know if she was standing or lying on the ground.

She wasn't even sure if she was still alive.

It took a few seconds for the furry-tailed rats to put away their instruments and the night to go back to something like normal. When it did, Gaia figured out that she was on the ground. There was something under her hands. Grass, but something else, too. Something gritty and crumbly. It took her a moment to realize that it was chalk—the chalk that had marked the body lines of the dead girls.

From somewhere behind her Gaia heard David laugh. "That's great," he said. "That's perfect. I'll go get the knife. You just stay put." His smashed nose turned "that's" into "dat's" and "great" into "gweat." It would have been funny if he wasn't about to kill her.

Gaia struggled to sit up, but the best she could manage was to roll onto one knee. The banjos might be packed away, but her head was still spinning. Everything hurt.

David didn't seem to be in much better shape. He limped as he crossed the field and stopped near the path for a moment to lean against a tree. He was banged up pretty good, but he was still going to kill Gaia. He knelt down beside the path and reached for the knife.

Gaia saw salvation coming from twenty feet away. David saw it, too, but he was slow. He barely managed to turn his head before Ed Fargo hit him like a freight train.

David was coming. He was climbing along Gaia's body, and he still had his knife.

a time to die

GAIA WOULD HAVE SCREAMED FOR

Ed to stop if she'd had the time. The collision happened with such speed that it looked more like a car accident than a wheelchair ramming.

Ground Rule Double

One of David's hands, the one reaching for the knife, was trapped under a wheel. Instantly every finger on that hand had snapped, one after another, like twigs. The metal frame of the chair caught him under the arm, rolled him over, and left him sprawling on the ground. His head hit the asphalt with a sickening crack, and Gaia saw every limb of his body go slack.

David was down for the count.

At the moment of impact Ed was thrown up and out. He flew almost twenty feet in a low arc before he thumped to the ground between a pair of pines. Freed of his weight, the chair rolled on another few paces, curved, then toppled on its side.

That was when Gaia hit the ground. The paralyzation had set in.

For the space of five seconds everything was still and quiet. Then the broken bodies started to move.

David was up first. Gaia couldn't believe her eyes.

She'd thought he was done. Unconscious. Useless. Yet he climbed to his feet, clutching his broken, bleeding hand against his chest. Who *was* this guy?

"Gonna . . . kill . . . you both," he grunted. He looked in the grass, located the knife, and lifted it in his good hand.

Gaia struggled to rise. She had to stop him.

She couldn't move. Gaia's muscles twitched and squirmed like bags full of snakes, and she was barely able to raise her head from the ground.

David looked at her, then looked at Ed. Slowly his split lips widened into a horrible, bloody grin.

"Which one first?" he said.

Me, thought Gaia. Come for me. But even her mouth had shut down. She could do nothing but watch as David decided who would die.

EVERY BRANCH GRABBED AT HIS

A Hundred Feet Away

coat. Every stone seemed to be out to trip his feet.

Tom Moore ran desperately through the woods. Loki wasn't the only one with fake identification, but it had taken Tom much longer than he expected to convince the police guarding the park that he should be allowed inside.

He pulled the gun from his coat pocket as he ran and thumbed off the safety. He only hoped it wasn't too late.

GAIA OPENED HER HAND AND CLOSED

it again. It wasn't much, but it was something. Her body was returning to her.

The Last Reserves

A dozen yards away, David limped toward the pilot of the overturned wheelchair. Ed had his hands under him and was dragging himself back as fast as he could. It wasn't fast enough. David would be on him in seconds.

Ed was about to die.

Gaia reached down and pulled at her reserves of strength. The tank was almost empty. She absently thought of what her father used to say when he had driven the family car long past the point the needle dropped to *E*.

Vapors. I'm running on vapors.

Slowly she rolled over onto her trembling arms.

Painfully she pushed her aching legs under her and climbed to her feet.

David glanced at her, then continued after Ed.

Gaia tried to go toward them, but she could barely manage a step. Her head swam, and her knees were weak. She wasn't going to be fast enough. There was only ten feet between David and Ed. There was at least thirty feet between Gaia and David. There was no way for Gaia to get to Ed in time.

"Hey," she called in a hoarse whisper.

David kept after Ed.

"Wasn't I the one you wanted?" Gaia's voice was a little stronger this time.

The gap between David and Ed was down to five feet. David raised his knife to strike.

"Hey, chicken!" Gaia screamed.

David froze.

"Are you afraid to fight me?"

David pivoted like a rusty screen door and looked at Gaia. "I'm not afraid of you."

"Then show me."

Gaia had trained herself to hold back. Even when she was fighting a mugger or a thief, she was careful to stop, not injure. She threw those rules away.

David staggered toward her with the knife held high. He pointed the glittering blade toward Gaia's face and swung the edge from side to side.

David was strong. David was fast. But by now Gaia

knew one thing for sure—David wasn't well trained. She leaned back her arm as if she were going to throw a punch.

That was all it took to draw David's attention. He leaped at her with surprising speed.

Gaia fell back. Her balance was gone. She was going to hit the ground—there was no stopping that—but there was enough strength in her legs for one last good kick. She pivoted on her left foot, kicking and falling at the same time.

David's right leg broke with a noise like a gunshot. A thin, high whine escaped his blood-smeared mouth as both he and Gaia toppled to the ground.

GAIA LAY ON HER BACK IN THE grass, biding her time. She knew David thought she was spent. Done. Gone. But she was just waiting. Overhead, the gloomy clouds that had covered the sky all day finally parted. Stars peeked through.

Seeing Stars

She'd never seen stars in the city. But they were up there now, sparkling down at Gaia as if they had come out just to watch the bitter end.

From somewhere nearby she could hear sounds of breathing. They weren't pleasant sounds. The breathing was kind of wet, as if the person making the noise was pulling as much blood as air into his lungs with every breath.

A hand grasped Gaia's ankle. Another closed on her knee. Something hard and cold pressed against the skin of her leg.

David was coming. He was climbing along Gaia's body, and he still had his knife.

Patience. Patience.

One of David's hands came down in the middle of Gaia's stomach with painful force. The other hand, the hand with the knife, slid along her arm.

It was strange. After a lifetime of feeling alone, or embarrassed, or just plain angry, what Gaia felt now was calm. She had done everything she could. Somewhere, way down in her brain, a voice was calling for her to get up. Get up and fight. But that voice was faint and far away.

Gaia was tired. Very, very tired. But maybe, just maybe, if she waited until just the right moment, she could finish this thing. And maybe she could live through it.

Tangled black hair came into view. Even from this close, Gaia could barely recognize the face as David's. His nose flattened like a pancake. His face painted over in blood. His lips pulled back in a snarl of rage.

Slowly David dragged himself beside Gaia. Then he raised the knife and held it above her chest.

"See?" he croaked through bloody lips. "See, I'm the best after all. I can beat you. I'm the best."

Gaia had no idea what he was talking about. David sat up straighter, raised the knife high, and plunged it down at Gaia. She raised her arms. Watched his eyes widen in surprise. And then it happened.

THE SOUND CAME THREE TIMES, all very close together. Hiss. Hiss. Hiss. It was like the noise of air being let out of a bicycle tire. Like water falling on a hot skillet.

Popped

DAVID'S SHOULDER ERUPTED. HIS body twitched around to the left, and blood poured out across his chest. There was a cracking, and for a moment Gaia saw something white exposed in the core of his wounds.

Splatter

Bone.

"I . . . ," said David. "You . . ." A bloody foam spilled from his lips. It hit her face with a sickening splatter. David toppled off of Gaia and fell still at her side.

For several seconds Gaia lay there, trying to understand what had happened. Something had hurt David. Something had stopped him.

She wasn't going to die. Not now. It seemed like an impossible thought.

Someone stepped into view at the edge of the clearing. Gaia turned her head for a better look.

She saw a tall figure in a trench coat. She saw the gun in his hand. She knew the face. Her uncle. Apparently he couldn't call or write, but he had an uncanny ability to materialize when she was in danger.

The figure at the edge of the clearing only stood there for a few moments. Then he turned and stepped back into the shadows of the trees.

Gaia closed her eyes.

IT TOOK ED NEARLY TEN MINUTES TO

Exit, Stage Left

get his wheelchair upright, get his battered self into it, and roll across the damp ground to Gaia's side. For every one of those ten minutes he harbored the unthinkable thought that she was dead.

And yet when he actually reached the center of the clearing, he was amazed to see Gaia sit up and push her ratty hair away from her face.

Total, utter, complete, euphoric relief.

Ed calmed his heaving chest before he let himself open his mouth. "Hey, Gaia," he called. "Your new boyfriend's the killer."

Gaia made a tired, gasping noise that might have been laughter on the planet Exhaustion. She stood slowly, swayed on her feet for a few seconds, then staggered over to lean against Ed's chair.

"Thanks for the update," she said. "How did you get in here?"

"Easy." Ed rapped his knuckles against the armrest of the wheelchair. "I got in while Sam was getting arrested."

Gaia blinked. "Sam got arrested?"

"Worked out great as a distraction," Ed said with a grin.

"Okay," said Gaia. She shook her head and swayed so badly that she almost lost her grip on the chair.

"What happened?" asked Ed. "I couldn't see what was going on. I was so afraid. . . . I mean, I was afraid he was going to . . ."

"Kill me?" Gaia nodded slowly. "He almost did. We'll leave him for the police."

David suddenly moaned. His broken, bleeding hand scrabbled at the grass.

Gaia pulled back her foot and kicked him again. The moaning stopped.

Ed looked at her and shook his head. "You know, sometimes I can't tell if you're really brave or just perpetually pissed off."

TOM KNEW HE HAD TO GET MOVING.

Broken

Once Loki and his operatives had figured out that Tom Moore was here, they wouldn't pass up the chance to bag him when they had it.

He turned to leave and heard movement behind him. Quickly he pressed himself against the dark trunk of an elm and waited.

A man was coming across the field. It was a tall man, a man Tom had no trouble recognizing.

Loki walked straight across the trampled field. He paused a moment beside the broken form on the ground. Then he knelt, grabbed the boy by the hair, and delivered a sharp slap across the face.

David groaned.

"Wake up," said Loki. Another slap. "Open your eyes."

The eyelids fluttered.

"She shot you?" Loki said. "She used a gun?"

The boy on the ground said something. From his place by the trees, Tom couldn't hear the words, but he could hear Loki's reply.

"Home?" Loki shook his head. "I'm afraid that boat has already sailed. You're worthless to me now."

The boy spoke again, and this time Tom could make out his words.

"I'll tell," he said. His voice was high and raw, like a child who had been crying. "I'll tell them everything."

"Yes." Loki released his grip on the boy's blood-soaked hair and stood. "Yes, I'm sure you would."

Tom knew what was coming next. He turned away from the scene and started to make his way through the woods. He had gone no more than a dozen steps before he heard the gunshot.

There have always been hor-
ror stories about first dates,
blind dates, setups, hookups, and
probably a bunch of scenarios
I've never even heard of.

   But this has to be one for the
record books.

   This is the type of thing that
could only happen to someone as
undateable as me.

   At least I didn't kiss him.

CHASE

To Nall

When I was very little—I mean braids and teddy bears little—my mother used to read to me from *Little Women* every night before bed. She used to read to me from a lot of books, but *Little Women* is the one I remember the best. Like everyone else who's ever read the book, I wanted to be Jo. Jo was cool. Jo was a writer, even though women weren't sup-posed to be writers. Jo spurned men. Jo took care of everybody. And above all, Jo wasn't pretty—she was awkward and unkempt and a tomboy. In short, I probably wanted to be Jo because I already *was* Jo. I was never going to be the beautiful, admired, gracious Meg or the sweet, meek, victim Beth. And Amy? I pretty much just wanted to kick that annoying lit-tle twit in the head.

But the one thing Jo had that I wanted most was her sisters. (Except Amy.) She would have done anything for them and they for her. There was this bond between

them that was like nothing I had
in my life. My parents were great,
but it wasn't the same. I wanted a
confidant, someone to have adventures with, someone to share my
daydreams and my nightmares with.
Someone who would understand. I
wanted that unconditional love and
friendship that was all over the
pages of *Little Women*.

But as many times as I asked
and begged for a little sister,
the answer was always the same.
"Maybe someday. . . ," my mother
would say, a sad, wistful look in
her eyes. I know she wanted more
kids, but I also know that she
and my father had a seriously
complicated life, what with Loki
sneaking around and pretending he
was my father so he could take me
out of school and coach me and
try to brainwash me. They probably wanted to wait until things
calmed down. Well, they never
did. And then she was killed.

So the closest I ever came to a
sister was Tatiana. I'm not saying
we ever approached anything like

unconditional love, but I would
say we had an understanding. We
lived together, we shared a room,
and our parents were clearly in
love (or so I thought). It was
impossible not to draw the conclu-
sion that we might be sisters one
day and that in some ways we
already were.

You see, we were in it
together. (Again, so I thought.)
We bonded over our superspy parents and the constant level of
mind-bending insanity in our
lives. I thought we were on the
same side—that we would be there
for each other no matter what. And
I could almost see a future where
we'd become really close. It felt
like it was almost destined, you
know? I mean, where else was I
going to find someone who had as
screwed up a life as I did?
Someone who understood it all.

But as usual, I was wrong.
Tatiana betrayed me in a way I never
would have thought possible. She
tried to kill me. Betrayal doesn't
get much more serious than that.

So much for sisters.

Maybe it's true, what they say. Blood *is* thicker than water. You shouldn't trust anyone but your family. Your true family. Your blood.

Huh.

The only blood relative I have that I *know* is alive is Loki. The evil, psychotic, scum-sucking maggot monster of death.

Sometimes the irony of life just makes the head spin.

She couldn't
remember the
last time
she hadn't
gotten worked

unstimulating

up and
focused and
generally
jazzed during
a fight.

IT WASN'T A UNIQUE EXPERIENCE FOR

Gaia Moore, wandering the streets of
New York City with nowhere to go. It
wasn't even a unique experience for
her to believe her father was dead,
that she was next, that around every corner she passed
could be the gun that held the bullet that
would end her life. It was just that it had been
so long since she had been so entirely alone. Weeks,
even. Months.

There was no one left.

Gaia pulled her collar up against the cold breeze
that blew harder and more bitingly with each passing
moment. It was late spring already, but then,
Manhattan never seemed to adhere to the *Farmer's
Almanac*. The island had taken on the general attitude
of its inhabitants and had mastered the ability to give
an "Up yours!" to even the likes of Mother Nature.
And so here was this winter wind on the heels of a
warm spring day. At least it kept the throngs of people
off the streets and inside, watching their rented
movies and eating their delivery food. Fewer inno-
cents for Gaia to trample. She turned a corner and
bent into the wind.

Just above the soft worn cotton of her jacket, Gaia
made sure her eyes were free and peeled. Natasha had
been captured and was now in the custody of the
CIA. At this very moment she was being questioned,

interrogated, maybe even beaten (one could dream). But Tatiana was still out there somewhere. She could be anywhere. And she still had orders to kill Gaia.

Not if I kill you first, Gaia thought, her rage bubbling over from her heart into her thoughts. It was still hard to swallow, the fact that Tatiana was in on it. The fact that everything they'd been through together had been a lie. That she'd actually been snowed by a little blond DKNY-sporting fake. In the beginning Tatiana had acted so helpless, like she didn't know how to fight, like she didn't understand the simple art of tracking someone. How many times had Gaia risked her own neck to help Tatiana? And she'd actually been proud of the way Tatiana was coming along. How she was learning to take care of herself, kick some butt of her own. Even if she was also turning into a materialistic, party-animal Friend of Heather. But it was all an act.

"It doesn't matter," Gaia spoke into the collar of her jacket, her warm breath heating her cheeks and mouth. So she'd lost Tatiana. Big deal. She'd lost more important people in her lifetime. Much more important. And if she bumped into the girl right now, she'd kick the crap out of her first and ask questions later. One question, actually. The only one that mattered.

Where is my father?

Yes, Natasha had claimed that he was dead. And Gaia had no reason not to believe her. Except, of course, that everything else the woman had ever said or done had been a lie. At this point Gaia gave her father a fifty-fifty chance of still being down with the breathing folk. But she was a hundred percent sure that Tatiana knew the truth. And those were good odds to be working with.

`If she only knew where the hell the girl was.`

"All alone, no place to go, all alone, no place to go."

Gaia paused for a moment, taken off guard by the rambling words of the homeless man who suddenly blocked her path. He looked at her with wild, blank eyes, shaking a battered blue-and-white coffee cup in front of her, the piddling change inside rattling pathetically. He was bundled inside about four flannel coats but somehow still looked impossibly cold. He shuffled toward her, his gooey gaze settling somewhere around the bridge of her nose.

"All alone, no place to go, all alone, no place to go. . ."

She knew he was just one of the thousands of unlucky people who had been driven insane by a life on the streets, but for a moment it felt like he was looking right through her skin into her heart. Somehow he was extracting the exact words she was trying to keep from eating away at her.

"All alone, no place to go, all alone, no place to go. . ."

"All right, all right!" Gaia said. She stuffed her hand into the depths of her jeans pocket and came out with a quarter. "Here," she said, slapping the coin into the cup. The man didn't acknowledge it—he simply took up the refrain once more.

"All alone, no place to go, all alone, no place to go. . ."

Gaia started to run.

She ran to feel the wind on her face, to get her blood pumping, to hear the roar of the cars and people passing by in her ears, to drown out the man's ceaseless words.

"All alone, no place to go, all alone, no place to go. . ."

She ran and ran, without even realizing that she was headed for Ed's building until she was standing right in front of it. The tears that had been ripped from her eyes by the stinging wind made little streaks across her temples, tightening the skin. Gaia pulled in a breath and hugged her jacket to herself. She stared at the door.

This was it. This was the place she always used to be able to come to when there was no place else to go. Ed had been the one person who was there for her, without fail. But she'd screwed that up, too, hadn't she? She'd screwed everything up.

Trying not to think about the comfort that lay just beyond those sleek glass doors, Gaia turned her steps toward Washington Square Park. It was time to admit the inevitable. If she was going to get any rest tonight, which she'd need if she was going to track down Tatiana tomorrow, then she was going to have to scare herself up a park bench. Washington Square Park was downtown's Motel 6 for runaways and druggies. The only difference was a person didn't need to lay out any cash to get a bed.

Gaia slipped into the park by the west entrance and started along the circle. A large woman dozed, sitting up, on the first bench, surrounded by dozens of shopping bags full of clothing and rags and heaven only knew what else. There was a shopping cart tied to the bench by a red bandanna, and a kitten was curled up in the child's seat among a bunch of tangled scarves. On the next bench was a scrawny kid wearing barely enough clothing to keep him comfortable on a hot summer's day, shivering away even as he slept. Gaia averted her eyes and swallowed back her pity. He was probably an addict who had left a perfectly good home behind him somewhere, and at that moment Gaia couldn't feel sorry for him. All she could think about was the warm bed out there with his name on it.

Finally Gaia came across an empty bench, and she glanced around to make sure the immediate area was creep-free. Satisfied, she lay down, her face toward the back of the seat, and curled her arm under her head.

Don't think about anything, she told herself. *You can deal with it all tomorrow.*

Soon Gaia felt herself starting to drift, and she silently thanked the stars for her ability to fall asleep anywhere. But just as her thoughts were fading to black, the entire bench shook from the force of a powerful blow. Gaia sat up straight and looked right into the stubble-covered face of a square-shouldered, square-jawed, totally strung-out junkie. His eyes were lined with red and his breathing was ragged. He bared his teeth like a rabid dog.

"This is my bench, girlie," he said, gracing Gaia with a cloud of breath that smelled of rotten beer.

"Leave me alone," Gaia said, starting to lie down again. She was definitely not in the mood.

The junkie walked around to the front of the bench, grabbed the back of Gaia's jacket, and yanked her to the ground. Her shoulder hit the asphalt and her head bounced against the hard ground. Quickly Gaia rolled over onto her back, grimacing. She scrunched up her nose and tried not to breathe.

"Look, when I got here, the bench was empty," Gaia said. "You don't look like the brightest guy in the world, but I'm sure you've heard of finders keepers."

"F'you won't give up the bench, I got no problem takin' it from ya," the guy said.

Gaia rolled her eyes. For once, she didn't feel like fighting, but she'd already had more than enough of the grandstanding banter part of the evening. She had a feeling that this was the type of guy who could stand here and trade threats until he passed out, but there was no telling how long that would take. Besides, the sweet taste of sleep was still clinging to her, and she wanted to get back there. So she decided to take the shortcut. She reached out and shoved him.

The junkie staggered back, surprised, then narrowed his eyes and threw a wide, arcing punch. Gaia easily blocked it, grasped his arm, and turned into him, jabbing her elbow back into his stomach. He doubled over slightly, and she brought her skull back into his with a crack. When she spun away from him and took her fighting stance, he already looked pretty beaten up. Gaia was about to let down her guard when he let out a battle cry and rushed her, tackling her right to the ground.

Gaia tried to push him off her, waiting for her adrenaline to kick in, waiting for that rush of energy, but it didn't come. She was just tired. And not a little bit bored. As she contemplated this, the junkie got one good punch into her gut and another to her jaw that sent stars across her vision. Gaia had had enough. She propped her calves under his torso and lifted, flipping him up and over her head onto his back. He let out a groan as he fell, and Gaia got to her feet to hover over him.

"Are we done yet?" she asked.

He waved his hands in front of his face and winced. "We're done! We're done! Please don't hurt me!"

"Fine," Gaia said, trying not to show how relieved she was. "Just get the hell out of here."

The junkie stood up, keeping his distance from Gaia, then ran off awkwardly into the night. Gaia trudged back over to her bench, feeling heavy and low and disappointed. She couldn't remember the last time she hadn't gotten worked up and focused and generally jazzed during a fight. And right now she felt about as alive as she did in her highly unstimulating math class every day. What was wrong with her? It wasn't like she hadn't been in places as depressing as this before. She'd spent almost her entire life in them.

But this time was somehow different. When she reached inside and tried to summon up some kind of motivating emotion—anger, vengefulness—all she felt was... broken.

Gaia lay down on the bench again, her brow furrowed as she put her head down on the pillow of her bent arm.

Don't think about anything, she told herself again. *You can deal with it all tomorrow.*

Then she closed her eyes and let sleep finally come.

Safe House

TATIANA'S HAND SHOOK VIOLENTLY as she attempted for the third time to master the simple act of inserting a key into a lock. She blamed her shivering on the fact that she hadn't expected the sudden shift in the weather and so hadn't dressed for it. She also hadn't expected, however, to see her mother get dragged off by a couple of huge men in black spy gear.

"Damn it. You must focus," she said to herself through her teeth. If her mother could see her now, she'd be ashamed. Tatiana had to pull herself together. Her mother was counting on her.

Finally Tatiana gripped her right hand with her left to steady it, and mercifully the key slid into the lock. There was a moment of suspense as she turned it, but the lock clicked and the door swung open with a slow, `angry creak,` as if it had just been woken from a deep slumber. Tatiana had the right place. She was home.

She slipped through the door and quickly punched the code her mother had made her memorize into the keypad on the near wall, the red light flashing menacingly as she worked. After hitting all the numbers, Tatiana pressed her thumb into the enter key and squeezed her eyes shut. The alarm let out a loud beep, and when she opened her eyes again, the red light had turned to green. Tatiana closed the door behind her and fastened all five safety locks. She leaned back against the door and allowed herself to breathe. She was safe. Alone, but safe.

Peeling off her lightweight jacket, Tatiana decided

to explore her new abode. In the semidarkness she found a light switch and flicked it on, illuminating the small living room with the weak light from a single overhead fixture. She'd been hearing about the Alphabet City safe house ever since she and her mother had arrived in New York City, but she'd never been here. The moment she saw the place in the light, she felt an almost painful longing for the lofty space of the Seventy-second Street apartment.

Your mother is most likely in a jail cell right now, she told herself. *Quit your whining.*

She breathed in the musty, sooty smell of the air and took a few steps into the tiny square living room. The walls were plain and white, and an old but comfortable-looking corduroy couch stood to one side. A table next to it held a single glass lamp with a dingy shade. Tatiana walked over to the one piece of artwork on the wall—a framed print of Renoir's *The Luncheon of the Boating Party*—and lifted it from the nail that held it in place. Just as she'd been told, there was a square, gray safe door built into the wall. Tatiana quickly dialed in the combination, which she'd also committed to memory, and the door popped open, letting out a hiss of air.

There were stacks upon stacks of bills inside— American dollars, Canadian dollars, Mexican pesos, British pounds, and Russian rubles. Tatiana grabbed a few twenties from one of the bundles of dollars, then pulled out a stack of passports. As she flipped through them—there were at least ten with her picture, each from a different country—she smirked sadly at the names her mother had given her. Annie Whitmore, Corrine Deveneaux, Marianna Alonso, Marcella Tuscano.

I could just disappear, Tatiana thought, allowing the seduction of such a thought to momentarily send her pulse racing. She gazed at her picture on the Italian passport and imagined it—imagined herself on the white sands of the Mediterranean, sipping something fruity and letting her bare back bathe in the sun. But as quickly as the image came, she squelched it. She wasn't going anywhere without her mother. Not now. Not ever.

She took the last items out of the safe, a nice, sleek .45 pistol and a full clip, then crammed the passports back inside. She shoved the clip into the gun, savoring the menacing click as it locked into place. After making sure the safety was on, Tatiana slipped the gun between her waistband and her back. Then she closed the safe and hung the painting again. She had to check the rest of her provisions.

The kitchen, just to the left of the living room, which was lined with avocado green cabinets and held a large brown refrigerator, clearly hadn't been redecorated since the seventies. Tatiana walked over to the pantry and checked inside. The shelves were stocked with canned soups, pasta sauces, packets of instant oatmeal, and cans of soda and juice.

She walked back across the living room to the bedroom, which took all of three steps, and flicked on the light. Two twin-size beds, draped with blue blankets, stood on either side of a single nightstand. Inspection of a small dresser against the far wall revealed drawers filled with plain underwear, bras, T-shirts, and sweaters in Tatiana and Natasha's sizes. The closet held a few pairs of jeans, assorted footwear, and two heavy winter coats. On the top shelf was a wide array of wigs, hats, and sunglasses. Tatiana pulled down a long, dark wig with natural-looking waves and smiled morosely. Her mother had certainly been prepared.

Still fingering the coarse hair of the wig, Tatiana sat down on the closest bed and tried to remain calm. She tried not to let herself picture the events of the evening over and over again. Reliving the nightmare was not going to help her deal with it. It wasn't going to bring her mother back to her. There was only one thing that would. She had to make Gaia talk. Gaia was the only person who knew where her mother was—who the men were that had taken her.

From their uniform fighting tactics, it was clear they belonged to some government agency, and considering Tom Moore's affiliation with the CIA, Tatiana assumed it was them. But that meant nothing to her. It wasn't as if she was privy to all the CIA's secret interrogation facilities. As much as she hated to admit it, she needed Gaia. Unfortunately, she knew that the self-righteous, egotistical **bitch-on-a-mission** was never going to help her.

What Tatiana needed was a plan.

Taking a deep breath, Tatiana gathered her blond hair on top of her head and pulled the wig on over it. It was tight, but all the better. She tugged at the temples, then walked over to the full-length mirror that was attached to the back of the door, suddenly hyperaware of the cold steel against the skin of her back. When she saw her reflection, she smiled slowly. It was perfect—a total transformation.

Tatiana pulled her gun out of her waistband, hoisted it, and aimed it at her reflection, her arms straight and locked at the elbow. She barely even recognized herself. Whatever her plan might turn out to be, Gaia would never see her coming.

GAIA KEPT HER HEAD BENT, EYES

focused on the grimy sidewalk as she emerged from the subway station on East Sixty-eighth Street. It was rush hour, and she was

So Blind

bombarded on every side by harried commuters, juggling their coffee cups and briefcases and reeking of musky aftershave and freshly sprayed perfume. Gaia's intention had been to remain inconspicuous, but among this crowd there was no way to keep from sticking out like a prune in a bushel of apples. She stepped to the corner and looked left and right, trying to pick out anything suspicious. Any signs of Tatiana.

The three guys who always hung out by the tiny newsstand across Lexington were there as usual, checking out the latest issue of *Boobs* magazine and sneering as they hovered over the centerfold. Mr. Han, the Vietnamese grocer, stood outside his shop, guarding his fruit with a watchful eye. A bus zoomed by, kicking a cloud of exhaust directly into Gaia's lungs. Yep. Everything was status normal.

The light changed and Gaia crossed the street, fully aware that she was taking her life in her own hands simply by appearing in this neighborhood. It was the one thing, besides school, that she and Tatiana had in common. The girl would have to be an idiot not to look for Gaia here. If Tatiana knew anything about her mark, she had to know that Gaia would come back to the apartment to look for clues. And as a morning breeze tossed a tangled clump of hair across Gaia's vision, she almost hoped she *would* bump into Tatiana. It would be nice to get this over with.

When she arrived at her building, Gaia nodded quickly at Javier, the doorman, then hopped into an open elevator. As she slowly made her ascent, she wondered exactly how long it would take the CIA to break Natasha. They were probably using all the standard tactics—sleep deprivation, starvation, threats against her daughter—to try to get her to talk. But Natasha was trained by some of the best in the world. She could cope with torture. Gaia knew it could take days, weeks, months before the government was able to get the information Gaia needed. She didn't have that long.

The elevator pinged and the doors slid open. Gaia cautiously peeked into the hallway and found it deserted. She crept along the wall to the apartment she had been sharing with Natasha and Tatiana for so many weeks. Pressing her ear up against the door's flat surface, she heard nothing but merciful silence. Gaia slid her key into the lock and opened the door.

The moment she stepped inside, she knew instinctively that the place was deserted. It felt cold and still, almost as if no one had inhabited its rooms for years. As she stood and looked around at the living room she'd kicked back in and the kitchen she'd snacked from, Gaia was filled with a hot, suffocating shame. How could she have let Natasha and Tatiana fool her into thinking they cared? How could she have been so blind?

She thought of all the times Natasha had scolded her for being late, of the concern she'd shown for her and her father. But suddenly she saw the bigger picture. Natasha had laughed at her in these rooms. She'd manipulated her and had enjoyed doing it. Poor little Gaia. Poor little naive daughter of Tom. And all the while Tatiana had been in on it. Tatiana had been laughing at her, too.

Gaia hated that she'd allowed it to happen. She hated that she had been so gullible. But not anymore. She was in control now. Now it was her turn to laugh. Gaia locked the door behind her and set to work.

And just as she had done earlier, when she'd been looking for clues to the attempts made on her life, she turned the apartment inside out. She started with Natasha's room, ripping through the clothes in the closet and checking every nook and cranny for hidden compartments, false walls. She knocked along the surfaces, searching for hollow spaces, but there was nothing. The shelves were stacked with shoe boxes and bags. Gaia pulled every one down and emptied them on the floor in a pile, but the search revealed nothing except the fact that `Natasha was clearly obsessed with her feet.`

Frustrated, Gaia checked under the bed, pulling out every single drawer and overturning them, emptying silky nightgowns, cashmere sweaters, and slippery scarves onto the bed. She could vividly see Natasha in this room, getting dressed, smirking her triumph in the full-length mirror, thinking of how easily she'd seduced Tom Moore. Gaia felt hot tears spring to her eyes. This was the first woman her father had trusted

21

since her mother had died. How was it that her father, who had been a spy for over twenty years, was so damned gullible? How could he have let her mother's memory be marred by someone like Natasha?

A sliver of anger worked its way into Gaia's heart, but she wiped her tears and tried to suppress it. This was not her father's fault. There was no use wasting time wishing things were different. Wishing he hadn't let his guard down. Gaia herself had mistakenly trusted many an enemy.

She dropped the last empty drawer on the bed, then checked under each one for documents that might be taped there and inspected lamps and phones, looking for wires. By the time she was done, the bedroom was chaos, the bathroom a total wreck of smashed eye shadows and broken bottles.

But there was nothing. If Natasha had been hiding anything in this room, she was damn good.

Gaia rushed into the hall and paused for a moment, listening for any sign of life, but didn't hear a sound. She attacked the room she shared with Tatiana with the same ferocity, ripping her precious clothes from the hangers and pawing through her school-books. She yanked bags and boxes out from under Tatiana's bed and emptied her CD collection onto the floor. But again there was nothing.

Gaia sighed and pressed her palm into her fore-head. Maybe this was pointless. Maybe she was just wasting her time. Her blood rushed through her veins as a little voice in her mind taunted her for being so stupid. Natasha wasn't an amateur. She wouldn't keep the secrets of her master plan right under the nose of one of her primary targets.

Still, Gaia wasn't quite ready to give up. Her father was depending on her. Alive or dead, she had to find out where he was, and as far as Gaia knew, Natasha and Tatiana were the only ones who had that information. She hit Natasha's room again, and the moment she walked in, she realized she hadn't checked the nightstands. She dropped to her knees in front of the closest one and yanked the small drawer out. It flew open and then stuck stubbornly. As much as Gaia jimmied and tugged, the drawer wouldn't come free. Gaia pulled out the paperback novel, the pad of paper and pen, and the sleep mask inside, dropping it all to the floor at her knees. She shoved her hands into the empty drawer and felt along the plywood surface.

"Come on," Gaia said under her breath, starting to feel desperate. A trickle of sweat ran down from her temple along her cheek. "Come on. . . ."

And then her fingertip hit something. Something sharp. Gaia's heart leapt into her throat. She ran her fingertip along the slim edge of what had to be a small envelope, from the feel of it. She pulled out her hands and crouched, tilting her head to one side and trying to see into the back of the drawer. Sure enough, she spotted the folded edge of a brown envelope that was wedged into the seam between the back of the drawer and the bottom. Gaia reached into the drawer again, grasped the envelope with both hands, and yanked as hard as she could.

The envelope came free and Gaia tumbled backward into the pile of shoes and boots behind her. Her heart slammed against her rib cage in excitement as she looked at the envelope. Across the front five capital letters were printed: *ABCSH*.

There was something heavy inside. Gaia tipped the envelope over her hand, and into her waiting palm fell a single brass key. It lay there, cold and unhelpful, but Gaia felt like she'd achieved a small victory. It was a clue. It had to be. The key had been just hidden enough and the message on the front of the envelope was just cryptic enough to reassure her that she was on to something.

Gaia slipped the key back into the envelope and stuffed it into her back pocket. She returned to her room, grabbed her duffel bag from under her bed, and stuffed some clothes into it at random. She slung her messenger bag over her shoulder, took one last look around at the destruction she'd caused, and headed for the door.

She had no idea where she was going, but she couldn't stay here. Aside from the possibility of being murdered by Tatiana in her sleep, this place had too many bad memories. Memories of how for weeks on end, she'd been sleeping with the enemy.

It was time to start over. Something Gaia was growing more and more accustomed to.

ABCSH, ABCSH, A. . . B. . . C. . . S. . . H.

Another Enemy

Gaia stared at the corner of the chessboard, the squares and playing pieces blurred before her. She'd come to the park hoping that a nice solid trouncing of Mr. Haq would help calm her nerves, help her focus, but all she could think about was the letters. They danced in front of her mind's eye like one of those animated lessons from *Sesame Street,* but they refused to form themselves into any kind of order that would yield an answer.

ABCSH. . .

What did it mean? And what did it have to do with her father?

"Girlie?" Mr. Haq said. "Girlie? Your move!" He snapped his stubby, calloused fingers in front of Gaia's dazed face.

She blinked, and her eyes settled on the board.

"I got you this time, eh, girlie?" the old man said gleefully, rubbing his palms together. "You not yourself today. I on top of my game." He snickered and Gaia sighed. She could take him in five moves, no problem, but she couldn't see the point. This was totally useless. The game had done nothing to calm her down. She had to get out of here. She had to go... somewhere, she just didn't know where. All she knew was that she felt like she had millions of tiny little Ping-Pong balls dancing around under her skin. She couldn't just sit here any longer.

"I have to go," she said, standing up.

Mr. Haq's tiny, dark eyes widened as he tilted back his head to look up at her. "You forfeit? You can't forfeit! You never forfeit!"

"First time for everything," Gaia said flatly.

"But I have you! I have you!" Mr. Haq wailed in protest, gesturing wildly at the board. "You can't just leave because I have you!"

"Sorry," Gaia said. She shouldered her messenger bag, grabbed her duffel, and hurried away, followed by the continued sounds of Mr. Haq's protesting wails.

Gaia crossed over to Waverly and started to walk east with less than no clue as to where she was headed. She immediately regretted forfeiting her game. At least as long as she was sitting there, she was *somewhere*.

Somewhere familiar. Now she was headed right back to nowhere.

If only she knew what her next move should be. If only she had some idea of where Tatiana was. But by now she could be in another state. She could be in another country. Gaia had waited too long. With each passing moment Tatiana gained an advantage. She was slowly slipping through Gaia's fingers.

Gaia continued to wander, letting the Walk and Don't Walk signs define her path. When she hit the corner of Second Street and Second Avenue, she heard the sharp start of a scream that was quickly cut short. Gaia's senses went on the alert as she looked around, searching for something amiss, wondering if she'd just imagined it. But then something caught her eye. A few figures struggling right in the center of the ages-old cemetery across the street.

Gaia dashed into traffic, ignoring the angry horn of a large meat truck that had to skid to a stop, and tossed her bags over the iron fence that surrounded the cemetery. She scrambled up and over the barrier. As she ran toward the fray, she saw that two average-size men were trying to pull the purse off a middle-aged woman who was struggling on the ground. The strap was wrapped around her body and under her arm, making it difficult for the guys to get it free. But they soon would, and who knew what they would do to the woman once they had what they wanted?

"Hey!" Gaia called out, bending at the waist.

The two men looked up in surprise, and Gaia used the moment to rush straight at the slightly taller guy, shoulder first. He didn't even have a chance to throw out his arms. Gaia hit him hard, and he let out an "Oof!" before tumbling to the ground with her in a mass of tangled limbs. Gaia was just getting her bearings to pummel the crap out of him when his buddy came up behind her and got her in a headlock. He yanked her away from his friend, and Gaia felt her eyes bulge as her windpipe was cut off. She choked and sputtered, grasping at the guy's arm with both hands.

"Don't go nowhere," her assailant said to the woman on the ground.

Gaia tried to shoot her a look, telling her to run, but she knew that her widened eyes, probably just made her look panicked. The woman wept and pulled her leg toward her. It was twisted unnaturally and was probably broken. So much for running.

"Yo, Tino, we got a spark plug here," the headlock guy said.

Tino, who had a nice scar that cut from the corner of his eye all the way down to the corner of his mouth, scrambled to his feet and fixed Gaia with a menacing glare. He slowly cracked his knuckles, then came at her, fast. But at the last second Gaia pushed her feet off the ground, used every muscle in her abs to bring up her legs, and double kicked Tino right in his nasty face.

The force of his momentum worked against him, and Tino crumbled to the ground, knocked out. The guy behind Gaia loosened his grip in surprise and she ducked out from under his arm, turned, and landed a nice right hook across his nose. His hands flew up to cover it, and she punched him once in the gut and kicked him in the groin. When he fell to his knees, she finished him off with an elbow jab to the back of his neck.

He hit the ground in a fetal position, unconscious. Gaia looked down at her handiwork—two knocked-out thugs in short order—and waited for a nice sense of satisfaction to come over her, but it didn't. She was still antsy. She was still made up of Ping-Pong balls.

"Are you okay?" Gaia asked the woman, who was now leaning back against a headstone.

She turned amazed eyes on Gaia. "I need to take a self-defense class," she said.

Gaia frowned. "I think your leg is broken. I'm gonna go get some help." The woman eyed her two attackers warily. "Don't worry about them," Gaia assured her. "They're down for the count."

She jogged over to her bags, grabbed them up, and this time found the open gate to exit the cemetery. A block and a half away she spotted a parked patrol car and told the officer behind the wheel that there was a woman hurt back at the graveyard and that the two guys who'd hurt her were still there. He picked up his radio and called it in.

"Don't move," he told Gaia as he turned on his siren. "We'll want your statement."

"Right," Gaia said. And the moment he peeled away, she took off in the other direction.

ABCSH. . . ABCSH, her brain started up again. What was it? What *was* it? She wished she had someone to talk to—someone to bounce this clue off and see what they came up with. Someone to brainstorm with. But there was no one left. Ed hated her. Sam hated her. There was no one else who knew about her psychotic family—her psychotic life. And there was certainly no one she knew who was up on espionage. No code crackers in her immediate acquaintance.

Except, of course. . .

Gaia stopped in her tracks so fast, the woman behind her walked right into her.

"Excuse me!" the lady snapped as she righted her bags and shuffled around Gaia.

But Gaia was in the midst of an epiphany—a bona fide brainstorm. *Loki.* As long as Gaia had lived, every awful thing that had ever happened to her had been perpetrated by Loki. Gaia had always thought it was just a little too weird that her father had fallen into a random coma the same day Loki had become comatose himself.

Gaia stepped out of the foot traffic of the sidewalk,

her mind reeling. What if Loki's men *had* caused her father's coma? What if Loki *was* responsible for her father being kidnapped from the hospital and taken who knew where? That would have to mean that Natasha was working with Loki's men. . . and maybe even Loki himself.

I haven't checked up on him since he was put in the hospital, Gaia thought. *Not once.*

Gaia had never had a chance to find out who Natasha and Tatiana were working for. Were they employed by some unknown agency—some new adversary—or were they just more of Loki's operatives? Was it possible that Loki had woken up and somehow escaped? Was it possible that he was calling the shots once again?

It was a slim chance, but it was the only lead Gaia had. If Loki was out there somewhere, she needed to know. At least she would have some idea of what she was up against. And if he was still safely tucked away in his coma, then she would know for sure that she and her father had another enemy.

With an actual purpose, an actual destination in mind, Gaia finally felt her nerves start to relax. She rolled back her shoulders and headed for the subway.

Gaia is starting to crack. I
can tell. She's been wandering
the city without purpose all day.
The longest she has stayed still
was the half hour she spent at
our old apartment. I imagine she
was tearing it to shreds. It
doesn't bother me, however. I
know she didn't find anything
there. My mother is nothing if
not careful.

Since then she has been
through Central Park, across
Columbus Circle, through Midtown,
down Fifth Avenue to Washington
Square, where she played a game
of chess for five minutes, and
then into the East Village, where
she found a fight. Of course. For
a moment I was concerned that she
was headed for the safe house—she
came very close to that neighborhood—but then she suddenly
stopped. She stared at nothing
for a few moments and got on the
subway. And all this time she has
never looked behind her. She's
had a crazed sort of look in her

eye all day, and she never even suspected I was following.

Like I said, she's cracking up.

And I could have killed her so many times. So many times I almost pulled out the gun and ended it. It was as if the weapon was calling to me, taunting me, telling me to finish her off. It is, after all, what my mother wants.

But I can't. Not yet. Without Gaia I will never find out where my mother is.

There has to be some way to get to her. Some way to trick her into meeting with me. Someone I can use as a decoy. But as far as I can see, I have only two not very attractive options.

One is Ed, but I will not put him in the middle of this. I could not bear it if he were killed. He is the one mistake I have made in all this time. I was not supposed to care for anyone, but I do care for Ed. Until I met him, I did not believe that any person in this world could be truly good. I didn't believe in friendship or in pure intention. But Ed is different. He is a good person, and he does not deserve to die just because he was stupid enough to fall in love with Gaia and be friends with me. Maybe that is his one flaw. His stupid heart.

But even if a small part of me wanted to be with him, I realize it is better that we were never really together. I would only break his heart like Gaia has so many times. Because once I'm done with Gaia, I'm gone.

Two is Sam. But Sam has no reason to trust me. In fact, he has every reason not to.

So I'm back at the first square. Too bad Gaia is such a friendless loser. It just makes my job harder. I have to think. There has to be *someone*, doesn't there? There just *has* to be. . . .

Was he going
to have to
date FBI
chicks and
cops and, **normal**
like,
girl
vampire
slayers or
something
for the rest
of his days?

"JAKE! JAKE! DUDE, WAIT UP!"

Blister Busting

Jake Montone heard his name but didn't bother slowing his steps as he strode down the middle of the crowded hall at the Village School, all the underclassmen instinctively moving out of his way. He wasn't in the habit of stopping for anyone. Except maybe the occasional beautiful girl. But Carlos Bernal could catch up with him.

Besides, he didn't want to break concentration. It was tough to find a person in a crowd without appearing as if you were looking for someone. It took a special kind of control to cover up riveted attention with removed indifference.

"Hey, man, we have a problem," Carlos began when he fell into step with Jake, only slightly out of breath.

"Oh, yeah? What's that?" Jake asked. His eyes scanned the hallway, his mouth lifting ever so slightly whenever he caught the admiring glance of a lovely lady. He could have any girl in this place if he wanted. Unfortunately, that fact made him not want any of them.

"Rob Tesca has mono," Carlos announced, covering his mouth with his hand and pretending that he didn't want to laugh. Jake could tell he enjoyed being the bearer of this bad news.

"What?" Jake blurted, looking fully at Carlos for the first time. His hair was extra gelled today, and he looked like he'd just walked off the set of *Happy Days,* with his tight white T-shirt and the chain hanging off his jeans. The kid even had dimples.

"How the hell does a guy like Rob Tesca get mono?" Jake asked, the tendons in his neck tightening.

"Dude may be butt ugly, but he does do well with the ladies," Carlos replied, swerving around a klatch of gossiping freshmen and glancing behind his shoulder to check them out. "So what are we gonna do? The team is already hemorrhaging."

"Tell me about it," Jake said.

The intramural karate team that Jake had formed on arriving at this new school was not getting off to an auspicious start. A bunch of guys had shown up for the informational meeting, but it turned out that eighty percent of them had gleaned their martial arts expertise from hours of blister-busting Street Fighter tournaments they'd been having since the sixth grade. The talent pool in this place was so shallow, it wouldn't even wet a person's socks.

Jake caught a glimpse of a blond ponytail from the corner of his eye and almost paused, but it turned out to be one of those perky chicks who were always giggling every time he walked into a room. Not the blond he was looking for.

"So, anyway, what are we going to do?" Carlos asked.

Jake stepped out of traffic and paused near a row of lockers, rolling his eyes and expertly appearing as if he was simply fed up with the crush of people.

"I got an idea," Jake said, glancing left at the locker that belonged to the blond who he *was* looking for. The blond who, conveniently, could also solve this new problem.

"Yeah? What?" Carlos asked, gripping one strap of his backpack with both hands. "I'm all ears."

It was an unfortunate turn of phrase for a guy who was, in fact, mostly ears. Jake glanced from one of Carlos's big flappers to the other slowly, and Carlos reddened. It wasn't that Jake *wanted* to embarrass the kid. He actually kind of liked Carlos and his perpetual kinetic state. But if he were forced to reveal that Gaia Moore was the person he was thinking of to take Rob's spot, that she was the person he'd been scanning the halls for all day, that she was owner of the locker they'd just stopped next to, then he'd also be forced to admit something that he was not willing to admit.

That he couldn't stop thinking about her. That he wanted to spend more time with her. That the karate team was the perfect excuse.

"Why are we stopping here?" Carlos asked when he regained his happy-go-lucky self. "The bell's gonna ring."

"No reason," Jake said, shrugging one shoulder. He looked down the emptying hall, and there was no sign of her. Apparently Gaia had decided to take a vacation day. Jake tried to ignore the hot infusion of disappointment in his chest.

"Let's go," he said to Carlos, just as the bell rang.

He was not disappointed that he hadn't gotten to see her before homeroom. He wasn't. He just needed her. No. The *team* needed her. That's what this was all about.

And the fact that he'd been looking for her before he even knew the team needed her? *Eh.* That just meant he was psychic.

THERE COMES A POINT IN EVERY MAN'S

Friendless

life when he has to ask himself, How did I get here. . . ? This, Ed Fargo, is that moment.

"Uh, you gonna move?"

Ed glanced over his shoulder at the scrawny little pale-faced, red-eyed Internet addict behind him and stepped out of his way. A group of four other such indoor beings, all of whom were probably still mourning the death of *The X-Files,* followed the kid out of the cafeteria line and over to a table in the corner.

See? Even geeky freshmen who haven't seen the sun since their diaper days have someone to sit with. You, however, have reached a point, as a senior, where you do not. How did you get here?

Taking a deep breath, Ed shuffled over to one of the smaller tables by the wall farthest from the lunch line, kicked a chair away from the table, and slumped into it. He placed his tray down in front of him and shrugged out of his backpack, tossing it into the empty chair to his right. It wasn't like anyone was going to be using it.

Ed picked up his plastic fork and stared at it `as if it held the meaning of life between its tines.` But his brain was actually trying to avoid finding the inevitable answer to his more pressing question by focusing on the inanimate object.

"I wonder why plastic forks grip pasta better," Ed muttered to himself, sticking the utensil into his noodles.

Unfortunately, this little quandary could only occupy his brain for so long, and the answer to the more important quandary finally came to him.

You got to this point because of Gaia, his brain voice said.

Ed's jaw clenched. No. That wasn't fair. It wasn't only Gaia's fault that he was `friendless.` It was Heather's, it was Tatiana's, it was. . . hormones. (Not to mention the fact that all his skate friends had scattered the moment he'd landed in his wheelchair and hadn't returned when he'd stepped out of it.) He'd spent the last few years, and the last few months especially, alienating everyone he knew in order to focus all his energy on women. Now all the women had up and left him, and he was friendless. It served him right.

A burst of laughter caught his attention, and he glanced over at the table in the center of the room that had welcomed the Friends of Heather at lunch hour every day of every year since they were but `breastless, brace-faced fourteen-year-olds`. Heather was no longer there, of course, but today Tatiana was missing as well. If she'd been there, then Ed might have sucked it up and gone over to sit with them and listen to them pick apart Jennifer Aniston's latest red carpet wear for forty-five minutes. At least then he wouldn't be sitting alone.

Of course, come to think of it, he might be better off where he was.

He realized, as he took his first bite of spaghetti, that he hadn't actually seen Tatiana all day. And Gaia was out as well—he'd noted that before the first bell. The dual absence couldn't be a coincidence. With those two, a simple flu was easy to rule out. They were probably back at home, kicking the crap out of each other. Not that he'd ever known Tatiana to be violent, but the way those two were acting around each other lately, it wouldn't have surprised him in the least.

Where the hell were they?

"Oh dear God, I have to get a life," Ed muttered, dropping his fork. He tipped back his head and covered his face with his hands, letting out a groan.

Enough with the Gaia obsession. Enough with the Tatiana "friendship" that could become something more. It had become clear to him over the past week or so that there was no way to be friends with Tatiana without constantly encountering Gaia, and he was never going to get over the girl if she was in his face all the time. And he had to get over her. It was for his own good. For his mental health. For his very survival.

Somehow, somewhere, there had to be a `normal girl` for Ed Fargo. Someone who didn't come with the lovely peripherals of gun-wielding psychos, vengeful thugs, and emotional issues too countless to list.

Why couldn't he find such a girl?

"Um. . . are you okay?"

Ed let his arms drop down and hang at his sides but barely moved his head. From the corner of his eye he could see a petite, pretty Asian girl in a pink-and-yellow T-shirt, with two short pigtails, tilting her head to look at him. She had a curious smile and a tiny diamond nose piercing.

"Yeah, I'm cool," Ed replied. He sat up straight and squeezed his eyes shut against the head rush.

"Oh, cuz you looked like you were a little. . . you know. . . floopy," she said, crinkling her nose. She was still holding her full lunch tray. She had a well-worn Birdhouse skateboard tucked under her arm.

"You skate street?" he asked semiblankly.

Her whole face lit up. "Yeah! And some vert," she said, setting down her tray and pulling out the board to show him. "This is my deck."

Ed frowned thoughtfully as he checked out the bird graphic on the bottom of the board, chipped away from hours of good, hard use.

"Nice," he said.

She grinned. Ed noticed that she had a nice smile. "Can I?" she said, gesturing at the chair across from his.

Ed barely lifted his shoulders. "Sure."

"I'm Kai," she said, shaking up her chocolate milk, her fifty rubber bracelets slipping up and down her arm.

"Ed," he replied.

"I've seen you skating down by Washington Square, right?" she asked.

"I've been known to," Ed replied, staring down at his food.

"You ever been to Extreme Skate up in Rhode Island?" Kai asked.

"No," Ed replied.

"Omigod, you have to go," Kai said, tearing into her salad. "I go every year, and it's the coolest jam on the East Coast, I swear. It's so not commercial, and when I was twelve, I entered the best trick contest and

I totally won, but not before I slammed, like, fifteen hundred times. . . ."

Ed smiled, but he felt himself starting to drift as Kai continued to talk about her many skateboarding exploits. He wondered where Gaia was at that very moment. Did she ever even think about him anymore? Did she realize she'd ruined him for life?

What if he would never be attracted to a normal girl again? Was this it for him? Was he going to have to date FBI chicks and cops and, like, vampire slayers or something for the rest of his days? At this point Ed wasn't even sure if he would recognize a normal girl if he found her.

"Are you sure you're okay?" Kai asked suddenly, ducking in toward the table to get into his line of vision.

"Yeah! Sorry," Ed said, pushing his hands through his thick black hair. "You were talking about Rhode Island. . . ?"

"Exactly! Like I said, you totally have to go. . . ."

Kai didn't seem fazed by his zone-out. Which was good, because it was probably going to happen again. He glanced around the cafeteria, looking in vain for some sign of Gaia or Tatiana, but they were definitely nowhere in sight. Something was going on. He could *feel* it. And he was going to find out what it was.

It wasn't like he had anything else to do—those girls had already destroyed his social life.

". . . we could go over to the park after school and I could show you, if you want," Kai said.

But Ed barely heard her. He was too busy planning the trip up to Seventy-second Street after school and what he would say to Gaia when he found her.

THE NURSE BEHIND THE COUNTER IN

Still Alive

the ICU looked up as Gaia walked out of the elevator and smiled a patented comforting smile, probably perfected after years of dealing with the families of the almost dead. Gaia glanced away, avoiding eye contact as she approached the woman. She didn't feel the need to be comforted. At least, not for the reason this woman thought she did. The patient Gaia was coming to see could stay in a coma until the hell he'd come from froze over, as far as she cared. She was probably the only person who'd ever come here hoping for "bad" news.

"Can I help you?" the nurse asked, lacing her fingers together as Gaia placed her bags on the floor in front of the chest-level desk.

"I'm here to see L—uh, Oliver. Oliver Moore," Gaia said.

The nurse's heavily lined eyes widened in surprise

and she stepped off her stool. "Really?" she said, sounding oddly happy. "Are you family?"

Gaia swallowed back the bile that rose in her throat. "Yeah. I'm his niece," she said, going for a smile but looking more like she wanted to throw up.

"Well! This is wonderful!" the nurse said, coming around the desk, her white sneakers squish-squashing as she walked. "Oliver never gets any visitors. We were beginning to wonder if he had anyone left. You see, the doctors like to have people come in and talk to our comatose patients. We always see better results when loved ones spend time talking and reading. . . ."

Gaia watched the nurse's face illuminate at the idea that poor old Oliver finally had someone who cared.

"Follow me," she said to Gaia as she squish-squashed toward the closed door to one of the rooms.

Gaia briefly considered turning around and bolting. The idea of actually laying eyes on the man who had made her life a relentless pit of pain wasn't appealing. But if there was one thing Gaia knew, it was that she should always make sure to see evidence with her own eyes. Whenever she was simply *told* something, nine and a half times out of ten it turned out to be untrue.

She picked up her bags again and followed the nurse over to the door she was now holding open. Gaia trudged up next to the woman and stood on the threshold, filling the empty doorway. There, lying flat on his back, was the man who was the spitting image of the father she'd loved and lost more times than she could count. Somewhere out there, if he was `still alive,` her father looked like an exact replica of the man lying before her. Hair combed back from his head, sensors pressed into his temples, arms placed neatly at his sides, machines beeping away all around him, stubble covering his strong chin.

In spite of all the hatred she felt, a huge lump welled up in Gaia's throat. She swallowed it back, ashamed of herself for displaying any kind of emotion at Loki's bedside. The nurse looked at her with pity in her eyes, and Gaia wanted to shake her and tell her the sorrow wasn't for Loki. No one should ever be sorry that this man was near death.

Okay, you've seen him, Gaia told herself. *Now go.*

"Talk to him," the nurse said softly. "It's okay."

No! Just leave! Gaia thought. But her legs wouldn't obey. As always, she was inexplicably drawn to Loki. And seeing him here like this. . . it somehow made her feel closer to her father.

The nurse slipped out, closing the door behind her and shutting out the light from the hallway. As soon as she and Loki were alone, Gaia's stomach clenched down to the size of a gum ball.

Swallowing hard, Gaia placed her bags down on the chair next to the door. She made her feet take the few necessary steps to the bed and stood there, her abdomen pressed into the metal railing that ran all around her uncle's resting place. He looked so vulnerable, lying there. Yet her fingers itched to circle his throat and squeeze out whatever life he had left. After everything this man had done to her and her family, he deserved to never wake up.

Like Dad, Gaia's mind blurted, as much as she tried to stop the thought from taking form. Loki and her father had always had that weird twin connection. They'd both fallen into comas at the same time. If it was really true that her father was dead, shouldn't Loki be, too?

Gaia's thoughts and emotions overwhelmed her. She pulled the second chair over to the bed and sat down, her knees weak. This was crazy, coming here. She should have known better. She should have left when her instincts told her to. But now it was too late. Everything she hadn't wanted to think about was hitting her full force.

Her father, her mother, Natasha and Tatiana's betrayal, her loneliness, her confusion, the fact that the only blood relative she might have left was not only evil but half dead in the bed in front of her. And the fact that it was now confirmed: She and her father had a new enemy. Someone other than Loki was out for their blood, and the only people who knew who that enemy was were Natasha and Tatiana. Gaia was back at square one.

"I don't know what to do," Gaia said, her throat

dry but her eyes full of tears she refused to shed. "I don't know what to do anymore."

The heart monitor bleeped away, and Gaia stared across the bed toward the shuttered window. Suddenly she laughed at herself. What was she doing here?

Gaia looked at his monitors. Lines peaked and dropped, dots jumped around. It all meant nothing to her. Nothing except that Loki was still breathing. And her father, for all she knew, was not.

"He's probably dead, you know," she heard herself say. Her gaze flicked toward Loki's face. "That should make you happy. I mean, that's what you always wanted, right? To kill your brother? To get your revenge? Well, I'm sorry you didn't get to do it yourself."

She glared at his face, waiting for a reaction she knew would never come. There was nothing more unsatisfying than trying to pick a fight with a guy in a coma. For once Gaia had nothing to punch, nothing to kick, no one to accuse. She had no recourse. And suddenly she felt very, very tired.

Gaia leaned back in her chair until the back of her head was resting on the top of the vinyl-covered cushion. It was warm in the hospital room, and the rhythmic beeping of the monitor was mesmerizing. Gaia could feel herself starting to slip into sleep and told herself to get up and go. She wouldn't keep vigil at her uncle's bedside.

But she was so tired. And she had no place to go.

And this chair was a hell of a **lot more** comfortable than that awful bench she'd slept **on the** night before. Maybe if she just took a little nap, **she** would wake up refreshed and be able to think more clearly.

Gaia had hardly even decided to let herself go when she fell into a deep, dreamless sleep.

GAIA AWOKE WITH A START. SHE

looked around the hazy hospital room, momentarily confused but searching for the cause of her sudden consciousness. Her heart was racing from being jarred out of a resting rhythm, and she felt like someone had shouted in her ear or shoved her to wake her up. But there was nothing. Nothing but a prone Loki.

No Loki in Loki

Gaia sat up and stretched, letting out a wide yawn and enjoying the feeling of her muscles awakening— her joints cracking. However long she'd been out, it had been a good sleep, and as she blinked away her grogginess, she realized it was time to blow this Popsicle stand. Now that she was certain Loki was no threat to her and her father, she had to focus on Tatiana. She had work to do.

Standing up, Gaia started to gather her bags, but

then she saw something that made her stop short.

Loki's fingers moved. Gaia took an instinctive step back from the bed. Her eyes darted to the monitors, but as far as she could tell, nothing had changed. Maybe she'd just imagined the movement.

I did. I just imagined it, she told herself, watching the display of Loki's heartbeat as the line jumped and squiggled and faded away.

"G-Gaia?"

A sizzle of anger ran over Gaia's skin the moment she heard his voice. He was awake. The rat bastard was awake. And he was saying her name.

"Gaia. . . where. . . how did you. . . ?"

And then he started coughing.

At first Gaia simply stood there, but the longer she did, the hoarser his coughing became. It racked his chest and sent his pulse skyrocketing. When he reached shakily for the protective bar around his bed, Gaia snapped to and rushed out the door.

"Hey! I need some water in here!" she shouted, causing the nurse to jump out of her chair.

Gaia waited for the nurse to scurry into action, then returned to Loki's room, watching as the coughs shook his body and praying that he wouldn't choke before she had the chance to tell him how much she hated him.

The nurse rushed in with a pitcher of water and

poured Loki a cup. She leaned over the bed and helped him drink, supporting his head with her hand. Gaia cringed just watching someone else touch the bastard. If only this woman knew what he had done.

"Better?" the nurse said when Loki had downed the water.

Loki nodded and lay down again weakly.

"His throat will be very dry," the nurse said, turning to Gaia. As if Gaia cared. "All those days with nothing to moisten it."

"Right," Gaia said. "You don't seem that surprised he's awake."

"Well, there have been indications in the past few days that something like this might happen," the nurse said. "More color in the cheeks, strengthening of the brain waves." She turned around and smiled at Loki, who was staring up at the ceiling with a confused expression. "But I wouldn't be surprised if you're the reason he's coming out of it now," the nurse continued. "Familial support has a very powerful effect on coma patients."

How about the familial support from the niece who wants you dead? Gaia thought.

"I'm going to go alert his doctor," the nurse told Gaia, handing her the water pitcher. "You should talk to him, but try not to excite him. He's still very weak."

Then, with a joyous I'm-so-happy-for-you glance, the nurse hurried away.

"Gaia," Loki croaked the second the nurse was gone.

Gaia didn't move. He turned his head and looked up into her eyes. Gaia didn't want to look at him, but something in his face made her pause. She couldn't tear her gaze away. It seemed like his eyes had softened. The hard, sadistic laughing that had always been present was gone. He gazed at her with admiration, with love. At that moment there was no *Loki* in Loki.

It's just the medication, Gaia told herself, turning away to place the pitcher on the nightstand. *He's totally drugged, that's all.*

"Well, you should get some rest," Gaia said, wiping her sweaty palms on her cargo pants. "I'll just leave you alone."

"Gaia, wait!" he exclaimed in his hoarse voice. "Why am I here?"

The sizzle of anger returned, this time heating Gaia's very veins. "You were in a coma. You woke up," she told him, grabbing up her bags. "The nurses will fill you in."

"But I. . . I don't remember anything," he said, blinking rapidly. "I don't. . . understand. How did I get here? When?"

After you tried to kill me and *Heather* and *my father,* Gaia's inner voice shouted.

"Look, you were in a *coma,*" Gaia said bitingly. "It may take you a little while to remember some things, but you will. Take care."

"But Gaia—"

"I am not going to help you. Not this time," Gaia said, her eyes flashing dangerously. "Not after everything you did. And don't give me any of that 'But I'm your uncle' bull, because I'm done falling for it."

She turned to leave and had her hand on the door handle when he spoke again.

"But Gaia, I *am* your uncle. It's me, Oliver!" From the sound of his voice he was near tears. Gaia's heart pounded in her chest. "Please don't leave me here. I don't understand what's happened!"

He collapsed in another coughing fit. Gaia turned slowly to find him reaching out for the water, unable to grasp it from his position, his arms shaking from the strain of stretching them. She narrowed her eyes.

Don't believe him, she told herself. *Believing him has gotten you into trouble so many times. . . .*

But then, from what she understood about human physiology, any trauma to the brain can change a person's emotional makeup. And a coma can cause trauma to the brain.

It can't be, Gaia thought.

But what if he *was* just Oliver? If he really was Oliver, she couldn't just leave him here to rot alone. If he really was Oliver, maybe he could help her.

Gaia dropped her things and poured him another glass of water. He drank it thirstily and collapsed back into his pillow. As he fought for his breath, Gaia watched him carefully. Loki was, after all, a fine actor.

He'd fooled her many, many times. And Gaia didn't want to be fooled again.

"Gaia, please don't leave me here," Oliver said, his chest rising and falling fast. "Take me home with you."

Gaia crossed her arms over her chest and dug her fingers into her biceps. "I don't have a home."

His eyes traveled past her then, and he seemed to notice her bags for the first time.

"But. . . what about your father?" Oliver asked.

Gaia's jaw clenched and her eyes stung. How was she supposed to answer that question? Especially when she didn't even know who she was talking to—someone who would rejoice in the news or someone who would be devastated?

"He's. . . missing," Gaia said finally.

Oliver quickly looked away, blinking rapidly as he stared up at the ceiling. Because of the line of work Tom was in, the fact that he was MIA wouldn't come as too much of a shock. But to a brother, if that was who he was, it was still upsetting.

If he's Loki, he deserves an Oscar, Gaia thought.

When her uncle turned to look at her again, his expression was resolved. "Where. . . what city are we in?" he asked.

"New York," she replied.

"I have a place, then," he said. "A place we can go." His frail fingers grasped at the metal guardrail closest to her. "I can't stay here, Gaia. I don't trust hospitals."

He swallowed with difficulty and pulled in a breath. "Ever since I was a little boy. . ."

Gaia felt an infinitesimal tug at her heart. She knew the feeling. And she knew what Oliver had gone through as a boy—all that time in and out of medical facilities, all those tests. If he was Oliver, he had every right to be petrified.

Still, how could she even think about taking him out of here? If he was actually Loki, she'd be unleashing some major evil.

"I know you have no reason to trust me. I don't remember what got me here yet, but I do remember the things I've done to you in the past. . . as Loki," Oliver said. "But I'll prove to you I'm not Loki. . . somehow. And if I don't prove it, you have every right to kill me."

Damn straight, Gaia thought.

She took a deep breath and looked into the man's desperate, scared eyes. Suddenly she knew she was going to do it—she was going to break Loki or Oliver, whoever he was, out of here. Maybe it was a serious lapse in judgment, but the fact remained that whichever personality had emerged from the coma, he was still the only person she knew who might be able to help her find her dad. If he turned out to be Loki, well, then, he was right—she would just have to deal with him.

Gaia walked over to the door, opened it a crack, and glanced out. Another nurse had taken charge of the desk while the first woman was off paging Loki's doctor. There was a doctor talking to a harried-looking couple outside another of the rooms. It wasn't Fort Knox, but it wasn't going to be easy. She closed the door again, silently.

"They'll never let me take you out of here in this condition," she said, glancing skeptically at his frail body. "We're gonna have to run."

TATIANA STILL COULDN'T GET USED TO

Dead Ahead

seeing all those dark strands of hair blowing in front of her own face. Every other time the wind kicked up and tousled her wig, she flinched. Not exactly the nerves of steel required for the spy game. But she'd been following Gaia all day, and since the girl seemed to be able to function indefinitely without food, Tatiana hadn't eaten, either. She leaned her shoulder against the big blue mailbox next to her and tapped her fingers on the dented metal, her stomach letting out an `irritated growl`. She was starting to get a little antsy.

"What the hell is she doing in there, having that long overdue personality change operation?" Tatiana muttered, glancing away from the hospital entrance long enough to check her watch. Gaia had been inside for more than two hours. A new record of stagnancy for the day. Maybe Tatiana could just duck into that bagel place and—

There she was. Not coming from the entrance, but from around the far corner of the hospital. And she was hustling. She was hustling with her arm around someone. Someone who was stooped over and shielded from view. Tatiana stood up straight, pulled her dark sunglasses down to the end of her nose, and narrowed her eyes.

Who the hell was Gaia smuggling out of the damn—

The patient glanced in her direction, only for a split second, and Tatiana's knees almost caved in. Tom Moore? Gaia's *father*? But how had she—? How had he—? She'd thought he was—

Then it hit her, and a dry heave caught in her throat.

It wasn't Tom. It was Loki, obviously. Tatiana and her mother had known for a while that Loki was being held in one of the city's many hospitals, but the name of the exact hospital was kept on a need-to-know basis. And even though it made absolutely no sense for Gaia to smuggle Loki out of the hospital, it made more sense than the idea of Tom being in New York. Tatiana knew for a fact that Tom was nowhere near the United States.

This can't happen, Tatiana realized, her heart racing. If Gaia and Loki had decided to team up, there was no telling what they might be able to do. And if the two of them compared notes, it wouldn't take long for them to figure out who Tatiana and Natasha were working for. Once they figured that out, Tatiana was as good as dead. Especially if she could have done something to stop it.

Gaia and her uncle scurried across the avenue and headed toward Tatiana but on the other side of the street. Tatiana ducked behind a lamppost, seething, swearing under her breath.

"I'll kill them," she said. "I'll kill them both."

Gaia and Loki turned a corner and started up the street toward the subway station, their backs to Tatiana. Suddenly a sleek black sports car pulled up to the curb right next to Tatiana's feet and the engine died. Tatiana squared her shoulders, walked around the front of the car, and waited for the driver to open the door.

A coiffed businessman of about thirty stepped out onto the street, his back to Tatiana. She reached around him, took his keys from his hand, and, before he could utter any sound of surprise, grabbed him by his jacket lapels and flung him to the ground.

As she sat behind the wheel and locked the doors, Tatiana absently noticed that now her hands weren't shaking. They weren't shaking as she inserted the key into the ignition. They weren't shaking as she cut the wheel and peeled out, slicing through four lanes of heavy New York traffic.

The driver stood up and yelled after her; countless cars screeched to a stop; curses were flung out like yesterday's meat loaf. But Tatiana didn't hear them. She didn't see them. She saw nothing but the tall blond girl and the sickly, stooped man, who were so helpfully stepping off the curb and into the street dead ahead.

You know what's unhealthy? Giving up stuff for a girl.

Like when I was in high school, my friend Frank quit the spring play because his girl-friend, Lily, was jealous because he had to kiss Maria Viola. Then five days after we all watched Frank's understudy, Calvin Carmichael, knock over the set and pass out from an asthma attack in the middle of act 2, Lily broke up with Frank for some kid from the debate team. Frank never acted again, never trusted women again, and took his first cousin Agatha to the prom. I haven't spoken to him since, but I'm sure he's still a shell of his former self.

It's because of the Frank and Lily story that I'm in New York at all. I had a girlfriend in high school. An amazing girl-friend. Her name was Anna, and she was perfect—smart, funny, legs that went on for miles. We always used to lie around and

talk about what it would be like
to go away to school together,
live together, and all that
stuff. But Anna wanted to go to
Notre Dame more than anything.
Her whole family went there.
Their den was like a shrine to
the place, with pennants and
jackets and photos, pillows,
blankets, and mugs. I applied
there, but I knew that I didn't
want to stay in the Midwest. I
knew I wanted to go to school in
a big city, see new things, get
the heck out of small-town USA.

And so, when I got my acceptance letters to NYU and Notre
Dame on the same day and immediately went for the one from NYU
first, I knew what I had to do. I
thought about Frank. I thought
about how I didn't want to make
that same mistake he had. So I
broke Anna's heart and I came to
New York.

The thing is, I never looked
back. Yeah, I still think of Anna
sometimes, but I know that I made
the right decision. And not just

because she got engaged to some
prelaw loser six months into her
freshman year (I got an e-mail
from her with their engagement
picture attached. They were both
wearing Notre Dame sweatshirts
and green turtlenecks), but
because I've always believed that
you've got to make your own deci-
sions. Like I said, you can't
give up stuff for a girl.

So what do you do when you've
given up not just your hobby for
a girl, but *everything*? You've
given up your friends, your pas-
sions, your education, your family, and approximately three full
months of your life? And then
what do you do if, after you've
given up all that, she decides
that you aren't worth trusting?
That everything you've done and
everything you've lost doesn't
even prove that one small thing.
How does one recover from that?

Need a few minutes to think
about it? That's cool, I'll wait.
It's not like I have anything
else to do.

And at that
moment, she
knew. She
knew,
without a
doubt,
that this
was truly
Oliver.

the

good

guys

OKAY, WHAT THE HELL AM I DOING HERE?

Quiver

Gaia asked herself, glancing at her uncle's profile as she half dragged him along the street. The light of day and the noise of the streets were like blaring wake-up calls from the intense emotional daze back in the hospital room. Sure, this man claimed his name was Oliver Moore, and he didn't seem to recall anything he'd done in the days before he fell into a coma. Sure, he looked pale and weak and his arms shook as he clasped her left hand in both of his.

But none of this changed the fact that she might have just sprung the most evil criminal on earth from the hospital. Loki was a chameleon. That was one of his strengths as a spy. And although Gaia's gut was telling her to believe that the person she was holding up was Oliver, her gut had betrayed her enough times for her to be doubtful.

She was so sick of doing this alone—of relying on her own instincts. If only she had someone here to tell her she was doing the right thing. Or the wrong one. Either way, she could deal. She just wanted to *know*.

"Oh God, no," Oliver said suddenly, stopping so fast, Gaia almost pulled him off his feet with her continued momentum. Oliver turned, spinning himself out of her grasp. He started to fall and grabbed at a grimy, overflowing garbage can to stop himself.

"What is it?" Gaia asked, glancing left and right.

She doubted the nurses had even noticed that Oliver was missing from his room yet, but if Loki's men had been keeping an eye on the hospital, they might already be tailing her. It was always better to be safe than dead.

Oliver looked at her, his blue eyes swimming and twitching, his mouth hanging slightly open. He slowly sank to the ground, every muscle in his body seeming to quiver.

"I—tried to—kill you?" Oliver stammered, tucking his chin.

Any color he had left drained from his face. Gaia felt her stomach turn over like a slowly folding omelette. Was he serious?

"Uh. . . yeah," Gaia said, trying to prevent the emotion she felt from creeping into her voice. "Lots of times. But we can talk about that later."

She grabbed his arms around what was left of his biceps and tried to haul him up, but he was like deadweight. His fluttering hand flew to his forehead and he squeezed his eyes shut.

"And that girl Heather. . . and Tom. . . my own brother. . . and that boy. . . that boy. . . Josh. . . I killed him at point-blank. . ."

And then Oliver started to weep. Sitting right there on the ground in the middle of a crowded sidewalk, with harried pedestrians looking him over warily as they hustled by. Gaia stood still, unsure of what to do—unsure of what she was witnessing. Everything that had happened before Loki had slipped into his coma seemed to be coming back to him, slowly and in agonizing relief. With each new victim he recalled, he collapsed in on himself a bit more.

So it was all coming back to him. But was it coming back to him as Oliver, or were his memories turning him back into Loki, the man who had actually committed those atrocities?

"Oh God, why did you take me out of there?" her uncle whimpered, covering his face with both hands now. "You must despise me. You have to despise me. . . ."

I do, Gaia thought. *Or I did. I despise Loki. So if that's who you are. . .*

Car tires screeched somewhere down the street and Gaia blinked. She had to snap out of this. They both had to.

"Look, we can talk about all of this later?" she asked, grasping his hands and hauling him to his feet. She wrapped her arm around his back, supporting his weight, and started to walk. "Right now we just need to get you inside, okay?"

Oliver didn't respond, but he did move with her, muttering under his breath. Mercifully Gaia could no longer comprehend his muddled words. If she heard him recount his memory of what he'd done to her mother, she might just give in to temptation and leave him right on a street corner to fend for himself.

"Come on. We have to cross here," she said, tightening her grip on his shoulder.

As Gaia stepped from the curb, Oliver paused again. Gaia stopped a few paces ahead of him, in the center of the road. She was starting to lose patience.

"Are you coming?" she asked him.

A fat tear rolled down the side of Oliver's nose and his chin quivered. He looked so entirely pathetic—so scared and remorseful. Gaia swallowed back a lump that threatened to rise in her throat. If this really was Oliver, he must be so confused. Of course, if he was Loki, he was just doing a really good job of snowing her. And he wouldn't be the first.

Suddenly Oliver, Loki, whoever he was swayed on his feet. Gaia took a step toward him, then froze.

The sound of screeching tires filled her ears this time, impossibly close. Gaia looked up to see a black sports car almost spin out as it flew around the nearest corner. The driver was obscured, but as the engine roared and picked up speed, it was clear he wasn't going to stop. Gaia was standing directly in the car's path.

Huh. In all the times she'd imagined herself dying, getting run over by a car was never at the top of the list.

"Gaia!" Oliver shouted suddenly.

Then, before Gaia could even turn to him, he'd run into the center of the street and shoved her out of the way of the speeding car, his eyes wild. Gaia hit the road on her butt, her palms scraping across the grainy asphalt.

When she looked up at her uncle, he was standing in the path of the car, his arms outstretched at his sides.

"No!" Gaia shouted, scrambling up.

As clear as day, she heard her uncle state, ever so simply, "I deserve to die."

And at that moment she knew. She knew without a doubt that this was truly her uncle, her father's brother, the man her mother once knew and cared for. He was one of the good guys.

Gaia glanced at the car, only yards away now and coming fast. A jogger jumped out of the vehicle's way, tumbling over the hood of a parked Jeep. The black car only accelerated. Whoever was behind the wheel either didn't know or didn't care that he had almost killed someone.

And that meant her uncle was next. Out of the corner of her eye Gaia caught a glimpse of long dark hair and dark glasses behind the wheel of the speeding car. Then she took off, using the few steps to gain as much momentum as superhumanly possible. She launched herself into the air and slammed into her uncle, wrapping her arms around him as they tumbled toward the far curb. They rolled over and over each other, legs entwined, arms flailing, until the curb stopped Gaia's back, sending a stabbing, body-shaking pain down her side.

The car didn't pause or slow. When Gaia lifted her head, it had already disappeared into traffic.

"Hey! Are you all right?" A burly man in an orange

Con Edison vest crouched over them on the sidewalk.

Gaia sat up slowly, touching a cut on her head and wincing as she glanced around at the crowd that had gathered. Her uncle started to cough, and Gaia helped him into a seated position, checking him over for broken bones. He was clearly shaken but still intact.

"We're fine," Gaia said to the little clutch of people. "Thanks."

"Wacko," the Con Edison worker said under his breath. "I tried to get his license plate, but it all happened so fast."

"Thanks again," Gaia said as the man stood up and walked off, shaking his head.

As the rest of the bystanders started to disperse, Oliver got his breathing under control. He looked over at Gaia and blinked rapidly.

"You saved my life," he said. "Why?"

Gaia shrugged. "You saved mine first."

Oliver looked down at his hands as if he couldn't believe they were there. "Back in the hospital, you said that Tom was. . . missing?"

Gaia's heart turned. "Yep," she said, pretending to concentrate on dabbing the blood from the scrape above her eye with the end of her sleeve.

"But he's alive," Oliver said.

"I don't know," Gaia replied.

Oliver let out a breath, and his shoulders slumped a bit more. "Well, wherever he is, I'll find him," he said. "I'm going to put a stop to all of this. Once and for all."

Gaia turned her head to look at him, and Oliver looked right back into her eyes. She wanted to believe him so badly—believe that he was really going to help her. But even if he really was Oliver, how long would he stay that way?

After all, Loki hadn't been born. He was a product of Oliver's bottomless self-hatred.

Good Progress

ED HAD NEVER SEEN SUCH A PATHETIC display of athleticism in his life. There were four girls on the two racquetball courts that the school gymnasium could accommodate, and they all sucked. He hadn't seen a good volley yet. Mostly one girl hit the ball at the wall, it came flying back, the other girl screeched and ducked out of the way, and then the first girl had to chase the ball down. Then the whole process started over again. The guys sitting in the bleachers above him seemed to find it entertaining, but all Ed could think about was the fact that these were forty-five minutes of his life that he would never get back.

And that if Gaia were here, she'd be putting all the other girls to shame.

Damn. He wasn't supposed to be thinking like that.

"Hey, Fargo!"

Ed turned around to find Jake Montone lumbering down the bleachers toward him with Carlos Bernal in tow. The skin on Ed's bare arms `flared with heat` at the sight of him, and he turned to face the courts again, feigning such sudden intense interest, he could have been a college racquetball scout.

"S'up, man?" Jake said, standing a couple of rows down from Ed so that he couldn't avoid looking at him in his gray T-shirt with the sleeves ripped off. Carlos waited for Jake down on the gym floor, keeping one eye on the racquetball players for his own safety.

"Nothing," Ed replied.

"Where's the little woman today?" Jake asked.

Ed pulled in a deep breath. "What little woman would that be?" he asked.

Jake laughed. "You know—belligerent chick with a nice big man-shaped chip on her shoulder?"

"Belligerent! Big word!" Ed snapped, in order to cover the surge of jealousy that threatened to overtake him. What the hell did this guy want with Gaia? And exactly how many guys did Ed's ex have lined up for herself, anyway? Sam, Jake. . . who was next?

"All I did was ask you a question," Jake said, an edge creeping into his tone.

"Well, all I know is she's not here," Ed said, lifting his feet and placing them on the step in front of him. "Out of curiosity, why do you ask?" he added, forcedly casual. It wasn't like he *really* wanted to know the answer. And it wasn't like he wanted Jake to think that he cared. But sometimes his tongue just felt the need to set him up for punishment.

"Not that it's any of your business, but I have something to ask her," Jake replied. Then he turned and loped down the rest of the bleachers, walking with Carlos over to the far court to take their turn with the rackets.

What do you have to ask her? Ed wanted to shout after him. *Is this like a help-me-with-my-homework-so-I-can-look-up-your-skirt question or a go-with-me-to-the-prom-so-I-can-put-my-hand-in-your-blouse question?!*

But Jake was right about one thing: It *was* none of his business. Ed knew this. He had to stop obsessing about Gaia and what she was doing and who she was doing it with. This behavior was going to get him nowhere.

Unfortunately, it was tough to teach an old Ed new tricks. And he'd spent so much time focused on Gaia in the last year, it was going to be difficult to break himself of the habit. Perhaps impossible.

Ed picked at a string sticking out from the leather upper on his sneaker, wishing he had something else, anything else, to focus on. He'd thought dating someone new would be the answer, but the further the school day progressed, the clearer it became that there was no one out there for him. This school was just too damned small. He'd been friends with every girl in it since his paste-eating days. And sure, there was a whole big city out there, but what was he going to do, go down to SoHo and pick up random chicks? The whole point of getting away from Gaia was to *keep* from getting his life threatened. Well, that was one of the points, anyway.

Maybe he should join a club. Or. . . or get a pet. Yeah, that was it. A dog. Or a nice cat. Yeah. Cats were cool. And then he could train it and feed it and it would cuddle up next to him at night and—

Yeah. Okay. Now he was thinking like a seventy-five-year-old woman. Good progress.

"Hey, Ed!"

He looked up from his sneaker to find Jennifer Niccols standing on the gym floor directly below him. Her curly brown hair was tied up in a high ponytail, and she was wearing a pair of short blue gym shorts that might as well have been underwear for all the area they covered.

"I need a partner," she said, flashing a toothpaste-commercial smile. "Wanna play?"

She took two rackets from behind her back and held one out toward him.

"I don't know," Ed replied, finding it difficult to

imagine himself out of wallow mode. Especially as far out as he'd have to be to get up the energy for racquetball. "I'm not really in the mood."

"Oh, come on," Jennifer said. She put the rackets down and climbed the bleachers until she was one riser in front of him. "What if I said pretty please?"

She cocked her head to one side and pretended to pout, reminding Ed of the time in kindergarten she'd proposed marriage to him in the Housekeeping Corner. Yet another girl he'd known for way too long. They were like brother and sister to each other.

Back then, of course, Ed had given in to her girlish wiles and ended up with his first kiss on the playground later that day.

He still blushed just thinking about it.

"Yes!" Jennifer said, noting the change in his coloring. She grabbed both his hands and pulled him out of his seat.

Ed followed her down the bleachers and picked up the racket, then swung his arm around and around, loosening up. It actually felt pretty good to move. Maybe this wasn't such a bad idea. Maybe smacking a ball around would get out some of his pent-up emotion. And maybe participating in gym would take his mind off his total lack of potential girlfriends for a little while.

But later he was definitely going to get a cat.

TATIANA LIFTED THE SMUDGED GLASS

of vodka from the bar, and half the contents sloshed over the rim onto her hand. She cursed under her breath and put the glass down again with a smack, attracting the attention of the surly bartender who was devouring the want ads at the other end of the counter.

Bra Strap

"You gonna drink that or wipe down my bar with it?" he spat, one cheek so full of chewing tobacco, he looked like he had mumps.

Tatiana narrowed her eyes, steeled herself to stop her shaking hands, and downed the rest of the drink. She closed her eyes and tipped back her head as it burned down her throat, then immediately felt better.

At least she hadn't done it. Or, in truth, at least she'd been prevented from doing it by the tag-team heroics of what was left of the Moore family. And at least there were seedy, no-name bars open in this city in the middle of the afternoon—bars that didn't bother to card as long as you had cash. At least she'd been able to ditch the car and disappear.

Tatiana took a deep breath and leaned her elbows on the rough edge of the chipped wooden bar. She couldn't believe she'd just come so close to eliminating Gaia—the one person who knew how Tatiana could get her mother back.

But why did Gaia get Loki out of the hospital? Tatiana wondered. *Why did she save one of her enemies from death?*

Tatiana lifted her hand to signal the bartender, and he quickly poured her another drink. As she took another hot swallow, she realized that only one thing in this life was certain—she would never figure out Gaia Moore. But that didn't mean she couldn't use her.

I have to get her to tell me what she knows, Tatiana thought. But if there was one thing that her near encounter with Gaia today had proved, it was that there was no way Tatiana could ever hope to take her. It wasn't as if she hadn't known this before, but watching Gaia throw herself across the street in front of a speeding car had just brought the point home for Tatiana. Gaia was practically a superhero. Tatiana couldn't rely on her own strength to deal with her. She had to find someone to help her—preferably someone with a little firepower. And that was the other reason that bars like this one were so handy—they were full of shady characters.

Tatiana lifted her finger again. The bartender sighed heavily, spat a wad of tobacco into a decaying glass, then trudged over to her.

"You ready to settle up?" he asked.

"Actually, I have a little trouble that I thought you might help me with," she said, calling upon the broken English she spoke only days after immigrating to the U.S.

Her trouble with the language made her seem helpless, and guys like this bartender were often more inclined to notice a damsel in distress.

He seemed to notice her for the first time and smiled back, his teeth yellow and gapped. Apparently he wasn't the type of person who saw smiles very often.

"What kind of trouble could a lady like you have?" he asked, clicking his tongue.

"It is my husband," Tatiana said, the lie dripping off her tongue. "He does not know how to stay at home, you know? I need to find someone who will teach him." Tatiana filled her eyes with meaning and stared at the greasy man. "Do you know of anyone who might help me?"

The bartender stood up straight and looked around the nearly empty bar. He picked up a damp rag and fiddled with it as he weighed whether or not to trust her. Tatiana leaned into the bar, letting the sleeve of her wide-necked sweater slip down slightly to expose her bra strap. The man's eyes were riveted.

"I may know someone, but it'll cost ya," he said.

"Money is no problem," Tatiana replied.

The bartender looked her up and down. "Be here tomorrow at noon," he said. "Brendan'll be here then. He's the one ya wanna talk to."

Brendan, Tatiana thought, smiling her thanks. She took a long, slow pull on her drink. *Let's just hope Brendan has a few friends. . . .*

I've decided to take this girl search very seriously. Why? Because one, I have no life and so I have time to take the search as seriously as I want. Two, if I find a girl, I will have a life and therefore will have remedied that problem. And three, I can't get a cat. I forgot that I'm allergic.

So where does one go to find cool girls in the city of New York?

1. Chelsea Piers. Pro: active chicks. Con: chicks who think that Chelsea Piers is the coolest place in Manhattan.

2. Bowlmor. Pro: chicks who can bowl. Con: chicks who can bowl better than me.

3. CBGB. Pro: musical chicks. Con: scary musical chicks.

4. The Guggenheim. Pro: cultured chicks. Con: boring chicks who can spend hours dissecting the meaning of a red blob on a canvas.

~~5. Washington Square Park.~~

6. The School of the Performing Arts. Pro: *Fame* chicks. Con: chicks with stage moms.

7. The Strand, half-priced-books section. Pro: chicks that not only read but know where to find a good bargain. Con: chicks that think you're Satan if you've ever been inside a Barnes & Noble.

8. Paragon. Pro: sporty chicks. Con: chicks who will spend two hundred bucks on a backpack.

9. The observation deck at the Empire State Building. Pro: international chicks. Con: too *Sleepless in Seattle*.

10. Port Authority. Pro: opens up the field to chicks from Jersey and Connecticut. Con: also opens up the field to hookers.

Once Jake
knew what he
wanted, he
went **falling**
after it,
and usually
he got it.

GAIA STEPPED OUT OF THE SUBWAY station in the West Village and took a deep breath. The weak morning sunlight glinted in the window of a tiny shoe repair shop, and a man in a stained white apron blasted the sidewalk with water from

Chocolaty Goodness

a coiled hose. It was a new day. Gaia had come to school via a whole new route, leaving from Oliver's creaky, dirty brownstone in Brooklyn. Different subway platform, different train, different people. It was weird how seeing the world from a new angle could give a person a whole new outlook. And this morning Gaia felt strangely positive. She was going to figure out the meaning of the key she'd found at the Seventy-second Street apartment. She was going to find Tatiana. And Oliver was going to find her father. Everything was going to be fine.

As long as Loki didn't resurface. As long as Tatiana didn't find Gaia first and put a bullet through her head. As long as her father wasn't dead.

Gaia glanced across the street at the Village School and saw Jake Montone hanging on the steps with a couple of his meathead friends and a few Friends of Heather. Maybe one of them could help her find Tatiana. Maybe Tatiana had slipped up during one of their little gatherings and said something, *anything* that could give Gaia a clue. Of course, it wasn't like any of them were ever going to help her voluntarily. None of them would even *speak* to her voluntarily.

Unless she planned to intimidate each one of them, she was going to need a different in.

Suddenly Jake looked up and caught Gaia watching them. His amazingly light eyes grabbed her attention, even from that distance, and Gaia glanced away a second later than she would have liked.

"Damn," she muttered under her breath when she noticed the self-satisfied smirk that crossed his face. Ugh! He thought she was checking him out. Just what she needed—Mr. Ego thinking he had yet another admirer.

Gaia turned and ducked into Dunkin' Donuts with a sigh. Her positive mood had lasted all of ten minutes. Now she needed a double-chocolate doughnut and a nice big black coffee to take the edge off.

She joined the long line of half-asleep workers and scanned the shelves behind the counter, making sure there were double-chocolate doughnuts to be had. She smiled when a guy came out from the back wearing his maroon-and-orange Dunkin' uniform and carrying a whole new tray of `chocolaty goodness`. Maybe this really was her lucky day.

"Hey, Gaia."

Maybe not. She turned in line to find Jake standing behind her with that somehow constantly teasing smile on his face. So predictable. He thought she wanted him, so he came right after her. He was wearing a dark blue T-shirt and no jacket, even though everyone else in line was bundled up against the morning chill. He was bending and unbending a tattered copy of *Atlas Shrugged* in his large hands. Gaia noticed this, scoffed, and turned around again to focus on the task at hand—doughnut acquisition.

"What? Surprised by my choice of reading material?" Jake asked, inching closer to her as the line moved forward.

"Surprised you read," Gaia replied, her back to him.

Jake laughed. "Set myself up for that one."

"At least you can admit it," Gaia replied.

"So. . . you weren't in school yesterday," Jake said, angling himself so that he could see her profile as she stepped up to the counter. He leaned in near the cash register and rested his elbow on top of it, earning a fire-spouting glare from the lady behind the counter.

"Thanks for the news flash," Gaia said to him.

"Can I help you?" the lady asked through her teeth. She glanced at Jake again, but he didn't notice.

"I'll have a large coffee, black, and a double chocolate," Gaia said. Her stomach grumbled. "Make that two double chocolates."

Out of the corner of her eye she saw Jake smile but refused to give him the satisfaction of acknowledging it.

"And another black coffee," Jake piped up suddenly as the woman turned to fill the order. She rolled her eyes, made a big show of punching the extra coffee into the register, and hit total before grabbing a couple of large cups.

"I'm not buying you coffee," Gaia said to Jake as she fished in the pocket of her cargo pants for some cash.

"Nooooo," he said as if he were speaking to a four-year-old. He pushed away from the counter and pulled a sleek black wallet out of the back pocket of his fitted jeans. "I'm buying you coffee. And a couple of dough-nuts, apparently."

He slipped out a brand-new twenty and tossed it onto the counter. Gaia could actually smell the crispy scent of `freshly printed bills`. What was this kid, a Soprano or something?

"That's okay, really," she said, snapping up the twenty between two fingers and handing it back to him. "I don't really feel the need to owe you."

"You won't owe me," he said, throwing the money on the counter again. "God! I'm just trying to be nice. What are you, allergic to nice?"

Huh. . . maybe, Gaia thought, mulling it over. *That would explain a lot.*

The Dunkin' Donuts lady placed a waxy bag on the counter next to two steaming cups of coffee and, before Gaia could protest, picked up the twenty and started hitting buttons again. Jake smirked as he leaned past Gaia to pick up his cup. His arm grazed her cheek and she turned away from him, the contact sending an unexpected thrill the skittering down her side.

For a split second Gaia held her breath, then her face flushed purple. Because against her will she realized she was wishing that little skin brush had lasted longer.

Okay, you are not attracted to Jake Montone, she told herself, even though her fluttery stomach was insisting otherwise. *You're obviously just delusional from stress.*

Gaia snatched up her bag of doughnuts, slid past Jake, avoiding the merest brush of contact, and pushed the door to the shop open so hard it almost came off its hinges. The second she was outside, she opened the bag and broke off half of one of the doughnuts, still warm from the oven. She stuffed it into her mouth as she crossed the street against the signal.

Maybe if she kept walking, he'd take the hint. Maybe if she kept walking, her skin would cool down and her brain would start functioning again and realize that Jake Montone was so not her type. Not only that, but even if he *was* her type, this was no time to be thinking about guys on any level—unless they were guys who could help her find her dad.

"Hey!" Jake called out behind her.

Just let him get hit by a bus, Gaia thought.

"Hey! Don't I even get a thank-you?" He was closer now, coming up on her heels.

Gaia chewed and swallowed and turned to face him. "I don't remember asking you to buy me breakfast," she said. *See! You're looking right at him and feeling nothing. It was just a blip.*

He eyed that little white bag in her hand. "Using the term *breakfast* rather loosely."

Gaia rolled her eyes and was on the move again. What was he going to do now, lecture her about the four basic food groups?

"Waitwaitwait," Jake said, grabbing her arm. Gaia's heart thumped and she sighed. "I actually wanted to ask you something."

Oh God, he's not going to ask me out on a date, is he? I look like a hellion. Does he not have eyes?

Gaia had, in fact, showered for the first time in a number of days that morning, but she'd only had time to wrap her hair up in a folded-over ponytail, with straggly wisps sticking out in all directions. Her cargo pants were covered with stains and her white ribbed sweater had such deep creases in it, she wasn't sure if they were ever coming out. Add that to the fact that she was, as always, make-upless and jewelryless and that her denim jacket smelled like street urchin, and she was sure she didn't paint a pretty picture.

"I. . . uh. . . I wanted to ask you if. . . you would consider. . ."

Okay, whatever it is, spit it out, Gaia thought.

"If you would consider joining the karate team," Jake finished.

Gaia's heart squeezed, and she felt her face fall. *What?* But no. She was not disappointed. She was relieved, right? Thank *God!*

"You already asked me that and I already said no," Gaia replied. She clumsily opened the little flap on the plastic coffee cup top, spilling droplets on her hands, then took a sip.

"I know, but one of the guys got sick and I really need someone to take his place or we'll have to forfeit," Jake said. He raised his dark eyebrows. "Come on, Gaia. The team needs you."

There was a persuasive argument. "I don't think so," she said. She started off toward school again, double time.

"Come on! How could you not want to do this?" Jake asked, falling into step with her. "You love to fight. I could tell that day you—"

"That day I kicked your ass?" Gaia supplied.

"I think there was mutual ass kicking there, but yeah," Jake said.

"Look, I'm not a joiner," Gaia said as she climbed the front steps of the school. "It's just not me. And I'm not only being selfish here. Trust me. I am not a reliable teammate."

Or a reliable friend, or girlfriend or daughter. . .

"Okay, what's it gonna take to convince you?" Jake

asked, holding open the door for her. Gaia paused for a moment. Well, that was unexpected. Jake didn't seem like the door-opening type. She glanced at his unabashedly hopeful face, then slipped inside.

"What if I do your physics homework for a month?" Jake asked.

"Don't care about homework," Gaia replied, fishing out the second half of her first doughnut.

"What if I. . . get you an excuse note for gym for a month?" Jake offered.

"Like gym," Gaia replied, momentarily wondering how it was he could offer such a thing. She popped a piece of doughnut into her mouth.

"What if I. . ." Jake stopped in the middle of the crowded hallway to think. Gaia kept walking.

"What if I buy you Dunkin' Donuts every morning for a month?" Jake called out, his tone pleading yet confident. She was glad her back was to him so he couldn't see the sudden smile that lit her face. There it was again—that skitter of excitement.

Damn, Gaia thought. *Jake Montone? I'm having. . .* feelings *about Jake Montone?*

He was so the opposite of the guys she liked. So the opposite of Sam and his laid-back, unconscious sexiness. So the opposite of Ed and his self-deprecating humor and kindness. Jake was a guy's guy. He was confident and cocky and strong. In short, he was the kind of guy Gaia liked to take down a few pegs. But still, there was something different about Jake. Something that was causing these skitters. And if she was going to be perfectly honest with herself, those skitters were something she wouldn't mind feeling more often. It wasn't like there were many pleasant emotions to be had these days.

Gaia took a deep breath, her mouth full.

Don't do it, don't do it, don't do it, a little voice in her head chided.

But there were other reasons to say yes. The guy was offering a free month's worth of chocolaty goodness. Plus she'd get to kick the crap out of all those annoying guys on the team. Plus, skitters or no, Jake was pretty much the only person outside of Oliver who was interested in talking to her.

But she couldn't go to practices and meets right now. She had to focus on finding Tatiana and on finding her father.

"Gaia?" Jake said.

Then it hit her. The factor helped the pros edge out any cons. Jake and Tatiana. They'd been getting kind of buddy-buddy there before Tatiana had gone all psycho assassin on her. And he was friends with all the people who Tatiana was *really* close with. People who Tatiana might have confided in or at least slipped up in front of. Jake could be her in.

It was a slim shot, but it was still a shot. And maybe. . . Yes, if she started hanging out with Jake at karate practices, she could also find out what those skitters were all about.

Gaia turned around and looked at Jake, waiting a few yards away. "Okay," she said. "You've got a deal."

JAKE LEANED HIS ELBOWS BACK ON

Inexplicably Full

the bleacher seat behind him, watching while Gaia made fairly short work of Erik Chin, arguably the best fighter on the team, after Jake of course. Jake was going for casual and detached, but in truth, he had to concentrate to keep from leaning forward and, well, salivating. He couldn't keep his eyes off Gaia.

She was unbelievable—so focused, so powerful. She looked amazing out there. She looked— he had to admit it—*sexy*. What was *that* about? Up until now Jake had thought there were three requirements for sexy: skin, red lips, and some kind of visible lace. Now all of a sudden he was attracted to a sweaty disheveled girl in huge karate whites who never wore lipstick and was undoubtedly a cotton-undergarments-only type. He really needed to snap out of it.

Gaia sliced her hand across the back of Eric's neck, he fell to his knees, and she elbow-dropped him flat on his face.

"Oh! Ooooh! Augh!" Carlos groaned animatedly next to Jake, wincing and shielding his face from the awful sight. "I can't even look," he said, his left knee pulled up and away from the gym floor and the mat on which the fight was taking place. "Is he still fighting back?"

"He is," Jake replied, absently digging his thumbnail under the nail on his forefinger.

"Poor bastard." Carlos hazarded a glance again. Gaia picked Erik up over her head and tossed him behind her back.

"Is that even legal?" Carlos blurted as the rest of the team squeezed their eyes shut and muttered epithets.

"Not really," Jake replied, his heart pounding.

"So should we stop them?" Carlos asked.

"I'll tell her later," Jake said with a smirk. On top of the serious attraction he was battling, he was also having too much fun watching someone else get their nuts handed to them by Gaia Moore. He'd been the victim of many mockings after the first-day-of-school whupping he'd taken from the girl. Now at least he was no longer alone.

A couple of seconds later Gaia pinned Erik to the mat and held him there for a few moments longer than necessary. Erik's whole body was limp. It was clear to Jake that he wasn't even going to try to get up. He looked over at the bleachers, his eyes begging someone to just call the match already.

"Okay!" Jake said, sitting up straight and resting his forearms on his knees. It was a relief to release his kicked-back pose. "You can let him go now, G.," he said.

Gaia glanced up, her expression almost surprised, as if she'd just been yanked from a deep sleep. Jake's heart skipped a beat and he smiled. He knew the feeling. Whenever he got a good fight going, it felt like he was functioning on some other plane—a plane where he was completely focused, channeling all his power and energy into his movements. Coming down from that feeling was always a letdown.

Gaia released Erik and scrambled up. The karate uniform Jake had lent her puffed out around the belt comically and the legs had come unrolled, so that her feet were completely hidden in the white folds. Jake tried not to smile, but it was hard. She looked like a little girl who'd borrowed Daddy's pajamas. Large clumps of hair hung limply around her reddened face, loosened from her ponytail. She'd broken a bit of a sweat, and it made her skin shine under the fluorescent lights of the gym.

Erik staggered up and stepped to the middle of the mat, where he and Gaia bowed to each other. Then Erik reached out and grasped her hand, shaking his head in amazement.

"I've fought some of the best guys in this city, and I've never had a fight like that," Erik said with an impressed frown.

Gaia's smile lit up the entire room, and Jake's heart responded with another thump. But as quickly as the smile had come it was wiped away again, as if she'd caught herself doing something she wasn't allowed to do and had corrected it as quickly as possible. She cleared her throat as Erik walked back to the bleachers and looked up at Jake expectantly.

"Anyone else?" she asked.

Jake didn't even know what she was talking about. The words didn't penetrate his brain. All he could see was that glistening skin. That glow in her eyes. The little notch in her shoulder that was exposed where his uniform—*his* uniform—slipped slightly to the left. His throat, his heart, his entire chest suddenly felt inexplicably full.

There would be no more denying it. He was falling for Gaia Moore.

"Jake?" Gaia prompted.

"Uh. . . somebody fight the girl, would ya?"

He was relieved when Greg Marshall finally got up and started to stretch. At least the attention was taken off him as the rest of the guys started to place bets on how long Greg might last.

Now that Jake knew what he wanted, he had to figure out what he was going to do next. Because Jake

Montone was not the type of guy who ignored his urges and desires, who let them fester and stood on the sidelines and hoped and dreamed and fantasized. Once Jake knew what he wanted, he went after it, and usually he got it.

But Gaia Moore was an unusual case—a rare breed. This one would have to be approached with the utmost care. Jake smiled to himself as he watched her toss Greg Marshall over her shoulder like a salad. A protective athletic cup would probably be a good idea as well.

"LOOK, I'M NOT GENERALLY IN THE

Mr. Elephant Stench

habit of. . . you know. . . wasting my time," Brendan said in his thick Brooklyn accent. The thug Tatiana's new bartender friend had hooked her up with had turned out to have a goatee, a serious leather fetish, and a gang of buddies who he claimed were willing to do anything she asked. . . for the right price. Patience, however, was not one of his virtues. He glanced at his big silver watch and then shook his arm until the timepiece disappeared under the cuff of his black leather jacket once again.

As she stood waiting for Gaia to leave the school building, Tatiana attempted a patient smile and bit back the retort on the tip of her tongue. Apparently he wasn't in the habit of bathing, either—something that she had become acutely aware of in the hour and a half they'd been standing together, waiting for Gaia to make an appearance. Of all the things that her acquaintance with Gaia had forced her to do over the last three months, this little olfactory nightmare was the one that Tatiana would be least likely to forgive. "Just give it a few more minutes, okay?" Tatiana said in her sweetest voice, fluttering her eyelashes. "If you're going to do a job, you might as well do it right."

She laid her hand gently on his broad chest and trailed it down toward his waist slowly. Predictably, Brendan leered at her, showing the gap between his two front teeth, then returned his attention to the school.

If I ever actually have to kiss that, I'm definitely going to throw up, Tatiana thought. She sighed and rested her chin on her hand on top of the parking meter in front of her, training her eyes on the big metal doors across the way. Could she possibly have missed Gaia's exit? Did she ever take another way out of the school? Over the past few months Tatiana's most important assignment had been to learn each and every one of Gaia's habits. If she had some other mode of escape from the Village School, Tatiana didn't know about it, and that basically made her the worst spy of all time.

Suddenly the doors flew open and out walked Gaia with Jake Montone at her heels. Tatiana ducked down slightly while letting out a small sigh of relief. They both looked flushed and slightly sweaty, as if they'd just gotten out of gym class, but Tatiana happened to know that they had gym sixth period, which was over three hours ago.

"That's her," Tatiana said, even as her brain rushed ahead, searching for a possible explanation for Gaia's and Jake's disheveled appearance.

Tatiana bit her lip. They couldn't have been. . . fooling around in there, could they? That would certainly explain the fact that their clothes had that just-thrown-on look and that they kept glancing at each other uncertainly, almost furtively. Their heads were bent closer together than was necessary, and Tatiana was almost certain she actually saw Gaia smile.

An unexpected twist of jealousy bored through Tatiana's heart. Here she was, on the lam, in hiding with Mr. Elephant Stench, and Gaia had spent her afternoon rolling around in the reference section of the library with that hot piece of Italian ass. Could this situation be any more unfair?

"That girl?" Brendan said, pointing ever so conspicuously. "It's too easy."

"Don't underestimate her," Tatiana said under her

breath, grabbing his hand and pulling it down. "She's full of surprises."

Jake laughed as he and Gaia rounded a corner, and Tatiana saw Gaia look up at him in surprise, with just a hint of pleasure in her eyes. There was definitely something going on between those two. Most likely, they were too moronic to notice it yet, but Tatiana knew, and that was all that mattered. Now she had her in. She wasn't close with Jake by any means, but Tatiana was an expert at reading people, and she'd hung out with him enough to know how to play him. Jake was definitely a knight-in-shining-armor type. The kind that loved to help, to be the better man, to be honorable, if only to pump his own manly-man ego. If Tatiana could just get him to believe that she was a damsel in distress, he was all hers.

"Well, Natalie," Brendan said, using the fake name she'd given herself, "this little job should not be a problem."

"Like I said, don't be so sure," Tatiana warned, turning her full attention to Brendan now that Gaia was out of sight. "She's an expert fighter, and when you kick her ass, I want it thoroughly kicked." She stood up straight and adjusted the strap of her shoulder bag; then she looked him up and down quickly. He was big, but she had a feeling he was clumsy as well.

"You'd better bring a few friends," she said.

I've always been careful when it comes to girls. I don't get why people go out and date whoever just to date. I don't get guys who go out with girls just to fool around even if the girl has no brain and no interests and no personality. Those are the kind of guys that give the rest of us a bad name—that rep that all we care about is sex and seeing how far we can get a girl to go.

I'm into girls who have minds of their own. The kind of girl who has her own hobbies and her own friends and her own things she's into doing. I'm into girls who are smart and can have real conversations, whether they're about school or politics or football or movies or even fashion. As long as she has opinions about something, that's what matters. I like a girl who can challenge me, who isn't always there when I call, who has her own life. I like a girl who won't take shit from anyone and who never backs

down from an argument. I like a
girl who's strong.

That's the word, I guess.
Strong.

I've gone out with a couple of
girls who came close to my ideal,
but those relationships didn't
work out. They just sort of fiz-
zled and died. I don't know if it
was me or them, but it just
didn't work.

But I've got to say, I've
never gone out with a girl who
embodied all of these things and
could also kick my ass. Could be
interesting.

Jake was
looking right
through her
carefully
woven so
exterior
intoxicating
directly into
her emotions,
and she didn't
even mind.

"THIS CAN'T BE RIGHT. . . . THIS

Permanent Fatal Error

can't be happening!" A hot sheen of perspiration covered Oliver's forehead, and he used an old, graying handkerchief to wipe it away. He was still weak, and his fruitless search was only making him feel weaker.

The computer screen cast the only light in the small, cold office on the top floor of his Brooklyn brownstone. He didn't want the place to appear inhabited to the outside world. But the strain on his eyes had started up a headache hours earlier, and the longer he sat and stared at the glowing screen, the more his temples throbbed. He pulled up the collar on his thick wool sweater to cover his bare neck and shoved his dry, frigid hands under his arms.

The speakers let out another low beep and Oliver's heart leapt hopefully. Maybe this time. He hit the open-mail icon, and a list of new messages popped up in front of him. Five new messages. All of them errors. *Address unknown... permanent fatal error...*

Oliver pushed the heels of his hands into his eyes, watching the purple-and-red swirls caused by the pressure behind his eyelids. Where had all of Loki's operatives disappeared to? Oliver was sure he had their e-mail handles right. Each and every one of them should have been sitting at their terminals or carrying their BlackBerrys, awaiting his return. No. *Loki's* return.

Had they all just defected in the short time that Loki was away? Were his men so disloyal?

Whereas Loki might have felt angered by this flagrant lack of response, Oliver was still feeling relatively optimistic—he'd only just begun his search, and there were many stones still left unturned. And whereas Loki might have felt the need for a release to alleviate his stress, Oliver felt perfectly peaceful. Whereas Loki might have taken the coffee cup that was delicately perched on the saucer in front of him and thrown it across the room, Oliver gently lifted the cup to his mouth and calmly took a sip.

Just keep searching and eventually something will turn up, he told himself.

But with each passing moment Oliver was becoming increasingly more aware of how Loki might have reacted, and this gave him pause. It was only an awareness at this point, but it was an awareness that frightened him. As if any reminder of the old Loki behavior could incite temptation. As if Oliver could slip back into Loki at any time.

Even though he had awoken from his coma as Oliver Moore—a good person, a person who loved his country and his family, a person who would never hurt a fly unless he was forced—the atrocities he had committed as Loki were all slowly but surely coming back to him. Every person he'd killed and tortured, all the hurt he'd caused Gaia and Tom. Oliver had a good soul, but he also had the vivid memories of doing the most evil things possible, and in spite of all his remorse those memories made him feel powerful. And he liked that feeling. It was a feeling so intoxicating, it was difficult to resist.

But he had no choice. No choice but to resist.

All Oliver could do to get past those intense feelings was to focus. "Think of Gaia and Tom," he said quietly, his slow breaths starting to work their magic on his racing pulse. His fantasy of throwing the coffee cup across the room or causing any more damage was quelled. He opened his eyes and got back to work. He deleted the error messages and started typing e-mails to the next ten operatives on his mental list. Helping Gaia and Tom, if he was still alive, was the only way he could make up for everything Loki had done. And he would make up for it.

No matter what it took.

"YOU HAVE TO COME OVER FOR DIN-

ner to celebrate," Jake said, walking backward up Fifth Avenue and causing all the other pedestrians to sidestep around him.

"Celebrate what?" Gaia asked, with the trace of a smile. Ever since

Tomato, Garlic, and Basil

Jake had gotten on the mat at practice and pinned three guys in a row, he'd been exuding the bouncy energy of a five-year-old just released from a day in boring kindergarten. His green eyes were bright, he was sporting a constant grin, and there was a definite spring in his step.

"Celebrate the fact that we are going to make Central beg for mercy at that meet tomorrow!" Jake countered.

"We'll see," Gaia replied, pausing at the corner of Fourteenth to wait for the light to change. Rush hour had begun, and the four-lane road was packed with cars weaving in and out, jockeying for position. She didn't want to think about the meet tomorrow. She knew that if she got the slightest lead about either Tatiana or her father before then, there was a good chance that she wouldn't even be there. And then Jake would be little more than the next victim in the long line of people Gaia had let down.

"Come on!" Jake said, bending slightly at the knee. "My dad had the day off, which means early dinner, homemade sauce. . . freshly baked bread. . . mozzarella that melts in your mouth. . . ."

Gaia's stomach grumbled loudly enough to be heard over the rushing traffic. "Your dad cooks?" she asked, raising her eyebrows as the Walk sign lit up.

"My dad *creates*," Jake corrected her, starting across the street. "Don't ever let him hear you reduce it to mere cooking."

Gaia pondered this. She saw herself sitting down

for an actual meal at an actual table. Saw herself sitting across from Jake, talking, maybe even laughing.

You need to get a clue, Gaia told herself, wanting to laugh over the datelike quality the scenario in her head had taken on. *He's offering you food, not some kind of dear-diary moment.*

Which was good, considering she was not looking for a date and she would never keep a diary if her life depended on it.

"Say yes," Jake said with a grin. "You won't regret it, I swear."

"Okay, I'm in," Gaia said, trying to ignore the little flip her heart did over his smile.

"Cool. My dad loves company," Jake said, turning down Fifteenth Street.

Gaia followed, wondering why it was that Jake was only mentioning his father. *My dad had the day off. . . . My dad loves company. . . .* But she knew better than to pry. Jake's family life was none of her business. Besides, once you started asking a person about his life, he started asking you about yours, and she definitely didn't want to go there.

Jake walked over to the glass doors of a swank-looking gray brick building, and the doorman jumped to welcome them.

"Evening, Mr. Montone," the white-haired man said with a nod as he held open the door. "Miss," he said, smiling kindly at Gaia.

"Evening, Rick," Jake said.

They crossed a hushed, intricately tiled lobby to an elevator with mirrored doors. It opened the moment Jake pressed the button and ascended soundlessly to the seventeenth floor. Gaia was accosted by the vision of her ratty reflection in the foggy silver walls of the elevator. She made an attempt at smoothing down her hair and tried to straighten her clothes a bit. Jake's father might be a `company-lover`, but she didn't want him to think his son had picked her up off the street.

Unfortunately, there wasn't much she could do with herself before the elevator doors slid open again. She was just going to have to hope the man was blind or something.

As she and Jake got out of the elevator, Gaia's mouth started to water like Pavlov's dog at the heady scent that permeated the hallway. Nothing like the smell of `tomato, garlic, and basil` to get your appetite going.

"That's him," Jake said referring to the aromatic extravaganza created by his father. Jake pulled a large clump of keys out of his pocket and opened the door to apartment 17A.

"Dad! We're home!" Jake called out.

The scents were even more intense inside, and Gaia suddenly felt weak with hunger. Jake led her into a large, comfortably decorated living room/dining room, where the table was already set for two. He tossed his book bag and jacket onto the couch, and Gaia shrugged off her things. Jake took them from her and laid them out neatly across an armchair. Gaia stifled a smile. If he knew what her stuff had been through, he wouldn't have been so reverent about it.

"Who's 'we'?" a cheery male voice called out. It was followed by the appearance of Jake's father himself, a tall, stocky man with a bit of a belly, who emerged from the kitchen, wiping his hands on a half apron. His hair was black but peppered with gray and receding at the temples. He looked at Gaia and grinned the most welcoming grin she'd ever been graced with.

"Hello!" he said.

"Hey," Gaia replied, feeling suddenly shy. Why was it she could banter for days with evil thugs, but she went tongue-tied in the face of congeniality?

Allergic to nice. . .

"Dad, this is Gaia Moore. Gaia, Arturo Montone, M.D.," Jake said.

"Nice to meet you, Gaia!" the man said, shaking her hand. "You're a friend of Jake's from school?"

"Yeah," Jake replied. "She just joined the karate team."

"Ah. . . a fighter!" Jake's father said, impressed. "I like a girl who can take of herself."

"Uh. . . thanks," Gaia said, feeling it was her turn to speak.

"Well, I'll grill you more over dinner," Jake's father said with a wink.

Great, Gaia thought sarcastically.

"He's kidding," Jake said.

Dr. Montone smiled as Gaia let out a breath. She wasn't used to so much positive energy bombarding her like this.

"You sit," Dr. Montone told her, unexpectedly reaching out to touch her arm. "Jake, get her a place setting! Dinner's almost ready."

He bustled back into the kitchen, and Jake pulled out a chair at the gleaming redwood table. Gaia stood there as Jake walked over to a hutch and removed a plate, a set of silverware, and a place mat. When he turned around again, he stopped in his tracks.

"That chair's for you, you know," he said, glancing at the seat he'd pulled out.

Gaia flushed, feeling like a moron, and sat down hard. How stupid was she? Did she think he'd pulled out the chair for fun? Because of some kind of weird OCD complex? Of course it was for her.

As Jake set the place in front of Gaia, she suddenly became hyperaware of her hands. She didn't know where to put them. They went from the table to her lap to the arms of her chair and finally back to the table, where she folded them together awkwardly.

Searching for something to focus on to help her stop obsessing about her total discomfort, Gaia's eyes fell on a framed photograph on the countertop of the hutch. The woman in the picture was gorgeous—raven haired with huge blue eyes and a flirtatious smile that was the mirror image of Jake's. Gaia knew she was looking at Jake's mother and wondered again where she was. The woman's gaze was mesmerizing, and Gaia couldn't seem to take her eyes off her. But she suddenly felt Jake hovering behind her chair, ready to put down a drinking glass.

"Sorry," Gaia muttered, reddening. Why had she agreed to this? She should be scarfing down a dirty-water dog right now on the train back to Brooklyn. Gaia wasn't accustomed to being waited on.

"That's my mom," Jake said as he placed the glass down a little too hard.

"She's. . . really. . ." *Really what, Gaia? Is it really so difficult to think of something nice to say?*

"I know," Jake interrupted, walking around the table and sitting across from Gaia. "She was really beautiful."

"Was?" Gaia asked before she could rethink it.

Jake cleared his throat and looked down at his empty plate as his father clanged around in the kitchen. "She died when I was ten years old," he said. "Brain tumor."

Gaia's heart went cold. He had said it so simply, but there was so much pain and emotion wrapped up in that statement. And Gaia knew all of it. She knew the anger he probably felt toward his mother for deserting him. She knew the guilt he probably felt over

110

that anger. She knew how he would probably give up his life for one more day with her.

"I'm sorry," she said. "I didn't mean to—"

"It's all right," Jake said, an edge in his voice.

Gaia stared into his light eyes, which were suddenly filled with defiance. She knew that feeling. He was daring her to be sympathetic—daring her to pity him. Oh, how she hated it when people gave her those sorry-ass looks when they heard about her own mother.

"What about you?" Jake asked suddenly, crossing his arms over his chest. "What's your family like?"

There it was. Ask a person a question and it comes right back to bite you in the ass.

I don't think I can answer that one without a graph and a couple of pie charts, Gaia thought, swallowing hard. But Jake was watching her expectantly. She had to say *something.*

"My mom died when I was little, too," Gaia offered, hoping that sharing this one piece of information might at least take that sorrowful-yet-hard look out of Jake's eyes.

"Really?" Jake asked. "How?"

"It was an accident," Gaia replied quickly. Now it was her turn to become entranced by her plate.

"You know what sucks?" Jake said.

This conversation? Gaia thought. "What?"

"The fact that everyone always says they understand

how you feel about it but they never can," Jake said. "No one ever can."

Gaia's heart pounded painfully in her chest, and she looked up into Jake's eyes. In that one moment there was a connection that even Gaia couldn't deny. She knew something about him that no one else could come close to knowing and he about her. And the really strange thing was, it didn't bother her. It was as if Jake was looking right through her carefully woven exterior directly into her emotions, and she didn't even mind. She actually felt kind of. . . free.

"Exactly," Gaia said quietly. "I know exactly what you mean."

"HEY, RED! LOOKIN' HOT!"

Tatiana tilted her head to the side so that the red curls fell between her face and the Neanderthal who was catcalling to her from the doorway to **No Harm** the twenty-four-hour Dunkin' Donuts around the corner from the Village School. This whole wig thing was turning out to be an interesting sociological experiment. That was the third guy who'd come on to her since she'd left the safe house twenty minutes ago. Maybe blonds

112

had more fun, but redheads definitely attracted more moronic come-ons.

She rounded the corner, grabbed the red curls on either side of her head, and yanked down on the wig, fitting it more snugly against her skull. It was dark out now, and if anyone saw her approaching the school, there was no way they would recognize her with the mass of hair shielding her face. Still, she wanted to get this over and done with.

The front door was always unlocked, even this late, so that overachieving teachers could come and go. The janitors were also at work inside somewhere, but Tatiana was sure very few people were left. It was her only chance to get in and out undetected.

She opened and closed the heavy metal door as quietly as possible, producing only a tiny click as it shut. She crept up the stairs and peeked around the corner to the main hall, left, then right. Every other fluorescent light was illuminated, casting an eerie glow over the deserted hallway. Tatiana took a deep breath and walked quickly, silently to the stairwell.

When she opened the door to the second floor, she heard movement and hushed voices to her left and paused. Damn kiss-ass teachers. How much money could they possibly be getting paid? Certainly not enough to keep them here this late. She trained her ear on the sounds and relaxed. They were definitely coming from the front hall—the opposite direction of where she had to go. She slipped out of the stairwell and slid along the wall this time, ready to duck into a classroom if anyone happened to decide on a bathroom run.

Jake's locker was at the end of a row, directly across from another stairwell. Tatiana pulled the folded note out of her jacket pocket and shoved it into one of the three chevron-shaped slats in the door, wondering if they'd been expressly designed to accept secret admirer cards and Dear John letters. She heard the paper flutter to the floor inside and turned to go, mission accomplished.

But just as she was registering the fact that she was home free, she heard footsteps running up the stairs right in front of her. Suddenly Megan appeared beyond the cut-glass window in the wooden door, her face downturned as she dug in her backpack, looking for something. Tatiana had nowhere to hide. She had only seconds to think. She whipped off her wig and smiled. At that moment Megan opened the door and looked up.

"Omigod!" she blurted, jumping back against the door and bringing her hand over her heart. Her moment of surprise gave Tatiana a chance to stuff the wig into her pocket. "Tatiana! You scared me!"

"Sorry," Tatiana said. "I guess this place *is* kind of deserted. What are you doing here?" *Besides completely screwing me over?* she added silently.

"Oh, the spirit club meeting went late," Megan explained with a smile. She resumed the search of her backpack. "We were making signs and stuff for the karate meet tomorrow." Finally Megan pulled out a tube of lip balm and quickly applied it to her lips, then smacked them together. "You know, when Tara came up with this whole idea of equal opportunity pep, I was all for it, but keeping up with all these teams and their meets gets kind of exhausting."

"I know," Tatiana said sympathetically. "Well, I'd better get going. . . ."

"What are *you* doing here?" Megan asked, tossing her hair over her shoulder and completely ignoring Tatiana's attempt to bail. Two little lines appeared just above her nose, rendering her the picture of concern. "You haven't been in school for a couple of days."

"Yeah. . . there's been some family stuff going on," Tatiana said, knowing Megan would eat up the idea of being let in on a private drama. "I'd rather not talk about it."

Megan raised her eyebrows. "Oh, I totally understand," she said. "But. . . why are you here, then?"

There is nothing worse than a girl with a nose for gossip, Tatiana thought.

"I came to get some stuff out of my locker," Tatiana lied easily, tilting her head to indicate the locker just behind her. "I want to keep up with my homework."

Megan's face scrunched up in confusion. "That's Jake Montone's locker," she said. "Yours is downstairs."

Tatiana had to concentrate to keep from rolling her

115

eyes. Of course. How could she have forgotten the many times that Megan had tracked her down at her locker to chat and giggle and exchange lipsticks? Not only that, but Megan was completely obsessed with Jake. She probably knew not only where his locker was, but his combination, his favorite food in the cafeteria, and the number of freckles on his arms.

"Okay, you caught me," Tatiana said, thinking quickly. If Megan kept such a keen eye on Jake, then she would notice when he found the note in the morning, and she was smart enough to put two and two together and realize Tatiana had left it. It was time to tell a version of the truth. "I was leaving a note for Jake."

Megan's eyes lit up with interest. She walked over to a locker a few doors down and started spinning the lock.

"Really?" she said provocatively. "You and Jake Montone, huh?"

"Yeah," Tatiana said, forcing a blush to her cheeks. "But. . . don't tell anyone, okay?" she added. "I mean, I think Gaia sort of has a crush on him and I wouldn't want her to find out that I was here. . . ."

"Please," Megan said. "Like I would really talk to Gaia Moore."

That, at least, was one thing Tatiana had going for her in this whole mess. Megan might love to gossip, but she'd rather wear `acid-washed jeans` to school than be caught talking to Gaia. And even if she did tell all her friends about the note, the news would never get back to Ms. Moore. No one bothered to let the girl in on anything.

"So. . . have you guys. . . you know. . . ?" Megan said, her interested tone barely masking her jealousy.

Tatiana smiled. There would be `no harm` in having a little fun with the girl.

"I will say that the boy is not shy," Tatiana said with a loaded grin. "And that whole phrase about the size of a guy's shoe. . . ? Totally true."

Megan groaned and blushed the color of Tatiana's hidden wig. "You're so bad!" she said.

You have no idea, Tatiana thought. "See you around," she said, fluttering her fingers at Megan. Then she turned and strode out of the school, hoping the girl would, for once, keep her big mouth shut.

HOW could I have been so careless? If my mother could see what
I have done in the past few days,
she would be in shock. I am not
acting like the daughter she
taught so well. I am not following procedure. I should have made
sure there was no one left in the
school to catch me. I should
never have taken that car on the
street. But I know why I have
become this way. I know why I
keep stepping away from protocol.

I have to save my mother. And
I am letting my emotions cloud my
judgment. It only makes it worse
that Gaia is involved. More emotions. More clouds.

I must take a step back and
make sure I do not make any more
errors. I must go over every inch
of my plan and strengthen the
weak links. Because this is one
mission I cannot afford to lose.

I am my mother's daughter, and
I have to start thinking like
her. If our positions were
reversed and I was the one who

TATIANA

was taken, she would have found
me by now. She would not have let
anyone or anything stand in her
way. Gaia would have talked, and
she would be lying dead right now
with a bullet between her eyes.
My mother and I would be
together.

And that is all I want. I want
us to be together, and I want
Gaia dead. Jake is my only hope.
I have to play this just right.
And I will. I will play it like
my mother would play it. I will
be cold, I will be smart, I will
be ruthless. I will be her.

And I will win. I must.

From: X22
To: Y
Subject: URGENT!

Our techs have picked up heavy activity from the private account of subject L. Subject L has been reactivated. Situation needs immediate attention. How is this possible? Please advise.

From: Y
To: X22
Subject: Re: URGENT!

This is not possible. Subject L has not been reactivated. Unknown agent must have broken his password, which we, I remind you, have yet to do. We must locate this agent, get the information, and terminate the agent. I have already assigned B team to the search. In the meantime, continue to monitor account activity.

Repeat: It is not possible that subject L has been reactivated.

How had
everything
impossible
gotten so
complicated?

WHEN GAIA LEFT JAKE'S APARTMENT

over an hour later, she was revel-
ing in the contentment brought
on by a good meal. Her stomach
was full, her head was clear, and

Epiphany

she was filled with a sudden sense of purpose.
Watching Jake and his dad participating in the familial
conversation over dinner had left Gaia with an intense
need to be around people she cared about. Unfortunately,
she'd managed to either alienate or completely lose track
of every last one of them. But there was one person she
might still be able to make things right with.

She swung a brown bag of leftovers as she pushed
open the door of Dmitri's apartment building. It
was time to talk to Sam.

He's had a few days to cool off, Gaia reasoned with
herself as the elevator zipped skyward. *And he under-
stands what my life is like. He has to understand why my
first instinct is always to be suspicious. . . .*

Of course, none of her reasoning could erase the
memory of the destroyed expression Sam had worn
when she'd accused him of setting her up for an
assassination attempt. He had looked as betrayed as
she had felt when a hail of gunfire was opened up
on her.

Yeah. He may take a little convincing, Gaia thought,
hoping for the best as she rang the doorbell. Maybe
she could bribe him with Dr. Montone's leftovers.

She heard footsteps, too heavy to be Dmitri's, and held her breath. She could practically *feel* Sam looking through the peephole at her. Hear him breathing. She counted silently while he thought over whether or not he wanted to open the door.

One. . . two. . . three. . . four. . .

Oh, come on, it can't be that *hard to decide.*

Nine. . . ten. . . eleven. . .

Gaia shifted from foot to foot and felt her body start to grow warm with embarrassment and anger. How could he leave her hanging like this? She felt like a complete and total idiot. Like the dork who went to the hot girl's house to pick up his dream date for the prom, only to find out she had already left with the quarterback and it was all a big joke on him.

Twenty-one. . . twenty-two. . .

This was completely uncalled for.

"Sam? I know you're there!" she said finally.

The door opened, causing Gaia's heart to skip an excited beat, and she braced herself for the wary look that was sure to be on Sam's face. But no one was there. She pushed the door until it hit the wall and saw Sam's back retreating toward the living room. She took a deep breath, squared her shoulders, and followed him. This was going to be harder than she thought.

When she got to the living room, Sam was shoving notebooks, pens, and a baseball cap, among other things, into his backpack. Gaia waited for him to acknowledge her. He didn't.

"Sam, look, I—"

"Dmitri's not here," he said, immersed in his frantic, rather violent packing. "He took off this morning. Said he'd be gone for a few days. Something about. . . staying under the radar."

Gaia barely had the wherewithal to assess this statement. She was too busy noticing how much concentration Sam was putting into not looking at her.

"I'm here to talk to you," Gaia said, reddening.

"Well, you'd better come back another time, then, because I'm on my way out," Sam replied. He zipped up his bag and finally looked at her, though his eyes were so hard, she could barely tell if they were focusing on anything at all.

Wow. He wasn't making this easy. The last words she could imagine herself uttering in the face of such coldness were *I'm sorry.* It was pretty clear they were just going to ricochet right off his icy exterior. He started to brush past her, and Gaia reflexively grabbed his shoulder.

"Wait!" she blurted, realizing that if she was going to get out an apology, it would have to be fast. "Sam, I wanted to say. . . I'm sorry."

Okay, that was weird. Usually she had to rev up for a good fifteen minutes before she could actually speak those words.

"Yeah, you told me that already," Sam said flatly, yanking his arm away. She felt like he had slapped her right in the face.

"Sam, you have to try to understand," Gaia told him, the area around her heart roiling with heat and emotion. "I just. . . I never know who I can trust. You know that I—"

"You should have known you could trust me," Sam spat, his eyes still hard. "After everything I've been through for you. . . ." He tipped back his head and groaned. "I am not going to do this," he snapped, his words piercing Gaia's heart. "I've had enough. 'I'm sorry' is just not gonna cut it, Gaia."

"Then what will?" Gaia asked.

Sam took a deep breath and let it out slowly. "I don't know. I don't know if anything ever will."

The huge meal Gaia had eaten started to rebel against her stomach the moment Sam turned his back on her and grabbed his jacket off a coatrack in the corner. She swallowed hard before speaking.

"Where are you going?" she asked.

"Out," he said, pulling on his jacket.

"Sam, I don't know if that's a good idea," Gaia said, trying to ignore the emotion coming off him like a tidal wave. "I mean, you might not. . . be. . . safe. . . ."

She trailed off as she realized that she was actually living with the one and only person who Sam was hiding from. Which meant that she was technically harboring his enemy. But then, he was Oliver, not Loki, so she wasn't really doing anything wrong per se. Gaia shook her head slightly to try to straighten it all out. How had everything gotten so complicated?

"I can't just sit in this apartment for the rest of my life, either," Sam said, his voice full of accusation. The underlying meaning: *"And I wouldn't have to if it wasn't for you."*

Gaia couldn't argue. After all, she knew where his former captor was and what he was doing at this very moment. She was pretty sure he would actually be quite safe out on the streets. She turned away from him and put her things down on the coffee table.

"Okay, so where are you going?" she asked, shoving her hands into the back pockets of her cargo pants.

"I found out there's some guy down in Alphabet City who might be able to get me a copy of my license so I can get access to my bank account and stuff," Sam said. "I can't keep living off of Dmitri. . . ."

Gaia suddenly felt stunned, like she'd just been in a head-on collision and time had stopped and she was just coming to. Everything Sam had said after the words *Alphabet City* was completely lost in the ether.

Alphabet City—the words scrolled across her mind.

AlphaBet City.

AlphaBet City. . . SH.

Alphabet City safe house.

That was it. It had to be. The key she'd found at the

apartment must be the key to a safe house that Natasha had set up in Alphabet City, the semiseedy area downtown east of the Village.

"Gaia? Why the hell are you looking at me like that?" Sam asked suddenly, yanking Gaia out of her mental happy dance.

Gaia snapped her mouth shut. She realized that she hadn't been listening to a word Sam had said. She was too busy having her epiphany. She looked at him, her face aglow with triumph. She could have kissed him for sparking the breakthrough she'd just had, but under the circumstances she was sure a kiss would go over about as well as a solid punch to the gut. Besides, she was anti–spontaneous kissing by nature.

"I have to go," she said, as close to giddy as she'd ever been in her life.

She grabbed up her bags and bustled by a stunned Sam, racing for the door. Sam was not going to forgive her now—from what he'd told her, he might never forgive her. But as much as she wanted him back in her life, she was going to have to deal with that later. Right now she was one step closer to finding Tatiana, and that took her one step closer to finding her dad. Armed with this new information, she had to get back to the Seventy-second Street apartment and make sure there was nothing she had missed.

She scrambled through the doorway and decided to take the stairs.

BY THE TIME GAIA RETURNED TO THE

brownstone later that night, all traces of her earlier optimism had been swept under the rug, taken out to the trash, and hauled off to a landfill in Staten Island. So what if she figured out what *ABCSH* stood for. What could she do with

The Spy Game

that information—knock on every apartment door in Alphabet City until Tatiana answered? Still, she forced herself to climb all three flights of stairs to Oliver's office. Maybe he'd have some good news for her to relighten her mood.

"I'm. . . back," Gaia said, trudging into the dark room and falling into the old moldy couch against the wall next to Oliver's desk. He sat hunched over his keyboard, the green glow of the computer screen casting an eerie array of shadows across his face. The tiny square of the screen's reflection danced in his eyes as he scanned the information he'd just brought up.

"This is not going well," he said, focused on the computer.

Gaia's stomach turned. So much for that.

"Nothing, huh?" she asked, slumping farther down in her seat.

"I've been working all day. . . trying to get in touch with Loki's men," he said, finally leaning back.

He let out a sigh and rubbed at his face with both

hands. When he looked at her, he blinked a few times as if he was trying to clear his sight. His eyes were glassy and rimmed with red, and his skin was the color of snow. Gaia looked around the desk and saw that there was nothing. No food wrappers, no glasses or plates—only one single coffee cup.

"Have you been up here all day?" Gaia asked, her brow creasing.

"I haven't moved from in front of this thing," Oliver said seriously. "I haven't even gone to the bathroom."

Okay. That was an overshare, Gaia thought. But still, she was impressed. Oliver was clearly determined to do everything he could to help her find her father. She allowed herself a slight smile. It was nice to have someone on her side. But he wasn't going to be doing anyone any good if he got himself sick through lack of food and. . . lack of bathroom runs.

"Maybe you should take a break."

"I'm not going to stop until I find Tom," Oliver said firmly, looking her in the eye with a suddenly clear and steady gaze. It was a tone that Gaia knew better than to argue with.

"Thank you," she said. "But tomorrow morning I'm going to get you some food."

Oliver smiled. "That would be good," he said. He returned his attention to the computer and leaned his elbows on the table at either side of his keyboard. "I just wish I had more to go on."

129

Gaia's mind instantly flashed to the key in the small pocket of her messenger bag. She pulled out the envelope and held it out to Oliver, her hand shaking ever so slightly. It was the only connection she had left to Tatiana and her father.

"I found this at our old apartment," Gaia said. "The one I shared with the two women who took my dad."

Oliver glanced at her and then took the envelope gingerly from her fingers. He dumped out the key and turned it over in his palm.

"It's old," he said, tossing it up and catching it. "Heavy."

"Look at what it says on the envelope," Gaia instructed. "I think it stands for Alphabet City safe house."

Oliver frowned at the scrawled letters. "A good assessment," he said. He glanced at her and smiled wanly. "I'd say there's hope for you in the spy game yet."

Gaia returned a wry smile. They both knew that she didn't want anything to do with the spy game, no matter how good she'd proved herself to be. It was outside forces that were always keeping her on the playing board. She let out a long sigh.

"The problem is, my stellar assessment doesn't do us much good," Gaia said, pushing her hands into her hair, then trailing them down her face. "It's not like I can go down there and try every single door in the neighborhood."

"No," Oliver said, clicking on a desk lamp and holding the key up to the light. "But that may not be necessary. With a key like this, there may be ways of narrowing down the door it matches." He slipped the key back into the envelope and placed it on the desk next to his mouse pad. "The Internet has been good for nothing all day, but this may prove to be an easier task," he said, smiling at her again.

Gaia took a deep breath. It was still odd to be in the same room with this man. Whether he was Oliver or Loki, his hands were still the hands that had killed so many people—that had taken loved ones away from her. She knew that no one else could help her, but knowing that didn't stop her from wishing things were different. No matter how hard Oliver worked, no matter how hard he tried to prove himself to her, it was still very hard to trust him. Almost impossible.

Look at him, Gaia told herself as Oliver started to tap away at the keyboard. *He's exhausted and hungry and weak and he still won't stop. That has to count for something.*

She walked over to the far wall, grabbed a dusty, rickety wooden chair, and joined Oliver at the computer. If he was going to be tireless, so was she.

WALKING EAST ON HOUSTON STREET,

Alphabet City

Jake pressed the note between two fingers in the pocket of his denim jacket. His palms were dry, his breath was normal, but his heart was pounding just a little bit faster than usual. He wasn't nervous, just. . . intrigued. This was by no means the first time a girl had left a secret note in his locker, but he had a feeling that this wasn't just any run-of-the-mill "I have a crush on you" meeting. For one thing, Tatiana hadn't been in school for days. For another, he'd had to cut class to make this little rendezvous. And now he was headed to Alphabet City, a neighborhood about as far from the one Tatiana lived in—both literally and socially—as you could get and still be on the island.

Something was up. Jake could feel it.

He turned up Avenue B and spotted the tiny coffee shop, Café Mille Lucci, that Tatiana had described in her note. He approached the pink-tinted window and saw her sitting in a booth, her face partially obscured by the neon Hot Coffee sign that was suspended from the glass in front of him. Huh. She didn't look sick or anything. This was just getting more and more bizarre.

Jake walked in and plopped down in the seat across from Tatiana's. Her face lit up when she saw him as if she hadn't spoken to another living soul in days.

"Jake! You came!" she said with a smile.

"Yeah," he replied. He didn't remove his jacket, and when the waitress approached, he shook his head at her. He didn't want Tatiana to think that he was getting comfortable. "So what's with the cloak-and-dagger? Where have you been the last couple of days?

Megan and all her friends can't stop talking about how worried they are," he added dryly.

It was true that Megan and her little friends hadn't stopped talking about Tatiana for the past two days, but he had a feeling they were less worried and more salivating for a scandal.

"I've just been. . . dealing with some family stuff," Tatiana said, averting her gaze.

Jake got that. And he knew better than to ask questions. Family stuff either meant, "I don't want to talk about it," or, "Ask me and I'll talk for days." He didn't want to offend, and he also didn't want to spend the next hour listening to Tatiana purge. The cleanup of emotional spillage was not his area of expertise.

Although if Gaia *had wanted to spill about her mother, I would have listened,* he realized, almost smiling. But Gaia was another story. Gaia was another *epic.*

"So. . . why am I here?" Jake asked. He didn't want to be blunt, but it wasn't like he and Tatiana were good friends. Sure, he'd hung out with her in a group, but this was the longest mano-a-mano conversation they'd ever had. Maybe she *did* have a crush on him.

"I was wondering if you'd do me a favor," Tatiana said, her eyes unabashedly filled with hope.

"What's that?" Jake asked, lacing his fingers together on the table in a double fist.

"I need to see Gaia," she said. "I was hoping you would help me set up a meeting with her."

Okay, that was unexpected. Jake's face scrunched in confusion. "Don't you guys, like, live together?" he asked.

"Not anymore," Tatiana replied. Jake couldn't put his finger on it, but something changed in her face when she said this. Like it put a bad taste in her mouth to even think about it.

"Well, can't you call her?" Jake asked.

"I can't do that," Tatiana replied.

Jake sighed and rubbed his forehead. He was losing patience with this conversation. If all Tatiana wanted was a favor, why hadn't she just called one of her real friends? Like Megan or one of the girls? Of course, none of those chicks were friendly with Gaia, but neither was Jake. . . at least not until recently.

"What did she do, stain your favorite sweater or something?" Jake asked with a scoff. He'd been around for some major catfights in his time, but never one where the two parties asked someone to set up a meeting. He felt like he was in the middle of some kind of CIA movie. God. Girls could be so dramatic sometimes.

Tatiana's eyes flashed. "This is a little more serious than that," she said. "It's life or death."

Jake's stomach sent up a warning. She sounded fairly serious. "What do you mean, 'life or death'?"

"I can't really explain," Tatiana said, looking down at her lap. She pulled in a shaky breath, and when she looked up again, her eyes were filled with tears.

The hair on the back of Jake's neck stood on end.

Something was really wrong here. Tatiana put her hands on the table, and he saw that her fingers were trembling. Whatever was happening between Tatiana and Gaia, this girl was really scared. Jake felt the sudden urge to protect her—his urge to be the hero kicking in.

"But Gaia can help you?" Jake asked.

"She's the only one who can," Tatiana answered, one tear spilling over.

"So what do you want me to do?" Jake asked.

"Just set up a meeting between the two of you and tell me where so that I can show up," she said, leaning forward and looking him dead in the eye.

Jake froze. Suddenly his protective instincts were shattered and replaced by nothing but suspicion. Tatiana was still teary, but there was something else in her eyes. Something. . . fierce. What the hell was he getting himself into here?

"No way," he said, sitting back in his vinyl seat, which let out a little hiss. He definitely didn't like the idea of setting Gaia up. Not when he had less than one clue as to what Tatiana was after. "I can't help you unless you tell me exactly what's going on."

Tatiana's back straightened, and Jake was reminded of the way his old cat used to arch her back when threatened. She had the same sort of battle-ready look about her.

"I can't do that," Tatiana said.

Jake stood up and hovered for a moment at the

135

end of the table. "Well, how 'bout you contact me when you can?" he said. He headed for the door but paused when he heard Tatiana's voice.

"If you change your mind, you can look for me in the evenings here," she said.

Jake rolled his eyes and walked out of the tiny café without a backward glance.

Outside, Jake turned his footsteps toward school and realized his hair was still on end and the he had goose bumps down his arms. Suddenly he was very worried for Gaia. There was something about that Tatiana girl he didn't trust. Something he couldn't quite put his finger on.

Whatever was going on between those two girls, Jake didn't want to get in the middle of it.

When I was young, my mother used to read the classics to me at bedtime. I used to drift off listening to the melody of her comforting voice as she read the Russian translations of books like *The Wizard of Oz, Alice's Adventures in Wonderland,* and *The Story of Doctor Dolittle.* Then one night she tried to read to me from her favorite book, *The Secret Garden,* but after she read the first few chapters to me, I started to cry. I was inconsolable. My mother thought I was just overtired and put me to bed. She tried again the following night.

But when I saw the book the next night, I started to cry again. I wouldn't let her read it. I took it from her hands and threw it across the room. My mother didn't understand what was wrong with me. She held me until I stopped crying, then pushed my hair away from my face and smiled down at me.

"What is wrong, little one?"

she asked me. "Why the tears?"

I told her that I thought it was a horrible book and that I didn't want to hear any more. I asked her to read me anything but that. I would even sit through *Little Women* again, which I hated, if she would promise never to read *The Secret Garden* again.

My mother was confused. Why did I hate the book she loved so much?

"Her mother and father died and left her all alone in that house in India!" I told her, unable to believe that she didn't understand how horrible this was. "No one even cared about her or came looking for her. She was all alone!"

My mother laughed and hugged me and promised me that the story got happier after that. That it was full of hope and life. But I couldn't get the image out of my head. What if my mother died and left me all alone? There would be no one left to care about me. No one would ever find me.

So my mother put the book back
on the shelf and started another.
And she promised me that she
would never leave me alone.
Never. She would always be there
to take care of me.

But now the tables have
turned. Now it's me who needs to
take care of her.

the sudden

flip her

heart

executed **victory**

when

Jake **hug**

tightened

his grasp

on her

COMING OUT OF THE BATHROOM STALL

In the Know

between sixth and seventh period, Gaia caught a glimpse of herself in the aging, scratched mirror that ran the length of the wall across the way. Dark circles had appeared under her eyes, her lips were chapped, and her skin was so pasty, she could have passed for a bottle of Elmer's. She sighed and put her bag down on the metal counter beneath the mirror. For once, though, her hair wasn't in knots.

Exhausted from the all-night Internet search, which had, at least, unearthed a few people in the lock-and-key trade who might be able to help her and Oliver, Gaia had spent the whole school day in a daze. This afternoon she was supposed to fight in that karate match, and she knew Jake was counting on her to help the team win. At this point she just hoped she didn't crawl onto the mat and pass out.

Gaia dug in her bag for some Chapstick, and the door to the bathroom swung open with a loud creak. She didn't look up until she realized that whoever had walked in was standing a few feet away, glaring at her. Gaia's eyes fell on a pair of three-inch-heeled black leather boots and she sighed. It was definitely an FOH.

Let the verbal diarrhea begin.

"So, Gaia, I have a question for you," she said. It was Megan. Gaia glanced at her, then continued her Chapstick search.

This should be good, she thought.

"What the heck did you do to Tatiana?" Megan asked, taking a few clicking steps toward Gaia. "I saw her last night, and she was *not* acting like herself."

Gaia lifted her face. Megan now had her full and undivided attention.

"You saw her last night?" she asked, pulling her bag off the counter and draping it over her shoulder, painful lips forgotten. "Where? When?"

"Here. Around seven," Megan replied, crossing her arms under her Miracle Bra-ed chest. "So why is it that everyone who gets involved with you drops off the face of the earth, huh? Sam Moon. . . Heather Gannis. . . now Tatiana. . ."

Heather hadn't dropped off the face of the earth, but now was not the time to argue semantics with this fairly brainless specimen. It made no sense— Tatiana lurking around school at an hour when she knew Gaia wouldn't be there. Unless she was planting something. Like a bomb, for example. But no. Tatiana would never be that careless. She would never do something that would attract so much attention. Not when she could take Gaia out quickly and quietly by simply following her after school. So what was the point? Gaia needed answers.

"What was she doing here?" she asked.

A slow, knowing smile spread over Megan's lips and she turned to the mirror, leaning in and turning her face from side to side, scrutinizing her perfect makeup.

"I promised her I wouldn't tell," she said, smirking.

Her eyes were dancing with the knowledge that she had information Gaia wanted. And Gaia was sure she was going to let it out. A person like Megan lived to let others know exactly how in the know she was. Gaia crossed her arms over her stomach and waited, eyebrows arched. This was the moment she'd been waiting for—the moment that one of Tatiana's so-called friends would slip up and expose her. But Gaia wouldn't give the twerp the satisfaction of begging for gossip.

Megan looked at Gaia out of the corner of her eye, then swung her blond hair behind her shoulders and turned to face her.

"All right, if you *must* know," she said, as if Gaia had been interrogating her, "she was leaving a note for Jake Montone."

She smiled and watched Gaia carefully, waiting for some kind of reaction. But Gaia was nothing if not good at masking her emotions—in this case shock, glee, and disappointment all rolled into one. A note for Jake. So he *did* know something. It seemed Gaia had chosen the right person to get close to in order to find Tatiana. A small victory.

Still, part of Gaia couldn't help wishing that Jake wasn't, in fact, involved. Part of Gaia just wanted him to be her friend. No espionage attached.

But there was no point in wishing for that now. Jake *was* involved, thanks to Tatiana. And Gaia knew what she had to do.

"Oh, don't feel bad, Gaia," Megan said with false sweetness. "You didn't really think that a guy like Jake would go for a hygienically challenged person like yourself, did you?"

But Gaia didn't even register the insult. She was too busy scanning her brain to see if she knew what class Jake had next. She brushed by Megan and out the door into the thinning crowd in the hallway. Damn. The bell was about to ring. It would have to wait.

But luckily, thanks to Jake himself, she would have plenty of time to pick his brain that afternoon at the karate match. Gaia smiled. Her fingers and toes were tingling with excitement over this latest lead, but she could squelch it for a couple of hours. This afternoon Jake was all hers. Maybe being a joiner wasn't such a bad idea after all.

"POINT! BLUE!" THE REF SHOUTED, thrusting his arm in Gaia's direction from the edge of the mat. The crowd in the bleachers cheered and applauded, and Gaia heard Jake's voice above the rest, shouting, "Yeah! That's it! Finish him off!"

Too Easy

The rest of the team was sitting on the bottom riser, but Gaia could see Jake from the corner of her eye,

standing in front of the others, completely focused.

Gaia waited in a fighting stance, feet spread apart, knees bent, hands fisted. She watched her opponent drag himself up off the ground. He was sweating, he was bleeding from the lip, he was gasping for breath. Gaia coolly blew a shock of hair away from her eyes. This really was too easy.

Most of the people Gaia fought had a lot more heart than this guy. Or a lot more desperation, more likely. Or just a lot more evil in their blood. Whatever the case, the difference between the street thugs and drug dealers and Loki operatives she'd fought in the past and this guy with his cropped hair and square jaw was clear. All those other people were fighting for a real reason—survival, revenge, loyalty. This guy was probably fighting because his girlfriend was in the stands somewhere, waiting for him to prove his manhood. Wasn't gonna happen.

"Finish him off!" Jake shouted again.

That was another new thing for Gaia. She couldn't remember the last time she'd had a cheering section for a fight. Her opponent approached her tentatively, his brown eyes begging her to just finish this already. Pathetic. But she could oblige. She was deathly bored.

He made a move to punch, and Gaia lifted her leg and kicked him clean in the jaw, not very hard. He fell on his ass, and the crowd went crazy.

"Point, blue! Match, blue!" the ref shouted, lifting Gaia's arm in the air.

Gaia grinned as her gaze fell on Megan and her pep squad, who cheered her victory, although with less enthusiasm than they had for Jake's win. Then her eyes traveled left and she saw Ed sitting there, clapping grimly. A cute Asian girl sat to his right, cheering and nudging him with her shoulder, trying to get his attention. But Ed didn't even flinch. His eyes were fixed on Gaia.

Her heart twisted painfully, and the smile fell from her face. The girl clearly had a crush on Ed, but he probably had no idea. Ed was clueless when it came to his own attractiveness. And the way he was looking at her. . . She couldn't tell if he hated her or was dying for her to acknowledge him. But it didn't matter. Ed was not going to be in her life. Not anymore.

She tore her eyes away and watched her teammates as they streamed over to her, gleefully whooping and clapping. Her win had also won them the meet, a meet that had been back and forth all afternoon. All she wanted in the world at that moment was to see Ed smile again—to see him happy—but there was nothing she could do about that at this very moment. She wasn't sure there was anything she could do about that at all. She had never made anyone happy in her life.

"That was amazing!" Jake shouted as he rushed over to her.

Gaia's eyes widened in surprise as he grabbed her up in his arms and spun her around in a victory hug. The contact itself was unexpected, but so was the sudden flip her heart executed when Jake tightened his grasp on her. She laughed against her own will, looking down at the smiling faces of her new teammates. For once she was a true celebrated hero. Maybe the victory was a silly one, but it felt good nonetheless.

Jake replaced her on the ground, and his smiling face was just inches from her own. But the second she looked into his eyes again, she remembered. This guy was getting secret notes from Tatiana. He might even know where the girl was hiding. This was no time to dwell on heart flips or on the thrill of victory or on the fact that Ed was stalking out of the gym right now, Asian girl in tow.

"We should go out and celebrate," Jake said.

"I'm in," Gaia replied, not missing a beat.

If Jake knew anything, she was going to find out what it was. And she was going to find out today.

Internal Warning System

"SO. . . SOLID FIGHT," JAKE SAID, taking two ice-cream cones from the guy inside the Tastee-Freez truck and handing one to Gaia.

She took off half the ice cream from the top in one bite, shedding sprinkles all over the ground as she turned away from the truck. They strolled into the south entrance to Washington Square Park. It had turned into a seriously warm afternoon, and Jake had his jacket slung over the top of his duffel bag at his side. Gaia had slipped on a thin white T-shirt after her postfight shower, and she was still flushed from the heat of the water. Jake had to concentrate to keep from staring at her.

"Solid fight?" she said, her mouth full. "What happened to 'That was amazing'?"

"I was in the moment," Jake said, shrugging one shoulder as he approached an empty bench. Her fighting *had* been amazing, but there was no reason to let her know exactly how much he admired her. There was something to be said for playing one's cards close to the vest.

"So. . . what? You have criticisms?" Gaia asked as she sat down.

"A couple, maybe," he said nonchalantly. "But we don't have to talk about that now. We should be celebrating."

"We are," Gaia replied with a smile, lifting her cone slightly, as if in a toast.

Jake smiled back, then looked out across the park. Was it his imagination, or was Gaia a bit easier to be with this afternoon? She seemed friendlier somehow—less closed off. Was it even remotely possible that the connection he'd felt the day before hadn't been one-sided?

Usually Jake would be up front about his feelings

and just say something direct, like, "So, do you want to go out with me or what?" But somehow he didn't think it was time for that yet. He wasn't sure it would go over with Gaia the way it had gone over with girls in the past. There was something about her that made him... nervous. He wasn't used to that feeling, and he wasn't sure what to do with it yet.

But there was something else he wanted to talk to her about, anyway, and this good-mood thing might prove to be beneficial. He was just turning to her to ask her what was up with Tatiana when she cut him off.

"So... have you seen Tatiana lately?" she asked.

Jake's internal warning system went off and he looked away again. That question was just a little too out of the blue to mean nothing.

"Why?" he asked the park, before taking another bite of his ice cream.

"Just curious," she replied lightly.

Jake shook his head. "What the hell is going on with you two?" he asked. "What are you doing, playing some elaborate game of Charlie's Angels?"

Gaia turned her intense blue eyes on him. "So you have seen her," she stated.

"Yeah, I've seen her," Jake replied, growing angry. "And she told me that she wanted to see *you*. Said it was a matter of life or death."

Gaia's face flushed from hairline to jaw and she crunched into her cone.

"What is up with you guys? I thought you were friends! You were living together, for Christ's sake!" Jake blurted, as miffed that the light, happy vibe was ruined as he was over the fact that no one was telling him anything. He chucked the rest of his cone into a nearby garbage can and ran his hands through his short, dark hair.

"Come on, Gaia," he said, clenching his jaw. "Tell me what's going on here."

Gaia took a long, deep breath and let it out slowly. Jake could practically see the gears in her head turning. She was deciding what to say to him. Deciding whether to trust him or not. Why was she so afraid? He hadn't known her for long, but he'd never done anything to earn her mistrust.

She turned toward him again, and for one moment Jake thought she was going to talk to him. Really talk to him. Tell him what was going on and ask him for his help. It was pretty clear to him by now that one of the two girls in this situation really needed it.

Come on, Gaia, he thought. *Trust me.*

"Just. . . tell me where she is," Gaia said.

Jake deflated.

"I don't know where the hell she is!" Jake blurted. "This is ridiculous," he said, standing and grabbing up his bag. "I'm not going to get in the middle of whatever it is you two have going on. I've got my own crap to deal with."

Gaia narrowed her eyes. She stood up and squared

off with him, `toe to toe,` as if she were going to challenge him to a fight.

"One word of advice," she said tersely. "Don't trust Tatiana."

Jake threw his arms up and took a step back from her, laughing sarcastically. "How am I supposed to know which one of you I can trust when neither one of you is telling me shit?" he said.

His heart was thumping painfully, and he realized with a start that he was actually hurt. Hurt that she wouldn't trust him. The knowledge only pissed him off even more. He barely knew this girl. How had he managed to let himself get so involved?

Gaia picked up her bag, slung it over her head, and threw back her shoulders. "You're just going to have to figure that one out on your own," she said. "It's up to you."

Then she turned on her heel and walked away.

Damn. Damndamndamndamndamn.

I'm doing it again. I'm doing it again, even though I know I shouldn't be.

I think Jake's telling me the truth. I think he really doesn't know where Tatiana is and I think he did just tell me basically everything that mattered from their conversation, whenever it took place, wherever it took place. (She wants to see me—a matter of life and death.) There is nothing about this guy that isn't earnest and honest, even if he is the cockiest asshole ever to walk the earth. But at least he doesn't try to hide it. He is who he is. No apologies. How can you not admire a person like that? How can you not trust a person like that?

And there it is. I trust him. I'm doing it again. I'm trusting someone again, even though I know I shouldn't be.

Damn.

From: 322
To: L
Subject: Re: Total Recall

Agent 322 active. I await your directive.

saw herself
running down
the sidewalk
and launching
herself at Gaia,
saw the **hatred**
look of surprise
in those always-
in-control,
ever-superior
eyes

OLIVER STARED AT THE COMPUTER

Nerves of Steel

screen, trembling with excitement and nerves. A response. He'd finally received a response. So Loki's agents were still out there. Some of them, anyway. Part of him wasn't sure whether to be elated or disturbed. Here was an agent of his own alter ego's evil at his disposal, ready and waiting.

Oliver reached for the mouse but then drew back his hand. After two full days of sending messages and trying to hack into Loki's unhackable system, this small triumph was something he'd begun to take for granted as an impossibility. Now that someone had answered his call, he wasn't sure he was ready to deal with it. Was he really capable of being an evil mastermind?

The answer, he knew, was yes. That ability was somewhere inside him. And the last thing he wanted to do was light that particular powder keg.

But Loki isn't you. You are not him, Oliver told himself. *He can't come to the surface if you don't let him.*

Oliver took a sip from the water bottle Gaia had left with him that morning and tried to focus on the task at hand.

He was going to have to play this just right. This could be the most important mission of Oliver's life. And agent 322 was his only hope of completing that mission—of helping Gaia and finding Tom.

But what if he couldn't do it? What if he couldn't pass himself off as Loki?

Oliver leaned back and pressed his fingertips into his skull just above his eyes, cursing his own weakness. He was petrified of failing. Petrified of losing the only family he had left. He hated it, but there it was. If only he could have just an ounce of Gaia's fearlessness right now, it would certainly help him through this.

What had happened to the nerves of steel he'd developed during his years in the CIA? What had happened to his confidence—his ego? Had Loki appropriated all of that and left Oliver lacking? Was the real Oliver Moore now this broken shell of a man?

His hands shook as he drew himself up straight and cleared his throat.

"Pull yourself together," he whispered firmly, jumping his chair closer to the keyboard. Saying the words aloud bolstered his spirits somehow. When a person needed a pep talk and there was no one else around, he had to create his own pep. He clicked the reply button. "They're counting on you."

His fingertips hovered briefly over the keys, and then he began to type.

Status: Urgent, immediate attention imperative.
Mission: Locate Tom Moore, alias Enigma.
Current intel: Last seen Lenox Hill Hospital ICU,

may have been taken overseas. Was unconscious at
time of extraction.
Response: Critical. Meet for exchange at location
23F, tomorrow noon. Deadline is nonnegotiable.

Oliver read these few words over a dozen times before holding his breath and clicking the send button.

It's fine, he told himself as the message was shot irretrievably into the ether. No frills. No pleas. No signs of any weakness. Direct orders were definitely Loki's MO.

His breath caught in his throat when, one second after the order was sent, the computer bleeped, indicating that a message had been received. Operative 322 was sitting at his computer this very second, awaiting Loki's command. Praying that 322 hadn't figured him out the second he read his directive, Oliver opened the new mail.

Mission accepted.

A laugh bubbled up in Oliver's throat, and he let himself give in to his triumphant mirth. He folded his arms on the desk and rested his forehead on top of them, suddenly exhausted, relief flowing out of him with every body-racking guffaw. He'd done it. He'd finally done it. Mission accomplished. He could finally, *finally* relax. He felt his bones settle and crack as he let his posture sag and his muscles uncoil. It had been so long since he'd slept. . . .

A loud ringing suddenly pierced the air, and Oliver jumped back, startled. Other than muffled street noise, there had been no other sound in the brownstone since Gaia had left that morning. Heart in his throat, he grabbed the receiver to the desk phone and fumbled with it before bringing it to his face.

"What?" he barked.

A pause. Oliver saw his life flash before his eyes. They'd found him. They were coming for him. He was going to pay for all of Loki's sins.

"I'm sorry, is this Roger Simms?" a male voice asked on the other end of the line.

Roger Simms. That sounded so familiar. Why did he know that name. . . ?

"Mr. Simms?"

It hit Oliver like a brick to the head. Of course! Roger Simms. The name he'd used when calling locksmiths earlier that day. He was really going to have to get some food in him right away. There was no room for brainlessness in this game.

"Yes, yes," Oliver said, gripping the phone. "I'm sorry. And this is?"

"Reginald Toth, sir, of Chelsea Antiques," the man replied, taking on a clipped tone. "I believe I have some information for you on that key of yours."

Oliver grinned and pulled a pen and pad toward him. First 322 and now this. He was definitely on a roll, and each rotation brought him that much closer to earning Gaia's trust.

If he could just have that, there was nothing else he would ever need.

GAIA DRAGGED HER TIRED FEET UP

All Business

the cement steps to Oliver's brownstone and pushed open the front door. Since leaving Jake in Washington Square Park, she'd spent the bulk of the afternoon wandering Alphabet City with her eyes peeled, and she was definitely ready to crash.

But the second she stepped inside, she felt her pulse start to race. Oliver was waiting for her. He walked right over to her from the front window, where he'd clearly been watching for her return. The man hadn't been down from the fourth floor since they'd moved in here two days ago. Something was obviously up.

Just let it be good, whatever it is, Gaia thought, even as her brain told her that was highly unlikely. She tossed her bag on the dirt-and-cobweb-covered floor and crossed her arms over her chest.

"I have good news," Oliver said brightly. A phrase Gaia hadn't heard in ages.

"What is it?" she asked, letting the arms drop. "Did you find my dad?"

"Very nearly," Oliver said. He walked excitedly from the front hall into the spacious, empty living room. The blinds were drawn and the sun was going down, leaving the airy space gray and murky.

"What does 'very nearly' mean?" Gaia asked, following him, her mouth watering with anticipation.

"I've finally made contact with one of Loki's operatives," Oliver said, smiling. "He should have information for me at noon tomorrow."

Gaia swallowed hard and looked away, trying to hide the distrust that was written all over her face. She didn't like the idea of trusting Loki's men. Not after everything they'd done to her and to the people she loved. The very idea, in fact, made her skin crawl with a million little bugs of doubt. But she knew it was the only way. She was just going to have to accept it.

"That's. . . great," she said finally.

"That's just the beginning," Oliver said, taking a few steps closer to her. He pulled a couple of squares of paper from his back pocket and unfolded them. "Information about your key."

The papers fluttered slightly as he held them out to her, and Gaia could relate—her heart was pretty much doing the same thing. She grabbed the sheets and looked them over quickly. There were names, dates, building code numbers, recall numbers, and on the last page Oliver had written in huge block letters:

Between Avenues A & D, East 2nd–East 5th.

Gaia's mind spun. "Does this mean what I think it means?" she asked, looking up at him.

Oliver smiled a knowing, almost cocky smile. He was proud of his detective work.

"It turns out that type of lock was used only in early–twentieth-century developments in the Meat Packing District and in Alphabet City. They were taken off the market when a fault was found in the pin system," Oliver explained. "If we're right about an Alphabet City safe house, then it's somewhere within those blocks."

Gaia quickly did the math, a grid of lower Manhattan appearing in her mind's eye. Sixteen city blocks. That was all the area she needed to search. Tatiana was somewhere within sixteen measly city blocks.

Oliver held out the key to her, and Gaia grabbed it from his hand, already plotting out the subway stops she'd need to sit through before she got where she needed to be.

"Thank you," Gaia said, folding up the papers and stuffing them into her pocket. Oliver didn't move, and

161

just before she turned to go, Gaia felt a sudden charge in the air. Like something was expected. Like he wanted something.

She glanced at him, and his softened eyes told the story. He was waiting for more than thanks. He wanted a reaction. He wanted elation. He wanted awe and congratulations. In fact, he was looking at her like he wanted a hug.

Gaia's stomach twisted with a combination of guilt, disgust, and pity. She knew this was Oliver standing before her, but the very idea of hugging him—of touching the body that played home to Loki—was physically repulsive. Her heart went out to Oliver but shrank from his evil alter ego.

She wasn't yet ready for contact.

"Thanks," Gaia said again, forcing a smile. "Really."

Oliver lifted his chin and looked away for a split second, and she knew he was consciously arranging his features. When he gazed at her again, he was collected—all business.

"Just watch your back," he said. "Natasha will have taken other measures to secure the safe house."

"Don't worry," Gaia replied firmly.

She clasped the key in her palm and headed for the door, her adrenaline running high. Whatever Natasha had in store for her, she could handle. The only thing that mattered now was finding Tatiana and finding out what she knew. The chase was on.

One Step Ahead

TATIANA WHIPPED A YANKEES BASEBALL cap out of her backpack and pulled it down low on her forehead, cursing Jake under her breath. She'd just spent two hours sitting in the café that time forgot, waiting for his curiosity to get the better of him and for him to come looking for her. The place had Frank Sinatra's greatest hits on an endless loop and sold nothing with caffeine other than `bad coffee and generic cola`. She'd picked Café Mille Lucci as her rendezvous point because all kinds of people were in and out of the place all day—young, old, poor, not so poor, every race imaginable. It was the perfect place to become just another one of the many. The only problem was, the atmosphere and the food sucked.

She stalked around a corner and almost leveled a scary-looking Hispanic man with track marks all up and down his arms. He shouted right in her face, but she quickly sidestepped him and kept walking, head down. Whenever she went to the café, she had to go wigless so that if Jake showed up, he wouldn't get more suspicious than he already was. But every time she left the safe house as herself, she was taking a risk. The last thing she needed was another Megan-type debacle. `She was supposed to be invisible here.`

"I shouldn't even have to *be* here anymore," Tatiana muttered, watching her feet as she walked.

She should have known that she couldn't count on Jake. At least Brendan was predictable and thus reliable. He was either in the bar or at the McDonald's down the street for about twenty hours out of every day. Maybe it was time she just got him and his stupid friends to kidnap Gaia from school. At this point it was probably the best plan she had going. Which wasn't saying much.

Tatiana took a deep, calming breath as she ducked around the last corner and her safe house came into view. All she had to do was get inside, sit down, chill out, and come up with a plan B. Jake might have failed her, but that didn't mean she was down and out. She wouldn't give up that easily.

A few doors down a group of men in puffy black jackets and do-rags stood on a stoop as always, chatting with each other and blowing smoke into the air. Tatiana abhorred this part of the day. Every time she walked past these guys, no matter what getup she was sporting, they hooted and howled and made smooching noises and lewd remarks until she was out of sight. She was just steeling herself for the onslaught when she saw something that made her stop dead in her tracks.

Gaia.

Tatiana leaned forward to get a better look at the

guy with the gold tooth who was gesturing with his cigarette. Tatiana's fight-or-flight reflex was telling her to get the hell out of there as fast as possible, but then her self-preservation kicked in and she realized that any sudden movement would draw big-time notice. Thanking God for her own split-second sanity, she slipped behind the corner newsstand and flattened herself against its rickety wall, waiting for her pulse to slow.

But it wouldn't. Gaia was here. Gaia was in her neighborhood. The little supersleuth had tracked her down. But how? *How?* It just wasn't possible. Tatiana had all the advantages in this situation, yet Gaia, as always, was somehow one step ahead.

Pulse pounding in her ears, Tatiana risked a peek around the side of the newsstand, and her jaw clenched. There she was, listening intently, her perfect brow wrinkled in concentration like that of a good little reporter. Oh, how Tatiana hated her. Hated her for her condescension, for her abilities, for her fearlessness, for the fact that she always had the edge. Her fingers curled into fists, and she saw herself stepping out of her hiding place, saw herself running down the sidewalk and launching herself at Gaia, saw the look of surprise in those always-incontrol, ever-superior eyes.

What she wouldn't give to be able to kick the living crap out of the girl right here and now.

Tatiana took a long breath and fought it. She fought the urge that was overwhelming every cell in her body. Because if she did what she wanted to do, it was her own ass that would get kicked. It wasn't fair, but it was true. It was just one more edge that belonged to Gaia.

Ever so slowly Tatiana pulled herself behind the newsstand again, her anger rushing out of her, leaving nothing but a sucking hole of loneliness in its place. Loneliness and fear—something Gaia would never have to face.

Tatiana thought of her mother. She was out there somewhere right now, probably in pain, probably scared and being as brave as possible, probably worried for Tatiana's life. And here Tatiana was, doing everything she could, but Gaia was still going to win. She was already well on her way.

It's not fair, Tatiana thought, feeling her resolve slipping away—feeling her strength escape her. *It's just not fair. . . .*

She knew that she needed to stay strong. She knew that the situation demanded it. But no one was here. Not a soul would witness it if she cracked. And for the moment she couldn't do it anymore. `Not alone.` It was too much.

And so while Gaia questioned every person on the street, coming closer and closer to her mark, Tatiana slid down the wall of the newsstand, pulled her knees up under her chin, and wept.

CURIOSITY KILLED THE MORON, JAKE

Two and Two

told himself as he approached the door to Café Mille Lucci, his brain trying to convince him one last time that this was a bad idea. But he couldn't help it. All he'd done all afternoon was go over and over his last conversations with Gaia and Tatiana, trying to put two and two together. The only problem was, he had yet to come up with four.

Someone was going to explain what was going on, and they were going to do it now. It was their choice to suck him into their little drama, so one of them was going to have to talk. And since he had a feeling it wasn't going to be Gaia, he'd decided to start with Tatiana.

He yanked open the door and readied himself for an inquisition, but the moment he saw Tatiana, he faltered. She was slouched in a booth, her back up against the wall and one leg up on the vinyl bench. Streaks of dried tears cut rivers down her face, and there were circles of smudged makeup beneath her eyes. Her gaze was unfocused and staring, and her skin looked sallow under the fluorescent lights.

Jake's mind flashed on an image of his mother before she died, when she was weak and tired and helpless and he couldn't do anything for her. When she would just lie there in that hospital bed, looking at him with those sorrowful eyes, and he was just a little kid who could do nothing. Suddenly every muscle in his body tensed up. He had to do something.

"Tatiana?" he said, walking over to the edge of her bench.

Her eyes slowly traveled up to meet his face, but she showed no sign of recognition. Okay, this was worse than he thought.

"Hey! Tatiana!" he said a bit louder, crouching by her sneaker that hung over the edge of the bench. "Are you okay?"

She inhaled, the breath choppy through an obviously stuffy nose. She looked off past his ear at some distant, probably nonexistent point.

"Hey! Can I get some cold water over here?" Jake called out over his shoulder.

An elderly waitress heaved a sigh and left her magazine at the counter to go wrangle up some ice water. Jake watched her progress with an ever-growing swell of impatience in his chest. When she finally handed him the glass, ice cubes tinkling, he gave her a sarcastic smile.

"Thanks a lot," he said tonelessly.

He dipped his fingers into the water, reached over, and flicked it into Tatiana's face. She blinked and shook her head and seemed to wake up.

"Jake!" she said, finally focusing. Then she sat up and started to cry.

"Hey! What the hell is going on?" Jake asked, sitting down next to her. Tatiana collapsed into him like a marionette whose strings had just been severed, crying quietly. Before he knew it, he found himself wrapping his arms around her, stroking her hair, and whispering a repetitive mantra of "It's going to be all right. . . . It's going to be all right. . . . It's going to be all right."

"You have to help me, Jake," she choked out through her tears. "Please. You're the only one who can."

Against his will, Jake was moved by Tatiana's total transformation from together, *über*-social queen bee to helpless victim. Whatever was going on between Gaia and Tatiana, this girl needed help.

"Okay," he said. "Okay. I'll do whatever I can."

Guys are so easy. They fall for sex, they fall for tears, they fall for the silent treatment, they fall for jealousy, they fall for disinterest. There are any number of things you can do to manipulate a guy. The key is knowing the guy well enough. Is he a knight in shining armor, a child, a lecher, a man who needs a challenge? Not all of the above tactics will work on all men—you have to mix and match.

Brendan, for example, is clearly the sex type. He isn't going to be swooping in to save any damsels in distress—he'd probably think that blubbering was funny. And he's not the type to waste his time with someone who isn't giving him the proper signals. So sex it was. And it worked.

Jake, on the other hand, is a total hero. He may put on a tough act, but he so wants to be the savior guy. It's written all over his face. So tears, of course, worked.

That's the difference between

me and Gaia—I understand guys.
Think she would ever break down
in front of Jake? Please. She'd
sooner die than admit she needed
to be saved.

And so I do still have an
edge. A small one, but an important one.

He was
trying to
make Gaia
jealous.... **stare**
Unfortunately,
it was
working.

BRENDAN WAS HUNCHED ON THE LAST

Undergarment Action

bar stool, one beefy arm resting along the edge of the bar, the other curled around a mug of beer like it was a bunny rabbit or a kitten—something to be cuddled and protected. From the lolling of his head and the constant movement of his lips, Tatiana could tell that he was sloshed, three sheets to the wind, completely blasted.

She clenched her fists and told herself to remain calm. These were the pitfalls of aligning oneself with shady characters like Brendan. All she could do was hope that he was cognizant enough to hear what she had to say and remember it. She unbuttoned the third button on her white blouse, exposing a hint of the lace bra underneath. Maybe a little `undergarment action` would rouse him enough to pay attention.

Tatiana walked over to Brendan and slipped onto the stool next to his, making sure her leg brushed his. He swung his big head to the left and grinned stupidly when he saw her.

"It's the siren," he said, lifting his beer mug and downing half the contents. He slammed it back down onto the bar, and Tatiana slid it away from him, placing it at arm's reach on her other side. He swiveled his bar stool so he could better see her. Tatiana watched, careful to control all visceral reaction, as his eyes slid down her neck to her cleavage. She leaned forward slightly to give him a better look.

"The plan is on," she said. She placed her hands on either side of his grizzly chin and lifted his face so that he'd have to look at her. It took a couple of extra seconds for his eyes to catch up with his chin. Tatiana smiled. "I need you to bring as much firepower as possible to the Hiro Dojo on West Eleventh Street tonight, nine o'clock."

Brendan's red-rimmed eyes swam. "That's where we're doing this?" he said, spitting a bit. "A freakin' dojo? What is this, *Karate Kid?*" He leaned back on his stool precariously and waved his hands around in the air. "Wax on! Wax off!" Then he collapsed on the bar, laughing at his own stupid joke.

Tatiana pressed her teeth together, waiting for him to finish convulsing.

"It's a believable location for my bait to lure our mark to," she said when he finally lifted his eyes. She raised one shoulder, thereby exposing a bit more breast, then reached over and trailed a fingertip along the back of his hand. "He's setting it all up. It'll be deserted, and he has a key." She looked flirtatiously into his eyes. "I'm good at what I do, Brendan."

He leered predictably. "I'll bet you are."

"So, you'll be where, when?" she asked him.

"Hiro Dojo, West Eleventh, nine o'clock tonight," he replied, looming so close, she could pick out the various alcoholic substances on his breath.

"Very good," she replied, smiling through her disgust.

"And when the job's done, I get my promised payment, right?" he asked, his hand falling clumsily on her upper thigh.

"Definitely," Tatiana replied. Holding her breath, she leaned in and kissed Brendan. His tongue fought its way into her mouth as he kissed her back violently. Tatiana silently counted to ten, then pulled away with some effort. Brendan nearly fell off his bar stool.

"I never break a promise," Tatiana said, the sour taste of him all over her. She passed him his beer in an effort to distract him, and he tilted his head over it, staring into its coppery depths. Tatiana headed for the door, fishing a roll of breath mints out of her bag.

322

"OKAY, OLD MAN," OLIVER SAID UNDER his breath, stopping his hands from trembling by stuffing them into the pockets of his gray trench coat. "Okay. You're fine. You can pull this off."

He stood in the darkest corner of the alleyway between Kavlav's Gyros and Song's House of Nails, trying to avoid breathing in the acrid mix of frying lamb and nail polish remover. The height of the buildings blocked out the sun, and the extra shadow cast by the Dumpster next to him provided a perfect haven. He had arrived fifteen minutes early for his meet in order to be there when 322 arrived. This was what Loki had always done to keep his operatives on their toes, so this was what Oliver had to do.

He heard a footstep, a crunch of gravel, and held his breath, telling himself not to peek. If it was his operative, he would know the protocol. There was no need to reveal himself if it was anyone else.

Noisy rustling in the garbage cans down the alley ensued, and Oliver knew he had time. Agent 322 wouldn't enter if there was a homeless person rooting through the trash. He would have to wait it out.

Naturally, his thoughts turned to Gaia. He knew she didn't fully trust him yet—had seen the way she looked at him with a protective veil over her eyes. She was probably wondering when Loki would resurface, whether she'd be able to tell the difference when he did, whether he already had. Oliver knew these suspicions were well founded—ingrained, even. He knew they were justified.

All he had to do now was erase them forever. He needed Gaia to trust him. She was all he had.

The banging and rustling stopped, and the footsteps gradually moved away. Oliver knew that the next few moments would decide his fate. If he could convince 322 that he was Loki, he would gain the information that would help Gaia. And once he had the information, she would know he was good. She would know that he lived to help her—that he was worthy of being called "uncle."

If 322 didn't believe him, however, all was lost.

More footsteps, quieter this time but authoritative. No timorous sneaking around. This was it. Oliver could feel it. A cold tingling sensation ran down his back. And there it was.

Scrape. . . scrape. . . scrape. The sound of a shoe sole being dragged carefully back and forth. The signal.

Oliver steeled himself and stepped out into the light.

"Boss," 322 said. He stood a few yards away, dressed in head-to-toe black, a baseball cap pulled down over his brow, exposing nary a hair on his head. His eyes were hidden behind dark sunglasses.

"The file," Oliver said flatly.

322 produced a large envelope from behind his back. He took the few steps necessary to close the distance between him and Oliver and handed over the envelope. He then took two respectful steps back and stood at ease.

Loki slipped open the envelope and glanced

inside. A few sheets of paper, an eight-by-ten photograph. A computer disk. He could hardly restrain himself from shaking the items out into his hand, but he found the strength. He cleared his throat and resealed the envelope.

"Good work," he said.

His words seemed to open a floodgate within the operative. "Where've you been, boss? The organization is a wreck. There have been so many defections. . . . How did you escape?"

Oliver's mind spun with possible explanations, lies, details. He could weave a plausible story in no time—one aspect of his CIA training that hadn't deserted him. He was about to unleash a web of deceit when he caught himself. No. Wrong.

"That's none of your concern," he snapped, causing 322 to go pale. "There may have been defections, but you have proved your loyalty here today." He tucked the envelope under his arm. "Your work will not go unnoticed. Now go."

The operative let a bit of a smile escape his lips, then he nodded once and slipped out of the alley. Oliver breathed a long sigh of relief. He'd pulled it off.

Clutching the envelope to his breast, Oliver strode from the alley and turned his steps toward the subway. He would wait until he was home to open the envelope again. There he would be able to peruse the contents safely and, hopefully, rejoice over his success.

Giving the Eye

GAIA STARED AT MRS. BACKER AS SHE walked back and forth in front of the classroom, lecturing about the Battle of the Bulge. Whatever the teacher was saying, she was very excited about it—gesturing, pausing for drama, throwing in her own sound effects here and there. "Boom! Argh! Move the line! Move the line!" Gaia was sure she would be riveted if she could remotely focus on what the woman was saying.

But she couldn't. All she could focus on was the fact that Jake had been staring at her for precisely thirty-nine minutes now without a break. He sat less than two feet away from her, and his eyes were riveted on her face, his chin resting on his arms, which were stacked on top of his desk. Greg Marshall's sizable frame blocked Jake from Backer's sight, making it all the easier for him to do this. To s t a r e . To drive her totally stir-crazy.

What the hell did he *know*? And why was he giving her the eye? Had she been wrong to trust him?

Gaia turned her head away from Jake toward the windows on the other side of the room and froze. Ed. He was staring at her, too. The second she caught his eye, he glanced at Jake, reddened, then turned in his seat to face the front.

Oh, this *is really fun,* Gaia thought, her heart convulsing.

But she couldn't deal with Ed's feelings right now. She'd talked to him, and he knew how she felt. Besides, Jake's unbreakable stare was a little too distracting to let her focus on anything else at that moment.

Gaia shifted in her seat, sitting up slightly and tapping her pen against the edge of her history book. Out of the corner of her eye she saw Jake's gaze follow her face. She colored slightly. What was this guy's *deal?*

It occurred to her that if she were to go completely against her instincts and *not* trust Jake, then he and Tatiana could be scheming against her. It was totally plausible that Jake knew *exactly* where Tatiana was. That he knew what her next move would be. That he would help her make it.

All of which would completely suck, considering the fact that Gaia was just beginning to like the guy.

Gaia sighed and glanced at the clock. Just over a minute left. Backer seemed to be coming to the climax of the battle, swinging her arms up over her head and down, her eyes bulging as she ranted.

There was one other angle to consider here. Maybe Jake was just an innocent do-gooder. Maybe he was simply a good friend. Tatiana could be feeding him some line about an estrangement between herself and Gaia. She could be playing him like a harmonica. And maybe, just maybe, Jake just wanted to help. Maybe he thought he *was* helping—both her *and* Tatiana.

Maybe Jake was really just a good guy. Somehow that was the easiest scenario to believe.

The bell rang and Gaia stood up, sliding her books into her hand. She hadn't taken one step when Jake's fingers closed around her bicep. Ah. So this was going to go beyond ogling. Gaia saw Ed pause by the door, jealousy and concern flitting over his face before he ducked his head and slipped from the room. Gaia ignored the sour feeling in her chest over the hurt she was causing Ed and turned to face Jake. She could deal with her warring emotions later. For now she had to deal with all her other problems.

"Are you going to let me go?" Gaia asked.

Jake started to speak, then stopped himself. He released her arm and adjusted his books from one hand to the other and rested them against his hip, watching the exchange as if it took great care.

"What's up?" Gaia asked, impatient.

Jake glanced at Mrs. Backer, who was straightening her desk at the front of the room. Then he tilted his head toward the door and started to move. Gaia followed him out into the crowded hallway, where he paused near the wall. He looked around, and Gaia did the same, then wished she hadn't. Ed was standing right across from them against the other wall, talking to the same girl he'd attended the match with the day before. She had obviously been waiting for him outside of class. Ed glanced in Gaia and Jake's direction, saw Gaia watching, then reached out and pushed the girl's hair behind her ear.

It was a shameless act. He was trying to make Gaia jealous because he was jealous of Jake. Unfortunately, it was working.

Focus, Gaia told herself. *You want Ed to move on. You practically told him to do this. You'll get over it.*

"Well?" she said to Jake impatiently.

Ed and the girl moved across the hall until they were standing right behind Jake. The girl started to twirl the lock on the locker about five feet away.

Perfect, Gaia thought sarcastically. *Now Ed's going to hear. . . whatever Jake's going to say.*

Jake lifted his chin and looked her right in the eye. "I was wondering if you'd meet me somewhere tonight," he said.

He was tense. He blinked about a hundred times. He reached up and scratched over his ear. Telltale signs that there was more going on here than he was saying.

Gaia's heart sank, but she didn't have time to dwell on it. This was it. Tatiana had gotten to him. Well, fine. At least she knew who her friends were, and at least it was almost over.

"Sure," Gaia said with an easy smile. "Where do you want to go?"

From: Y
To: X22
Subject: Subject L

Reactivation confirmed. Major breach. Have
assigned my personal team to subject L's movements. This is a debacle. This is unacceptable.
Any informant on the breakdown of communication
in this matter will be rewarded.

The responsible parties will answer for this
with their lives.

If there
was ever
a time
to play
the
superhero,
this
was it.

karate chop

ED GLANCED AT HIS WATCH AS HE

Ex waited outside the rest rooms at the Union Square Theater. It was eight fifty-five. In five minutes Gaia was going to be meeting Jake a couple of blocks away to do. . . whatever it was they were going to do. And Kai was in the bathroom, taking a very long time.

"Come on, Kai," Ed said under his breath. "What are you doing in there?"

The door opened and a pretty brunette walked out. She took the hand of one of the other guys waiting along the wall, and they walked toward the door together, laughing.

I'm evil, Ed thought, watching the happy couple. *Kai asked me to go to a movie and I set the whole thing up at this specific theater at this specific time just so I could spy on Gaia and Jake. What kind of date am I?*

Of course, Kai did live somewhere in this neighborhood, so it wasn't like the choice of theater was out of her way. Plus he wasn't totally certain that he and Kai were *on* a date. Maybe they were just two people hanging at the movies together. And if that was the case, he didn't have to worry about the fact that he was obsessively stalking his ex.

Uh-huh. Sure.

"Hey!" Kai said, emerging from the bathroom. "Ready to go?"

"Uh. . . yeah," Ed said glancing at his watch again.

Maybe he should just bag it. Maybe he should walk out the front door of this theater and make a right instead of a left. Walk away from the address he'd overheard Jake give Gaia that afternoon.

But he knew he wouldn't. He had to see what the two of them were doing. He had to know if she'd broken his heart just to date someone else.

"So, what did you think of the movie?" Kai asked as they pushed through the glass doors at the Union Square Theater and were accosted by the scent of roasting nuts and toasting pretzels from a nearby vendor.

"It was supremely bad," Ed said, surprised at his own ability to make normal small talk when his heart was racing. "I mean, that was on par with *Saving Silverman* and *Scooby-Doo.*"

"You didn't like *Scooby-Doo*?" Kai blurted, eyebrows raised.

"You did?" Ed asked over his shoulder as he crossed the street. "I just lost all respect for you."

"Please! You have to leave some room for movies you can laugh *at* as well as *with*," Kai replied, giggling. "There's value in that."

Ed tilted his head, trying not to be too obvious about looking around for a glimpse of Gaia or Jake. He was close enough to their meeting spot that he might catch one of them approaching.

"Huh. Never looked at it that way," he said. "In that

case, *Episode Two* is a classic and Hayden Christiansen is my favorite comedic actor."

Kai laughed and skipped to catch up with him. She linked her arm through his, and Ed glanced down at her pink-gloved hand, surprised. Huh. So apparently this *was* a date. And he was happy to note that, even in his slightly neurotic state of mind, Kai's gesture sent a little warm tingle through his arm.

Of course, the tingle was quickly followed by a massive wave of guilt. Kai was cool. She was talkative, happy, fun. She had this optimistic take on pretty much everything from the flatness of her soda ("Bubbles sometimes make me sneeze, which is, like, so rude in a movie theater") to the fact that she'd stepped in gum ("At least the poor usher guy doesn't have to scrape it up now").

This was new and different. A girl who saw the good. A girl who touched him without a huge internal debate. A girl he could actually *date* instead of fruitlessly pursue to the point of exhaustion and ultimate multiple heart-breakings.

A girl who was too cool to be used in the way that Ed was currently using her. Ed paused in the middle of the sidewalk. That was it. He couldn't do this to her. He wasn't going to go looking for Gaia in the middle of his first date with Kai.

"Why are you stopping?" Kai asked.

Ed looked north toward the park. "I was thinking. . . .

You want to go get something to eat at Coffee Shop or something?" Coffee Shop was on Fifteenth Street, in the opposite direction from the place Gaia and Jake were meeting. In the *healthy* direction.

"Actually, I kind of have to get home," Kai said, wincing. "My mom's a nutcase when it comes to school night curfews."

Ed smiled and pulled her a little closer to him. "Well, then, I'll walk you home," he said. "Where's your place again?"

"I'm on Sixth Avenue and Tenth," Kai replied. "We can cut down here."

She started off toward Eleventh Street, but Ed didn't move. "Uh. . . why don't we walk down Twelfth?" he asked.

"You feeling okay?" Kai asked. "Why go up to come back?"

Good question, Ed thought. *Can't answer, "Because if we go down Eleventh, we may see my ex with her new boyfriend, which I've just decided would be bad."*

"Come on," Kai said, tugging at his arm. "I want to stop at the market down here, anyway, and stock up on gum."

Just go. She's going to think you're a psycho, Ed told himself.

He fell into step with Kai and took the turn down Eleventh Street, his heart pounding, hoping his stall tactics had eaten up a few minutes. Maybe he had already missed the happy couple. Maybe he wouldn't even have to see—

Gaia.

Ed stopped short, causing Kai to almost lose her footing, when he saw Gaia walking along the other side of the street. Her shoulders were slumped forward and her head was down, but her eyes were on high alert. She was staring at the door to a building a few doors up from her—a dojo—and she was tense.

She was definitely not in a nervous I'm-meeting-a-guy frame of mind. She was in a defensive I'm-watching-my-back frame of mind.

"What's up?" Kai asked, her brow wrinkling. "Oh, no. Did those Sour Patch Kids just hit your stomach?"

"No. I'm all right," Ed replied, ripping his eyes from Gaia long enough to give Kai a reassuring smile.

Gaia looked around her before ducking into the alley next to the dojo. Something was up. Ed could feel his Gaia-danger radar going off. This wasn't a date—this was something else. Something not good. And Ed didn't even register relief over the fact that she wasn't in for a night of romance. His first instinct was to follow her—find out what was going on and whether he could help.

But where had that gotten him in the past? Almost killed a few times, that's where. And all his interference ever did for Gaia was annoy her. She could handle herself. And she *was* meeting Jake here. He could protect her. Not that Ed could ever imagine Gaia needing protection.

"You *sure* you're all right?" Kai asked skeptically. She popped her gum.

"I'm fine," Ed replied. He turned his back on the dojo and started walking again. Kai leaned over and rested her head on his shoulder as they strolled, and Ed took a deep breath.

I'm fine, Ed repeated silently—firmly. *I'm just moving on.*

GAIA CLIMBED THE CEMENT STAIRS
to the back door of the dojo, her thick-soled boots crunching through the thin layer of silt on the steps. As Jake had promised,

Yin-Yang

the place was deserted—no classes battling it out inside, not a soul in sight. A fading `yin-yang` symbol was painted on the wooden door at the top of the stairs. Gaia pressed her ear against it and heard nothing. When she turned the knob, the door swung open easily.

The place was pitch black. Gaia stepped into the large, airy room, moving only inches from the door. It was freezing inside, as if someone had left the air conditioning on full blast, but the hair on Gaia's neck wasn't standing on end because of the chill. Someone was here—she could feel it.

"Jake?" she called out.

Before her question stopped echoing, someone grabbed her from behind. Her arms were pinned back, and as much as Gaia struggled, she couldn't free herself.

So here it is, she thought. *Ambush time.* Apparently Tatiana had made herself some friends while she was on the lam. Some friends other than Jake.

"Ooh. . . feisty," a growling voice said in her ear, accompanied by the thick stench of scotch.

Gaia wrinkled her nose in disgust and stopped trying to pull away. The guy seemed to like the struggling. And besides, she had a feeling he wasn't going to kill her. Not just yet. Tatiana was here somewhere, and she was going to want to show herself to Gaia before she died. She was going to want to gloat over her victory.

Gaia's assailant shoved her into a chair and proceeded to hold her down while some other person used thick ropes to bind her. Her hands were tied around the back of the chair, straining her arm muscles, and her ankles were each tied to a chair leg. As they worked, Gaia strained her ears to hear whether there were more people in the darkness, and there were. At least two—maybe more.

The two men stepped away from Gaia, satisfied that she was going nowhere, and the lights flickered on. Gaia blinked against the sudden brightness. When she was able to focus again, she saw that five men, mostly in jeans and distressed suede and leather, surrounded her, each with his own special sneer and each with his own special gun aimed at her face. A couple of them looked strong, and most of them had the glassy eyes of total drunks. Gaia looked past them to the thick black velvet curtains that lined the two side walls, and then the door to the dojo's office opened and out walked Tatiana, her boots clicking on the polished wooden floor. She was wearing a short, dark wig, but it was definitely her.

Gaia felt her blood start to race in her veins at the sight of her. Before this night was over, she was going to wipe that smirk off little Tatiana's face.

Ever so dramatically, Tatiana stepped across the room until she was face-to-face with Gaia but a few yards away. She flicked her blue eyes to each of her thugs, smiling a bit more each time, as if to draw Gaia's attention to them—as if to say, "I've got you now."

Gaia took a deep breath, sighed, and adopted her most bored expression.

Tatiana's eyes narrowed. "You're going to tell me where my mother is," she said, her voice filling the room.

Gaia's lips twitched. "No. You're going to tell me where my father is."

"I don't think you're in any position to make demands," Tatiana snapped.

Gaia's smile widened. "I wouldn't say that."

192

"NOW!" JAKE SHOUTED.

Unarmed

He ripped away the black curtain that shrouded his face and stepped out into the dojo in perfect unison with nine of his closest, most powerful friends. He took in the scene quickly. Gaia was tied to a chair in the center of the room, Tatiana was looking at him, shocked, and five huge guys with guns were just turning around to take aim at the fighters who lined the walls. Jake and his friends had the gun toters surrounded, but they were also unarmed.

"Dude, no one said anything about guns," Jake's friend Thomas said through his teeth.

You read my mind, Jake thought, trying not to let his fear show. Who *were* these girls?

Suddenly Tatiana reached behind her back and pulled a gun out of her waistband, aiming for Jake.

"Down!" Jake called out.

He dropped to the floor and rolled into the legs of the nearest guy, taking him down just as he fired his first shot—into the ceiling. After that, everything was a blur and Jake was moving on pure instinct. The guy's gun went skittering across the floor and slid under the curtains. He struggled to get up, but Jake and his sparring partner from the dojo, Derek, made sure he stayed down. It was almost too easy. The guy was clearly trashed, and he didn't have much fight in him. A one-two punch from Derek, followed by an elbow jab to the back from Jake, and the dude had passed out on the floor, sleeping like a baby.

"No!" Tatiana yelled out over the sounds of fired shots and landed punches, the groans and grunts and shouts of the battle. "No! No! No!"

Jake glanced in her direction and saw that Christov had easily disarmed her before moving on to his next opponent. Tatiana was stomping her feet like a spoiled child.

Jake and Derek rose up into their fighting stances and surveyed the room. The big guy who'd arrived first with Tatiana was giving a couple of Jake's friends a hard time on the far side of the room.

"You help Tim," Jake said, feeling not unlike an army general giving orders. It gave him a bit of a high. If there was ever a time to play the superhero, this was it. This was his moment. "I'm gonna get Gaia," he added.

Derek nodded and ran across the room. Jake rushed over to Gaia and fell on his knees at her side. He yanked his switchblade from the back pocket of his jeans and went to work on the ropes that bound her wrists.

Jake Montone to the rescue! a little voice in his brain shouted. *Super-Jake! Jake the Great. . .*

"You carry a knife?" Gaia said, her voice strained.

"Only when I need to," Jake replied. "You all right?" he asked as he sawed at the ropes.

"Been better," Gaia replied.

Something about the way she said it made Jake's heart stop short in his chest. He pulled back a little and surveyed her body, making sure she wasn't hurt. There was a large stain of blood on the leg of her jeans, and it was spreading.

"Oh my God. You're shot," he said, grabbing for her leg.

"Leave it," Gaia demanded. "It's just a scratch."

One of the thugs went flying over their heads and landed on his back with a loud moan. Jake still couldn't believe this was happening. When Gaia had told him that Tatiana was setting them both up, he'd had no idea she was going to bring her own little army.

"Jake, please," she said. "Tatiana. . ."

He glanced around and saw Tatiana searching the guy who'd just been tossed—shoving her hands frantically into his pockets and feeling along his legs. She was looking for a gun.

"Got it," Jake said, his adrenaline pumping.

He sliced through the last threads of the fraying ropes and Gaia swung her arms free. Her eyes were trained on Tatiana, and Jake could tell she was salivating to get to the girl, but her legs were still bound. Jake stood up, grabbed the back of the chair, and ripped it off the seat, tossing the shredded wood across the room.

"Can you stand?" he asked Gaia.

Tatiana was now crawling around the room, feeling under the curtains. She was only yards away from the first thug's gun.

Gaia grunted her approval and struggled up. The moment her butt was up, Jake sliced the wooden seat in two with one expertly placed karate chop. The seat fell free of the chair legs and he was able to pull the two rods of wood out of the ropes around Gaia's ankles.

As soon as Gaia was free, she spun around, her eyes searching. She spotted something and dove past Jake toward the back wall. At the same moment Tatiana finally found her gun and whirled around as she stood, her wig falling from her head, her eyes wild.

"Gaia!" Jake shouted.

But he didn't need to alert her. She'd found her own weapon and aimed it right back at Tatiana. The two girls cocked their guns at the same time and stood there, chests heaving, at opposite sides of the room, an Old West-style standoff.

Okay, Jake thought. *This is not your ordinary catfight.*

He had no idea what was going to happen next, but he had the distinct feeling that it was not going to be good. His friends from the dojo, having made short work of Tatiana's little band of thugs, walked up behind him. They all stood there and watched the two girls in silent awe.

"You don't see that every day," Derek whispered just off Jake's shoulder.

"No, you don't," Jake replied.

"We're not going to solve this if we're both dead," Gaia said, her shooting arm as steady as a tree branch.

"No, we're not," Tatiana agreed.

"I don't want to shoot you," Gaia said.

There was a beat. "Nor I you," Tatiana replied.

She blinked. She was lying. In that moment Jake knew for absolute certain that Tatiana wanted Gaia dead. Gaia had warned him that this was the case earlier this afternoon when he told her about this meeting and had been honest about who was calling it. That was why he'd agreed to bring along his friends. That was why he was here. But he'd never fully believed it until that moment. Tatiana wanted to kill Gaia. The girl really was a psycho.

"So why don't we just both put down our guns and talk this out?" Gaia suggested. "I'll tell you what I know about your mom, you tell me what you know about my dad."

Tatiana took a deep breath. "Agreed," she said.

Ever so slowly both girls lowered their arms and crouched to the floor to put down their guns. Gaia winced in pain and grabbed at her leg, and Jake's heart flew into his throat. He glanced at Tatiana, and she saw her opportunity. She reached behind her, and Jake caught a glimpse of silver—the butt of another gun—tucked into the waistband of her pants.

197

"No!" Jake shouted, and took off across the room.

One step and Tatiana had the gun in her hands.

The second step and she was training it on Gaia.

The third step and he swore he heard the catch of the trigger.

He threw himself into the air, his eyes locked on Gaia's shocked face. The sound of the gunshot exploded in his ears, and then `everything went black`.

Tonight, I swear on my life, I remembered what it was like to learn to walk. The first time, that is. Not the last time, after I got out of my wheelchair. I swear, I vividly remembered being one year old and concentrating my little diapered ass off as I tried to walk to my father's outstretched arms. Only this time I was concentrating to walk away from someone. And it took everything I had.

It's unbelievable, that thin line between love and hate. That tiny little thin line is like a balance beam that's. . . well, impossible to walk.

But somehow I did it. I put one foot in front of the other, and somehow I made it to the end of the block and got Kai to her building.

And then I took that last monster step. I kissed Kai good night.

And it wasn't half bad.

She thought of
Jake's open,
honest face. . .
the way he'd
looked at **heart**
her as he
threw **monitor**
himself in the
path of the bullet
that was meant for
her heart.

GAIA PULLED THE METAL-AND-PLASTIC

Grub

chair over to the side of Jake's hospital bed and sat facing his side, watching the little line on his `heart monitor` jump up and down on the other side of the room. She slumped down in the chair, brought her hand to her mouth, and promptly started to chew on the side of her thumb. Jake's dad, after at least an hour of intense conversation with a CIA agent who had calmed him down while divulging nothing, had just headed down to the cafeteria for some coffee. Gaia had actually turned down his offer to buy her food. The very idea of tasteless hospital `grub` made her lose her appetite. She'd been spending way too much time in hospitals lately.

"Gaia?"

She sat up straight and saw that Jake was rubbing his eyes with his fingertips. He blinked a few times and looked at her, confused. "Am I dead?"

Gaia laughed—a loud, relieved sort of bark. "No. You don't die from getting shot in the shoulder."

"The shoulder?"

He attempted to move his arm and winced and groaned. His head, which had come up about an inch off the pillow, flopped down again.

"Why does my head feel like someone ripped it in half?" he asked, his face crinkling up in pain.

"Concussion. You should probably just stay down,"

Gaia said. She got up and quickly flicked the light switch off so that the glare wouldn't cause him more pain. "You were knocked out when you fell," she explained, returning to her chair.

Jake managed a wry laugh and closed his eyes. "That's graceful." He took a deep breath and let it out slowly, gradually relaxing the muscles of his face. Gaia watched him, her heart pounding. There was something she wanted to say to him, but she was, as always, having trouble with the words.

A few more of his calming breaths and his eyes opened again. They were cool and clear now in the semidarkness—the only light in the room seeped in from the hallway.

"How's your leg?" he asked.

"It's fine," she replied. "Like I said. . . just a scratch."

"Great. You get a scratch, and I get an arm that feels like a sack of flour," Jake said with another laugh.

Gaia reddened and looked down at her hands in her lap. "Yeah. . . about that," she said, picking at her nonnails. "I wanted to. . . you know. . . thank you." He said nothing, and she finally forced herself to lift her chin—to look him in the eye. "You saved my life."

"Eh," Jake said, blowing it off. But he smiled nonetheless.

"Really. I was stupid. I should have known she wouldn't let it go," Gaia said. "So thanks."

"Don't thank me yet. You're going to be carrying

my books for the next few weeks," Jake shot back with a smirk.

Gaia smiled and looked down again, unsure of what to say next. Her legs were itching to run. She'd done what she'd come here to do, and now she was free to flee the hospital. But something made her stay right where she was. She didn't want to leave Jake alone. If she were honest with herself, she would have to admit that she didn't want to leave him, period.

There was this new but unmistakable pull between her and Jake. If she could, she would have made sure he was with her wherever she went. Having him around made her feel. . . safe. . . calm. . . almost normal.

"Gaia. . . how did you know?" Jake asked slowly.

"Know what?" Gaia asked, her face reddening as if he could hear her thoughts.

"That Tatiana was going to have those guys there?" Jake asked. "I mean, when I told you that the meeting was for the two of you and not the two of us, you knew right away that she was setting you up for something."

"I just know her," Gaia replied, realizing he'd want more than that. "Why did you tell me she asked you to bring me there? I'm sure she wanted it to be a surprise," she added with a touch of sarcasm.

"I didn't trust her," Jake replied. "When it came down to the two of you, I just. . . I knew she was in trouble, but somehow I knew I had to believe you."

Gaia's whole body warmed, and she looked away again. For all of Tatiana's flirting and damsel-in-distress routines, Jake had still seen who she really was. Gaia knew there was something great about this guy.

"Thanks," Gaia said.

"Look, I don't want to. . . you know. . . stick my nose in or whatever," Jake said. "But those guys tonight were pretty serious. I wasn't expecting. . ."

Gaia swallowed hard. "To get shot," she said, fresh guilt welling up inside her. "I never meant for you to—"

"No. I don't care about that. I'll be fine," Jake said. He looked her in the eye, and Gaia could tell there were a million questions he wanted to ask. She just wasn't sure if she could answer them. "I just. . . want to know if you're. . . if you're going to be okay."

A smile pulled at Gaia's lips. *That* was the most important thing on his mind? "I will be," she said. "Now that Tatiana is in custody. . . I'll be fine."

"Good," Jake said. He leaned back and looked at the ceiling. "God! She lied to me. Right to my face. All those fake, freakin' tears. She's insane."

"Pretty much," Gaia replied.

"So. . . you said she's in custody?" Jake asked, using his good arm to push himself up into a half-seated position. He let out a little groan as he settled back in.

Gaia took a deep breath and nodded. "She's been turned over to the proper authorities," she said.

Jake simply stared at her for a moment. "You ever gonna tell me what that means?" he asked, raising his eyebrows.

For a moment Gaia sat in silence, listening to the beeping heart monitor and the sounds of nurses and visitors walking past the room. She thought of all the secrets she'd kept over the last year, all the people she'd lost, all the people she'd tried to protect to no avail. She thought of Jake's open, honest face, of that afternoon when he'd readily offered to bring his friends to the dojo to help, of the way he'd looked at her as he threw himself in the path of the bullet that was meant for her heart.

He cared about her. He wanted her to be safe. He wanted to be at her side.

Maybe it was time for a change in her life. Maybe it was time to stop protecting and let someone protect her. Let someone in. Let someone be a true friend.

And so she looked at Jake, smiled, and meant it when she said, "I will. . . someday."

THE HANDCUFFS WERE LIKE ICE
against Tatiana's bare wrists. The cold of the

Dim metal chair stung her skin, even through her

clothes, and she felt like she was being refrigerated from the inside out. Even her bones were shivering. Her head slumped forward, pulling the muscles in her arms, which were secured behind her back. She sniffled, trying to keep her nose from running. Trying to keep that one sign of weakness at bay.

I've failed, she thought, staring down at the blood spatters on the thigh of her jeans. *I've failed you, Mother. I've failed myself.*

She sat in the center of a dim, gray, cinder-block-walled room. A two-way mirror hung on the far wall; a single lightbulb swung overhead. The only two pieces of furniture aside from her own chair were a wooden table and a high stool that stood next to the leaden door. Tatiana had no idea where she was, but she'd never felt so alone.

I'm worthless. I hope they just let me die in here, Tatiana thought, feeling her bruises throb, the cut across her left cheek sting. She'd gotten that just after the gun went off—just after Jake had slumped to the floor—dead, for all she knew. Not that she cared about him. He'd betrayed her. He'd ambushed her. He was a traitor.

Gaia had launched herself over his prone body and landed a backhand across Tatiana's face that had exploded behind her eye and knocked her out for a few moments. Long enough for Gaia and the Karate Squad to tie her up. Long enough for Ms. Moore to call in the CIA.

If I ever see her again, I'm going to kill her, Tatiana thought. *Next time I'll get it right.*

A loud clang echoed through the room as the lock on the heavy door slid free. Suddenly alert, Tatiana snapped up her head. The interrogation was about to begin. She could not be weak in the face of her enemy. She knew they'd probably hit her with the good-cop, bad-cop routine. It was standard procedure. She waited for the appearance of a couple of suited CIA agents, ready and more than willing to break her. Tatiana would not be broken.

The door swung open slowly, and Tatiana's brain almost exploded at the sight before her eyes. Gaia Moore—hair slicked back into a neat ponytail, a clean black sweater over a clean pair of jeans, and her standard black boots. No sign of a fight anywhere on `her perfect little face.` She stepped into the room, her eyes locked on Tatiana's, and the door swung shut behind her.

Somehow Tatiana managed to stare right back at Gaia. Stare through the confusion, the shame, the pain, the anger, the hatred. Her blood boiled and raced and melted away the cold. She refused to be the first to look away.

Gaia turned and picked up the stool by the wall. She set it down about two feet from Tatiana and perched herself on top of it. Now Tatiana saw the benefit of the higher stool. Gaia could look down on her— she could feel taller and more imposing. Tatiana lifted her chin and met her eyes. She was not intimidated.

"I'm here to tell you that the CIA has decided to give

you a choice," Gaia said slowly, deliberately. Tatiana seethed at her superior tone but refused to let slip the mask of bored defiance on her face. "If you tell me where my father is, they will let you join your mother in confinement," Gaia continued. "If you don't tell me, they're going to throw you in solitary."

Tatiana's eyes burned with instant tears. Her mother. She would get to be with her mother. She longed with every inch of her being to see Natasha again. It was all that mattered. It was all she had left. She ducked her chin so that Gaia wouldn't be looking right into her eyes when the first tear fell.

"Think about it, Tatiana," Gaia continued. "Solitary means a room smaller than this one—darker than this one. All alone. For as long as you decide to remain silent."

Oh God, I can't do this, Tatiana thought, her mind racing as she stared at the floor. *What if I tell them everything and go to my mother and she turns her back on me? She'll know I failed. I could never handle that.*

But she also wouldn't be able to handle solitary. She'd hardly been able to handle being alone for the last few days. She'd go crazy if they locked her up by herself. She'd go mad.

"Well?" Gaia said. "What do you say?"

Tatiana looked up at her, vision blurred, the words on the very tip of her tongue. All she had to do was say it and she'd be in her mother's arms again. All she had to do was talk.

But then she saw the shame and disappointment that would be in her mother's eyes. She saw her mother turning away as she ran to her. And the pain of that simple image was excruciating.

Tatiana turned her profile to Gaia and squeezed her eyes shut. She wouldn't tell. Not now. Not yet. She had to think. And right now she was too tired, too confused. She needed some time to process everything.

"Fine," Gaia spat, shoving the stool away from her. "You have twenty-four hours to make your decision."

The door swung open again as Gaia approached it, and Tatiana felt her glare at her one last time. Then she stepped out, and the door swung shut behind her. The resounding clang sounded with the finality of death. Finally Tatiana tipped her head forward and gave way to silent tears.

THE MOMENT GAIA WALKED INTO

Hyperawake

the fourth-floor office at the brownstone, Oliver turned away from his computer and looked at her with a never-before-seen excitement in his light eyes. Against her will, Gaia's heart leapt crazily. Even after everything she'd been through that day—the good-bye with Ed, the fight, the hospital, the one-on-one with Tatiana, she was suddenly hyperawake.

"What is it?" she asked, dropping her stuff on the floor and crossing the room. She stood at his side and squeezed her arms over her chest. "What's going on?"

"We've got him," Oliver said, smiling up at her. "We've found your father."

Inside, Gaia jumped up and down. . . she yelped and hugged Oliver, tackling him to the ground. . . she did cartwheels and somersaults and danced a jig worthy of *Riverdance*. Outside, she remained the picture of intense concentration.

"Where?" she asked.

"He's in Siberia. . . in a hospital there," Oliver said, sliding a few sheets of paper out of a large manila envelope. He handed over a glossy black-and-white photo of her father in a hospital bed, either sleeping or unconscious. His face was covered with a few days' beard. As expected, he did look exactly like Oliver had when she'd first seen him in the hospital. Lying on top of the blanket that covered his legs was a copy of a Russian newspaper, the date as clear as day in the top-right corner. The picture had been taken two days ago.

Gaia felt her mouth go dry as her eyes traveled to the medical monitors to the right of her father's bed. They were alight with lines and squiggles and numbers. Her father was alive. Or was two days ago.

"Thank you," Gaia said under her breath. "You found him. . . . Thank you."

Oliver smiled slightly and handed over another sheet of paper. "This is the address of the hospital," he said. "You'll have to fly to Minsk."

"Great," Gaia said, turning for the door. "I'm gone."

"No!"

Oliver stood up from his chair, scraping it back so fast, it fell over and clattered to the floor. Gaia stopped short and closed her eyes. Nothing was going to keep her from leaving right this very second. How could he even suggest otherwise?

"Gaia, the second you book that ticket, there are going to be hundreds of agents on your tail," Oliver said, each of his words hitting her back like tiny daggers. "I promise you, you will never make it to Russia alive. Never."

"Well, then what am I supposed to do?" Gaia demanded, whirling around again, clutching the papers and the photograph in her hands. "Why give me this information if you expect me to do nothing?"

Oliver stepped over to her, reached out, and placed his hands on her shoulders. "I expect you to wait," he said, eliciting an eye roll and a sigh from Gaia. "Just two days. In two days I can get you a legitimate passport with a new name for you to travel under. I can have a whole history made up for the new you in case anyone decides to check."

He squeezed her shoulders, and Gaia looked down. She knew that he was right—that this was the only logical way to do things. But how could she? How could she wait two whole days?

"And I can have the same thing done for myself," Oliver continued.

Gaia raised her chin and looked into his eyes, her pulse thumping in her ears—her heart a tangled mess of conflicting emotions. Had he really just said what she thought he'd said?

"I'm coming with you," he added firmly. "You're not going anywhere alone. Not anymore."

Two days.

Forty-eight hours.

Two thousand, eight hundred and eighty minutes.

One hundred seventy-two thousand, eight hundred seconds.

And I'll be on my way to find my father. And this time I'm bringing him home. For good.

here is a
sneak peek of
Fearless™ #29:
LUST

I guess the only time most people think about blood is when it's gushing out of their veins and they need to find a Band-Aid— or an emergency room—to keep it from messing up the white carpet. But I'm thinking about it a lot lately. Little red platelets and big white corpuscles rushing through everyone's veins. Keeping us alive as long as it stays on its dark little course—but signaling weakness or death when it wanders off the path, out into the light, to spill on the ground.

Funny thing about blood—it also connects people. There it is, hidden inside your skin, yet it manages to call out to other blood, related blood, inside someone else's skin. You might have nothing else in common, but that red stuff really is thicker than water. There's nobody in the world I should have more cause to hate than Oliver. Or should I say, Loki. He has engineered more destruction— starting with my own mother, the

woman who created my own blood—than
anyone else in my life. So a bout
of postcoma confusion has forced
his pre-Loki, kinder and gentler
Oliver personality to emerge, and
suddenly he regrets his evil ways.

At best, I should feel indif-
ferent toward him. But because we
share blood, I find myself drawn
to him. I find myself willing to
try to trust him—this new,
remorseful Oliver—because our DNA
matches up so nicely.

Am I just a sucker? A girl so
lonely she'll cling to any sem-
blance of a family connection? Or
is this an instinct, speaking
through the layers of primordial
history, telling me the tide has
turned for Oliver?

Let's hope it's the latter.
Let's hope it's the blood
that's letting me forgive him.
Anyone else would get nothing from
me but my everlasting hate. Like
Natasha and Tatiana. The mother-
daughter team from the third ring
of hell. A couple of lying, con-
niving females who took my dad

from me and almost had me convinced he was dead. But he can't
be dead. My blood would tell me if
he was. They're still going to
pay, though. Maybe with their own
blood. If I get half a chance, you
can bet that'll be the case.

But that's so not a priority.
What's important now—what's got
to happen before anything else—is
I've got to find my dad. My real
blood link. Even closer to me
than Oliver. He's the one I owe
my loyalty to. And I'm going to
find him. Come hell or high
water, the blood pumping in my
veins is going to give me the
strength to reach around the
globe and find him. You can bet
on that.

She had to
remember
to keep her
distance

unfamiliar

this

terrain

time—

within her

heart and

out in the

world.

GAIA SAT SLUMPED IN AN UNFORGIV-

Dangerously Accurate

ing wood-and-metal chair as she cycled through the seven local stations one more time, looking for something that would amuse her and Jake in his hospital room. The television, which looked about twenty years old, was bolted to the ceiling and made a disconcerting fuzzy noise whenever a channel was changed, like the *cchk* sound at the beginning and end of a walkie-talkie broadcast. The static was only marginally less interesting than daytime TV.

"Is this *Judge Judy*?" Gaia wanted to know.

"No, that's a different show," Jake said, pointing to the screen. "It looks like a judge show, but then they bring in therapists and it turns into a corny lovefest where everybody's hugging and crying, even though tomorrow they're going to go back to throwing chairs at each other."

"You need better health insurance. This no-cable thing is a problem."

"Aren't you supposed to be in school?" Jake asked again. Gaia glared at him. Forcing herself to ignore the way his black hair fell on his forehead just right, even after a full twenty-four hours of lying in a hospital bed. And the way his green eyes sparkled as he asked the

5

question he knew would annoy her. And the muscles she could see even through the loose hospital gown he wore. If he got out of bed, she'd get a prime view of his butt. She forced herself to ignore that, too.

"Didn't I already sidestep that question?" she wanted to know.

"Yeah, that's why I have to ask it again. I'm in a weakened state. I'd think you'd be more considerate— it's tiring, all this verbal tangoing, you know."

"Whatever. I skipped again," she admitted. "I can't sit around in school. I'm too agitated."

"What? Because of this?" Jake shrugged. Gaia tried not to think about the fact that he'd been shot when he'd been ambushed along with her. *Because* of her. So what if it turned out to be nothing more than a flesh wound? He was hurt because he'd gotten in the way of people who were after Gaia. And that made her feel ill.

He wasn't the first person to end up lying on a metal cot with a tube in his arm because of her. And she felt a leaden certainty that he wouldn't be the last.

"No, not because of that," she said sheepishly, glancing at the bandages enveloping his powerful shoulder. "You know why."

"Because you're worried about those visas," he said, taking the remote from her hand and switching the TV off. "You're going to make yourself crazy, you know."

"Oh, I'm already there, so there's nothing to worry about," she told him.

6

"Yeah, but. . . I mean, you have to wait a couple days anyway, right? Why can't you just go to school and avoid getting in trouble?"

Gaia blinked at him. "What are you, a boy scout?" she asked.

Jake laughed. "No, I'm just saying you could pass the time at school as easily as you can pass it sitting here."

Gaia knew he was right. She didn't know why she had such an aversion to school. Maybe it was because she already knew everything that was being droned about at the front of the classroom. Her dad—her dad and her mom, actually—had made sure of that, making her take advantage of her sharp intellect from the moment she could read. Maybe she just hated being fenced in. Maybe she was worried that another strike would hurt the students around her.

Or maybe she just wanted to be here, at the hospital, with Jake.